BLOOD
of my
MONSTER

MONSTER TRILOGY BOOK ONE
RINA KENT

To every girl who was fascinated by monsters

AUTHOR NOTE

Hello reader friend,

If you haven't read my books before, you might not know this, but I write darker stories that can be upsetting and disturbing. My books and main characters aren't for the faint of heart.

Blood of My Monster is book one of a trilogy and is NOT a standalone.

Monster Trilogy:
#1 *Blood of My Monster*
#2 *Lies of My Monster*
#3 *Heart of My Monster*

For more things Rina Kent, visit www.rinakent.com

ABOUT THIS BOOK

I'm out for revenge. He's out to rule the world.

Kirill and I are as different as day and night.

We shouldn't have been in the same frame or universe.

But we meet under the strangest circumstances.

He's my superior in the military and the man who'll
introduce me to carnage.

His charm and exterior perfection shouldn't have tempted me.

Behind the smokescreen lurks a manipulative
emotionless monster.

And that monster might find out all my secrets, including the
reason why I'm pretending to be a man.

He might also lure me to the point of no return.

PLAYLIST

Blood in The Water—Joanna Jones as The Dame
Find You—The Phantoms
The Darker The Weather // The Better The Man—Missio
Villain—Halflives
Darkside—Oshins & Hael
Love You More—LIynks
Born For This—The Score
Gone Away—Five Finger Death Punch
Unsteady—X Ambassadors
Dark Things—ADONA
Tether Me—Galleaux
Guardian—Aether Realm
Animals—Architects
Private Eyes—Lenachka
Beautiful Crime—Tamer

You can find the complete playlist on Spotify.

BLOOD
of my
MONSTER

ONE

Sasha

I DIDN'T MEAN TO BE HERE.

Or maybe the right expression is: I shouldn't be here.

I connived and snuck into this establishment that has never catered well to women and probably never will.

Ironically, this is the safest place for me and the only environment where I can survive beyond the metaphorical ticking time bomb I've been carrying around for years.

My muscles ache, and I groan with each movement. I'm sluggish, lack energy, and I'm weighted down by heavy army boots. Every step forward is a struggle, every breath is scratchy and choked.

A buzzing sound echoes in my ears and I lean against the wall outside the toilets to catch my choppy breaths.

I raise my hands under the bright fluorescent lights of the grim, gray-colored corridor. The brightness adds a layer of gruesome visuals to my cuts, making them look redder.

The sight of blood thrusts me back to gruesome memories. A pool. Gunshots. Screams.

They sizzle through my head, lowering, then heightening in a sporadic rhythm until a screeching buzz fills my ears. My hands tremble, and my body goes so still that I could be mistaken for a statue.

It's over.

Breathe.

You *have* to breathe.

It doesn't matter how many times I repeat the mantra. My brain has already decided that he and I ought to live in the past, crushed between those corpses we couldn't save and the souls we left behind.

"Who do we have here?"

The distinctive voice speaking in Russian shakes me out of my surreal experience. I straighten, letting my unsteady hands fall to either side of me.

The hallway comes into focus again, grim with yellowish stains and dark walls that belong in prison instead of a military institution. The unnaturally bright lights make the view glaring, intrusive even.

My eyes move to the one who spoke just now. Matvey. He's a fellow soldier in my unit and a pain in the ass who displays seriously toxic behavior.

As luck would have it, he's accompanied by four other soldiers who stand on either side of him, watching me with unveiled disgust and humiliating disregard.

All twice my size, they have mean features and harsh gazes. They're wearing T-shirts and cargo pants that are probably a lot more comfortable than the combat gear I'm still in.

I was waiting for them to finish showering so I could hop in, which is something I've habitually done ever since I joined the army eighteen months ago.

Despite the factor of intimidation, I square my shoulders until they hit the wall behind me. I suppress a wince and stare Matvey right in the face. It doesn't take a genius to figure out he's the leader of their little group.

"If it isn't the weakling Aleksander," he taunts in his coarse, annoying voice. His four companions snicker, hitting each other on the shoulder as if it's the funniest joke.

My first thought is to knee Matvey in the balls and scream bloody murder at the others. But, alas, that would be no different than signing my own death certificate. At my current strength, I can barely defend myself against one of them. Five is total overkill and would cause me to end up in the hospital or be tucked neatly in a coffin.

Besides, we're from entirely different backgrounds. Most men here either have harsh lives or severe circumstances and only joined the military because it's sustainable income. Some even forge their real age for it. If they're not here, they would probably be in gangs.

Keeping my head up, I try to push past Matvey and speak in my pretend 'male' voice. "If you will excuse me."

"If you will excuse me," Matvey taunts and blocks my path with his burly physique. "Such a noble little boy with proper manners. I wonder if he has any balls between his legs."

The others burst out laughing. I try to remain calm, but I can't control the heat that flares up my neck and spreads over my ears.

"Let me through, Matvey," I say in a clear tone, glaring at him and standing my ground.

"Oh, he's scary, this one. *Let me through. Let me through.*" His grating voice causes my throat to close and bile to rise in my stomach. "You're too uptight for your own good, Aleksander. Relax a little, will you?"

He grabs my shoulder, and I stiffen. My flight mode zips through my limbs like it did the day I lost everything.

"Fuck. You don't only look girly, but you also feel like one." He strokes my shoulder, and even though our skin is separated by clothes, the predominant need to escape gets stronger.

"No wonder you're a weak little thing at camp." Matvey's hand tightens as if to prove he has the physical superiority and is able to inflict harm if he wishes to. "Anyone ever tell you the army isn't for weaklings?"

"I'm not a weakling," I snarl in his stupid face, resisting the urge to knee him in the balls.

The others snicker, taunting from the background, but I can't look away from Matvey. A maniacal grin spreads across his lips, stretching his features in a disturbing manner.

"Sounds like something a weakling would say."

"Maybe we should check the balls situation, after all, eh, Matvey?" one of his goons says.

The dangerous nature of the situation dawns on me in a sudden flood. I fling myself forward to try to release my shoulder from Matvey's hold, but he shoves me back against the wall so easily, I can feel the tears forming in my eyes.

I am a weakling.

It doesn't matter how long I slave through physical activities or try to build my muscles. The truth remains, I don't have these guys' strength. Not only are they men, but they've also been in the army longer than I have.

"Aww, are you crying, boy?" Matvey shakes me. "Should I call your mama to come pick you up? Oh, sorry, you don't have a mama, do you? Or a papa, for that matter. Poor Aleksander trying to be a man—"

His words are cut off when I grab his shoulders and raise my knee, hitting him in the nuts so hard, he's lost for words.

And expressions, apparently, because his face is caught in a blank state for a while. All the others freeze, too, probably not believing what just happened.

His hold loosens from my shoulder, and I use the chance to free myself and slip from beneath his limp arm as he wails and groans in pain.

"You fucking…fuck… I'm going to kill you!" he screams from

behind me, but I'm already running toward the exit. If I find the captain or even some other soldiers, I'll be safe.

Note to self: Never stay alone with Matvey and his gang again. Ever.

My muscles scream with exhaustion, and the boots weigh down my escape, but I still don't stop running.

Like back then, I know, I just know that my survival depends on how fast and far I run.

Just when the exit is within reach, I'm pulled by a firm hold on my nape, flung back, and tossed on the floor like an old rug.

The thud splashes all the way to my bones, and I groan, then grab a painful spot in my arm. Well, shit. It's either sprained or broken.

I have no time to focus on that when a shadow falls on me. I slowly stare up to find a very pissed Matvey hovering over me, his goons close behind him.

"You really fucked up, little fuck." He reaches for me, and before I can get away, he lifts me up with a savage grip on my jacket.

The material tears at the top, nearly revealing my chest bandage, and I dig my nails into his hand while I grab whatever I can of my jacket to keep it in place.

For the first time, I'm glad to be wearing my combat gear over my T-shirt and, therefore, won't be fully naked, even if he rips it.

But that would put my chest bandages into question.

His palm wraps around my neck, applying enough pressure to cut off my breathing. I wheeze, but little to no air sprinkles into my lungs.

My legs flail in midair while the other soldiers taunt, laugh, and snicker. Matvey slams my back against the wall and reaches for my pants.

"Let us see those miniscule balls."

I thrash, scratch, and scream, but only a haunting sound escapes my lips.

Each of Matvey's goons clutches a limb and glues it to the wall behind me, effectively stopping me from moving.

Matvey smirks when he sees the horrified expression on my face, then slowly releases my neck to dedicate his whole attention to my pants.

Please, stop it, is at the tip of my tongue, but if I say that, there's no doubt they'll take this further. They'll be enticed by my begging and will be tempted to prove that I'm indeed weak.

"Fuck you," I snarl, even as my voice chokes and the last of my hopes start to shrivel and die.

Matvey's response is a wide grin. "But you're the one who probably likes to take it up the ass, sodomite."

I sneer, wanting—no, needing—to poke his eyes out for being a bigoted asshole.

Matvey is every bit of the toxic masculinity that's wrong with this place. He believes that a man should be macho and show no emotions or else he's labeled subhuman. According to his stupid, uninformed logic, being gay is also a weakness. Which is what he and his friends have called me ever since I got here.

I'm neither a man nor gay, but I still feel the offense on behalf of everyone Matvey must've put through this discrimination.

Being a woman in a man's world is just as bad.

Which is part of the reason I cut my hair and joined the army as a man. My uncle helped me by bribing the physical examiner and a few other officials to keep my gender a secret and help me integrate into this institution.

If my gender is found out, I will be killed. Simple as that.

Now, if Matvey, of all people, discovers that bit of information, I'm fucked.

I push my whole body forward in one last desperate attempt to set myself free, but that only causes them to tighten their holds on my limbs.

Matvey is unbuckling my pants, and I can feel sweat covering my skin. Hyperventilation starts to set in, slowly but surely devouring my inner assertiveness.

In my twenty years of life, this is the second time I've felt this helpless and torn and that there was no way out.

The first was when I lost most of my family and had to run for my life.

The chain of current events plays in my mind's eye. Matvey will find out I'm a woman, he and his goons could assault me, and then they'll either report me to the captain, or they will demand sexual favors in return for keeping my secret.

Blackmail or being kicked out of the safest place for me. Hell, I could even be thrown in jail for lying to the military institution.

"You're an obedient little fucker, aren't you? Bet you're submissive and shit." Matvey licks his lips in a suggestive way.

"Your broken dick would testify otherwise." I glare at him. "Guess that makes you the submissive one, motherfucker."

I hear it before I feel it. His fist connects with my face, sending it flying sideways. Blood splatters on the wall, my lips feel twice their size, and my nose is instantly clogged.

Still, I laugh, like a maniac. The sound is so forceful and unruly that they all pause to watch me. "So macho and big but also so small. Maybe we should see *your* dick, Matvey."

"You fucking—" He raises his fist again and I stare him square in the eye.

I'm taunting and provoking him on purpose. If he's preoccupied with beating me to a pulp, seeing my nonexistent balls will be the last thing on his mind.

"What's going on here?"

All movements halt at the booming, commanding voice. If anything, it seems as if the world pauses for a fraction of a second as the newcomer strides in our direction.

My state of alertness slowly withers but then heightens again at the sight of him.

He's tall and muscular, but not as glaringly buff as the soldiers surrounding me. He has the type of physical profile that would fit an agile spy or a member of the Special Forces. In fact, judging by his black long-sleeved shirt and cargo pants, he's probably special ops.

They have their own camp, but during this period, they're our guests for special joint training.

My gaze lifts to his face, and I'm struck by his features. They're dark, sharp, and, most importantly, blank. It's like I'm staring into a nonexistent entity that's only projecting itself onto the physical world.

He's good-looking in a clean-cut, mystic way. The one thing that strikes me the most is that his external appearance reveals nothing of what's lurking inside him.

And the worst part is that he looks oddly familiar. His presence feels like an encounter that's hidden behind unresolved feelings and untouched memories.

Where have I seen him before?

Gravity pulls me down as the soldiers let go of me, and the asshole Matvey even grabs me by the shoulder as if we're best buddies before they all line up and salute. "Captain."

He's a captain? Also, how come these tools know him and I don't?

His black boots stop right in front of us, and he stares at me. I stand still and salute, feeling like a novice.

Get it together, me. I'm usually the most disciplined when it comes to military codes of conduct.

The captain strolls parallel to us, not offering the usual 'at ease' most higher-ups do after the salute. So we all remain in the same position, staring ahead and so stiff that I feel the ache in my joints.

That may also have to do with my busted lip and clogged nose, though.

The captain's movements are unhurried. If anything, they follow a methodical rhythm as he stops in front of each soldier to study his face.

I feel the stiffening of the one beside me before it's my turn to earn the same treatment. I continue staring into the distance, but he lowers his head, and his light blue eyes slam into mine. They're icy and so fair that they resemble an arctic wolf's.

Not only are they unnerving to look at, but I also feel myself trembling under their scrutiny.

What the hell?

I shake myself out of my daze and try to keep staring ahead. The key word being *try*. It's impossible to ignore his presence when he's so close; I'm forced to inhale him with every intake of air.

He smells fresh and clean, which is a rare occurrence in the training camp.

"I'm asking for the second and final time. What happened here?" His controlled words float over my skin, and the command in them bounces against my chest. His Russian is different from these guys' and anyone in the army.

Everyone speaks in a colloquial manner, but his words are more elevated, almost similar to how I was brought up.

My lips tremble, wanting to let it all out, but Matvey steps forward. "We were just joking among each other, sir."

Joking, my ass.

I must break my salute stance because the captain pushes further into my space, which makes me immediately go back into the correct position.

Jeez.

I forgot he was right in my face.

No, not forgot. That would be impossible to do. More like, I was taken aback by Matvey's audacity.

"Does joking include a bloody nose and lips, soldier?" He's asking Matvey, but he's still looking at me.

"Sometimes, yes, sir," Matvey replies confidently like the low-life he is.

"Very well." The captain finally pushes back, but before I can breathe properly, he swings his fist and punches Matvey across the face so hard, he reels back from the power of it.

A collective gasp echoes in the hall as Matvey's nose runs with blood and drips on the ground.

The captain lowers his hand, letting it nonchalantly hang at his side. "Then let's say I'm joking with you, soldier. I will also be reporting the five of you to your direct superior for insubordination so he can teach you that this institution doesn't tolerate these types of games."

Then, he turns around and leaves with long, even strides that steal my attention.

Matvey clutches his nose and curses, and the others fawn over him, trying to make the bleeding stop.

I don't wait to take the fallout of their anger and be trapped by them again. So, without allowing myself to overthink the situation, I follow the captain.

Maybe, just maybe, I've finally found someone to teach me how not to be a weakling.

TWO

Sasha

WHILE I LIKE TO BELIEVE I'M A PRACTICAL PERSON who overthinks before acting, there are times when I act out of pure impulse, not considering the possible ramifications, circumstances, or people's reactions.

This is one of those times.

My steps are lighter as I completely ignore the pain from the boots and the general discomfort caused by my blood-clogged nose and swollen lips.

I break into a jog to catch up with the mysterious captain's wide strides.

You know how some people are thrown into your path for a specific reason? I think—no, I'm certain that he's here for that reason.

He's nothing short of a phenomenon, an occurrence that I'm sure happens once in a lifetime, and if I don't seize this chance, I won't be given another.

His retreating back is getting farther and farther away, disappearing down the depressing hallway with the flickering fluorescent lights.

I can't help noticing how he walks with purpose. No, not walks. He's definitely striding, looking the part of a captain even when he's not on duty.

Just when he's about to round the corner, my mind goes into overdrive at the prospect of missing him—and my chance.

"Captain!" I call with all the strength I have.

He shows no sign of hearing me, and for a moment, I think I've lost him. That all my strength wasn't enough.

Then in one swift movement, he spins around, and I freeze in place. He's farther away than he was earlier, but I see him more clearly now, and I have no choice but to be sucked into his penetrating gaze.

The unforgiving harshness of his feral eyes pins me in place. It strikes me then.

He looks like a human weapon.

I don't have to see him in action to guess that he's both highly efficient and cold-blooded.

I shouldn't have any misconceptions about this man just because he saved me earlier. He would've done the same for anyone in my position, considering he's a higher-up.

It's a duty. Nothing less and nothing more.

He slides his gaze over the length of me, eyes tapering with an acute sense of…disapproval.

"Do you have a habit of not greeting your superiors, soldier?" His crisp, deep voice again.

I'm caught in a trance by the subtle authoritativeness in it and the lowering edge in his tone.

He raises a perfect thick brow, and I straighten, then salute. "Sir, no, sir."

Long silence stretches between us, and I think he'll turn

around and forbid me from following this time, but his voice carries in the silence again. "What's your name, soldier?"

"Private Lipovsky, sir."

"Full name."

A shiver goes through me. He could be asking for my name to report me or something, but I seal away my doubts as I answer, "Private Aleksander Abramovic Lipovsky, sir."

Another long moment of stretched silence. The few seconds that tick by feel like hours. As much as I try to hold my ground, I can't help the sweat that trickles down my spine.

The sound of heavy boots reverberates in the air and invades my ears as he advances toward me. When he stops an arm's length in front of me, I have trouble breathing.

Was silence always this unbearable, or is it only this way around the captain?

I'm not ready for when he speaks in that authoritative voice of his. It doesn't matter that he was also close to me earlier. There's an edge of intensity to his presence that's impossible to get used to.

"Why are you following me, Private Lipovsky?"

"I wasn't…"

"You weren't what?" Something changes in his tone. Though subtle, I can feel the escalation of his usual command, and my spine jerks.

It's not that I cower in front of figures of power. I've never acted or felt this way with my direct superiors. This captain, however, falls into a new category I haven't dealt with before.

"I wasn't, *sir*," I say in a lower range than my usual 'male' voice and pause when he tilts his head to the side, studying me so closely, it borders on intrusive.

"Care to explain why you're in the same space as me then?"

He's losing his patience. I don't have to see it on his face when I can hear it loud and clear in his voice.

If I don't make use of this chance, this moment will just go down in his memory as a faceless encounter.

"I lied, sir."

"You lied?" There's a note of amusement in his voice. No, not really amusement, but something along the lines of 'did you, now?'

"Yes. I did follow you, but only so I could ask you something, sir."

"You're not in a position to ask me anything."

"I know, and I'll understand if you turn me down, but I would rather be rejected than regret not taking this step, sir."

"Which is?"

I meet his eyes, deliberately, for the first time since I followed him. I'm metaphorically knocked off my feet by the sheer intensity that stares back at me, and I'm almost derailed from my mission.

Almost.

However, I take my time to breathe in steady intervals and force myself to recall what's at stake here. This isn't only about me.

The rest of my family is at stake here.

They're weak, hidden, and have no one to protect them except for me.

"Please train me, sir." I speak in a clear, determined voice.

"Train you?" he repeats. Although his tone is calm, there's something intimidating beneath the surface and that, indirectly, makes me doubt my own words.

I manage to keep my cool, though. "Yes, sir."

"Why?"

Neither his expression nor his demeanor changes, but that might not be as good as it seems. Especially since he looks no different than a sturdy wall standing erect between me and my goal.

While his question is logical, the answer isn't as easy to

come by. I doubt he's the type who likes ass-kissing, so if I say it's because I think he's strong, he'll call bullshit. Not only have I never seen him in action, but I also don't even know his name.

If I say because I want to be in special ops and potentially have the type of power that will help my family members, that would be no different than selling them out.

So I take a deep breath and go with the most direct route. "Because I don't want to be a weakling, sir."

"You don't want to be a weakling. Interesting." Usually, that last word would be accompanied by a note of curiosity. Not with the captain. Instead, it's coated with dark edges and somber amusement.

A combination that's odd at best.

"Does this have to do with your brutalized nose and mouth?" He juts his chin in the general direction of my face.

For some reason, that makes me self-conscious about my appearance and the weakness he must've seen in the scene from earlier. I wish I could dig a hole and bury myself in it, just to conceal the humiliation.

But then again, this isn't only about me. So I nod slowly.

"You have a voice, use it, Lipovsky."

Is this man…a dictator? It's not too late to backpedal, is it?

Under his scrutinizing stare, I say, "Yes, sir."

"You were cornered by your colleagues, beaten and shaken up a little, so you decided to ask for help. The way I see it, you're not fit for this place. It'd be better for everyone if you'd pack your things and leave."

At first, astonishment creeps through me, but then it's replaced by an acute sense of rage.

"With all due respect, you know nothing about my life or circumstances, and, therefore, you can't ask me to leave, *sir.*"

He doesn't miss the way I enunciate the word sir and stares at me so hard, I think I'll catch fire and burn in the pits of Hell.

"No, I can't. What I can do, however, is wait for the circumstances to align for the day you'll quit."

"I'm strong enough to be here."

He reaches for my stomach, and I'm about to step back, but he flicks my calf with his boot. It's not that strong, but it's sharp and fast. My legs give out from beneath me and I fall on the floor, catching myself with my hand at the last moment.

When I stare back up, he's looking down at me. "You don't even have a decent body balance, and you dare speak about strength? Give up, Private."

Humiliation beats beneath my skin, and the taste of bitter irony explodes in my mouth. This isn't the first time I've been in such a situation.

Give up, Sasha.

That's what everyone used to and continues to tell me. I'm physically, mentally, and emotionally weak. The more I fight against the tides, the lower I sink. But if I followed that logic, then I would never find the power to rise above this situation and regain the control that was robbed of me.

The captain starts to turn, erasing me from his immediate presence as if I were a pesky fly.

"No," I say hard enough that the word bounces off the walls surrounding us.

I see the exact moment the captain decides to give me the time of the day. Again. He stops in his tracks and faces me—fully.

Once more, I'm taken aback by his impressive physique and every bulge in his muscles. I realize then that he's the closest to a human killing machine that I've ever met.

He crosses his arms and stares at me. Only, it's different now.

There's no disdain, and while that should be a good thing, it isn't. In its place, there's a crippling sense of…challenge.

He might have told me to give up earlier, but now, he appears ready to force me to.

"No?" he repeats slowly, unhurriedly, and I'm sure it's an intimidation tactic.

This man is used to getting everything done his way, and any hint of rebellion is probably punishable in his books.

"No. Sir," I enunciate, and I swear a shadow passes through his eyes, too fleeting to catch or study properly.

"You're on your knees because you couldn't remain standing after a simple maneuver, and you have the audacity to tell me no?"

It's a question, but it sounds rhetorical. The words are injected with enough disdain to cause my skin to crawl.

I start to get up, but he shoves me back down with a mere hand on my shoulder. In this position, he's so close, I smell his aftershave, or shower gel, or whatever that smells clean.

"Have I given you permission to rise?"

"No, sir." I swallow, and the sound echoes in the surrounding silence.

Still, I stare into his frightening icy eyes, even as I feel frozen in place with no way out.

Yes, his eyes are frightening, but there's nothing scarier than my fate if I'm kicked out of the military.

And, most importantly, everyone else's fate.

"I might not have the power now, but I want it." I speak in a harsh tone, unable to control the emotions flooding through me. "I will work hard for it. I will be the most disciplined soldier you have if you just give me a chance."

"Give you a chance." It's not a question this time. A mere repetition of facts. "There are more competent soldiers than you. Why should I pick you?"

"I don't have the answer to that, sir, but I do know that I never give up."

He raises a brow, again looking at me in that funny way I can't put my finger on.

"Prove yourself first," he says with ease, as if the method is a given.

Confusion must be written all over my face as I ask, "How do I do that?"

"Now, that's the part you have to figure out yourself." He pushes back and gives me another stern glance. "Let's see if you have it in you to take a man's place, Lipovsky."

And then he spins around and leaves.

My brow furrows at his last words. He didn't say another man's place. He said a man's place.

I wonder why he phrased it that way.

Anyway, that's not important now that I finally have a chance to regain control over my life after the massacre that took away my everything.

THREE

Kirill

Cold sweat covers my skin as I sit on the hard surface of the military bed.

Deafening silence surrounds me, and I jump up, my feet making no sound on the floor.

The images from the nightmare redden my vision and play in slow motion in the dark corners of my subconscious.

Everyone and everything I cut from my life have been slowly returning to my immediate presence. Not in person, but as ghosts and shadows.

I stare down at the cuts and marks slithering over my skin, serving as a constant reminder of what happened before I got here.

The reason I escaped it all.

It's also the reason I have this fucked-up need to return and rule it all. Every last bit of it.

No one can control me if I'm the leader. No one can deny or order me to do anything. In fact, it'll be the other way around.

But that's neither for here nor for now.

I throw on some pants and a T-shirt, then slip out of the room and into the empty training camp. The soldiers were granted a night out, so they all fucked off to get drunk and get some pussy while they could. Including my own men, who usually follow me like wannabe shadows.

All the better. The empty darkness gives me the needed space that allows me to run and push myself to my physical limits. It's a sure way to recharge and erase the gory events from the nightmare earlier.

Or more like a memory.

Despite the bright moonlight in the middle of the sky, it's freezing. The cold air hits me deeper in my bones with every passing minute, but I've always found solace in the freezing weather.

Something about harsh natural circumstances allows me to blend with them and see myself as part of the ecosystem.

I'm an entity of destruction with no qualms about stomping on everything in my path.

My choices are unlimited, and everything I do will be labeled as a natural disaster.

I didn't choose to be this way, but it happened, and instead of fighting it, I embraced it. Fully.

Without any questioning.

Either that or I would've been collateral damage in a bigger and more dangerous game.

A groaning sound reaches me from the other end of the track, and I stop.

It comes again as a low "Ugh" in a very familiar voice.

I follow it discreetly, without making a noise. The night serves as my camouflage and the silence is my cover.

Sure enough, when I reach the source of the noise, I find a dark figure doing push-ups against the soil.

Only, it's not all dark.

The arms that peek through the T-shirt are pasty-white in the night, and his face is red with exertion.

His movements are disoriented, uncoordinated, and his limbs shake uncontrollably.

"109, 110, 111, 112..." With each whispered number, he grows weaker, his rhythm, breathing, and impatience all spiking up until he's a myriad of turbulent energy.

I lean against a pillar, legs and arms crossed. "You're doing it all wrong."

Lipovsky lifts his head to look at me, then stumbles and falls sideways, his frail muscles finally giving up on him.

For a second, he observes me from his position on the ground as if I'm some twisted form of salvation that got thrown in his path.

He did it a week ago, too, when he asked—begged—me to take him as part of my team with his nonexistent skills.

That was a bold move. And he's an insolent little fucker, considering the way he's staring at me without a hint of a salute.

This guy either has a death wish, or he simply shouldn't be in the military—as I previously tried to convince him.

It could be because of my stare or, although it's a very slim chance, that he finally realized his insolence because he finally stands with great difficulty and salutes. "Captain."

He looks rough at best in unflattering cargo pants and an oversized T-shirt that's soaked in sweat at the front and the back.

"If this is your way of proving yourself, then you might as well give up. My men do 200 in a steady rhythm without blinking an eye. No limbs shaking, no groaning or whining or looking like an amateur."

Lipovsky's eyes widen, appearing alarmed for a moment

before he remembers to school his expression. "I'm improving compared to my previous record, and I only compare my achievements to myself, sir."

No clue whether I should laugh or smack him upside the head.

I've met a lot of types in my years in the special ops, but he's the only one who's had this infuriating habit of talking back, even to a superior.

"That's a foolish way of saying you'll never improve. The past you isn't a measurement of success, and if you only do self-comparison, the world will move by you before you know it." I straighten. "On the ground, Private."

His eyes study me for a while, probably wondering if what he heard is correct.

"On. The. Ground," I repeat. "Continue what you were doing."

He's about to object. I can see it in his deep hazel eyes, a curious mixture of earth and forest. And since it's freezing winter here, they seem to be stuck in a different universe at an alternative time with nontraditional customs.

A protest lurks on the tip of his tongue, but he has the self-preservation mentality to slowly lower himself to the ground for push-ups.

"One," I count and he goes down. "Two."

"How many am I supposed to do?"

"Until I stop counting. Three."

He remains in the same stance, but there's a slight curve in his back.

"Four. Five. Six."

"Sir, may I speak?"

"You already are."

He glares at the ground. I see it because I'm in a bilateral position, where I can watch the entirety of him and his slim, bony body that shouldn't have been accepted into the military in the first place.

"My limit is 120, sir, and I already finished that. I've been adding ten a day for six days, so I can't go anymore." He strains with every word and his ass curves up.

I jam my boot on his back and push it down so that he's straight. "Your desire to join my team should be the deciding factor on whether or not you can go more. Seven."

It takes a moment, only a few seconds of heavy breathing and half groans and grunts, before he lowers himself farther.

I count faster and keep my boot on his back, then on his ass when he starts getting sloppy.

His face goes redder at that one and I'm tempted to keep it there just to fuck with his head. However, he's smart enough to slightly raise his back and draw my attention to it.

Once I switch my boot to his spine, he doesn't raise his ass again. Not even once.

He's on the verge of collapsing, though.

Good. He's obviously never pushed himself to physical exhaustion where he no longer feels his limbs, and that's exactly why I'm doing this.

He needs to realize that limits are only invented in his mind and could only serve as a self-made cage.

I'm twenty-eight now, so I can understand that, but a long time ago, when I was younger than him and had to deal with my father's games, I was as oblivious as this kid.

"Sir, I can't take it anymore." His voice and limbs tremble.

"Thirty-five."

"Sir…"

"Thirty-six."

"I'm—"

"Thirty-seven."

"I can't…" His voice chokes and he falls over, going limp all of a sudden.

Did he just...faint?

I tap his sweaty face once, then pause. That day, when I saw those soldiers cornering him, I heard sideways remarks. Things like:

He's so girly.

A weakling.

I bet he takes it in the ass.

A sodomite.

Usually, I would've walked away from such a scene, and in view of how persistent this shit has become since I saved him, I probably should've let him be.

But I didn't.

I wonder why. It probably had to do with the desperation on his face, and the way he intended to take the beating, no matter how brutal it got.

Now, I'm thinking about those soldiers' words again. More specifically, the girly part.

His skin is so soft, it's almost like butter beneath my fingers, and that's...fucked up.

Not because of the feminine part, but the fact that someone as delicate as he is, is hell-bent on joining the army. It's a place for brutes and outcasts like myself.

People who only know how to kill and need a license to do it freely and with a justified cause.

This is a nest for the orphans, the poor, and men who usually have no place to turn back to. Those who protect society are the very ones who were rejected by it.

I'm ninety-nine percent sure Lipovsky is a woman. The only reason I keep addressing him as a he is because that's the gender he chooses to display on the outside. In fact, he's making a lot of effort to avoid standing out.

He starts wheezing, his breathing morphing into an irregular rhythm. I grab him by a fistful in his shirt and turn him over so that he's lying on his back.

My boots are on either side of his waist, and I pause again at the sight of his face under the bright moonlight. Delicate, gentle features, small nose and mouth, soft facial curves.

Am I really the only one who sees the signs.

I'm about to release him when I sense something taut on his chest, right beneath the oversized T-shirt. I let his head fall to the ground and reach toward it.

A smaller hand grabs my wrist, halting me in my tracks. Lipovsky's eyes shine in the darkness, resembling a feral injured animal. I'm almost sure he'll start to snarl and hiss any moment now.

Like a powerless kitten.

He shakes his head once, whether in warning or suppliance, I'm not sure. This little fucker has the audacity to touch me.

I jerk my wrist from his hand and stand to my full height, but I don't change my position, so I'm glaring down at him. "Do you or do you not know that you fainted, sunshine?"

A red hue creeps up his neck. No shit. It splashes over the pale skin and spreads until it fully covers his ears.

Is he…blushing?

"I told you that I couldn't take it anymore, sir," he all but announces as if this is some sort of amateur training that he gets to quit whenever he wishes.

"Say that again." My voice has turned chilly, deadly almost, with no hint of coolness whatsoever.

Any smidge of red disappears from his face, and he meets my gaze with his weary one.

"Cat got your tongue?"

He purses his lips but has enough self-restraint to stop himself from talking and unavoidably earning himself a disciplinary punishment.

"You'll continue to do this training every day and you'll also add a muscle-building routine. Every night. Every morning. If

I find out you've missed any, you can kiss the military goodbye, because I could—and would—get you discharged, Private."

An expression of pure panic covers his features and his voice comes out a bit weak, apprehensive even. "I...can't leave."

"Why not?"

"I just can't. It's not safe for me out there."

"It's not safe for you here either, if you remain at this level."

He sits up, desperation coating him like an aura. "Please, sir, don't have me discharged."

"Begging is rather pointless. So instead of indulging in futile things, how about you do as you are told?"

He inches closer and grabs the threads of my boots in a fist as his eyes shine under the silver light.

I'm not sure if it's desperation, a last resort, or something in between.

"Sir, I—"

"Captain."

Lipovsky's words die in his throat as a new presence materializes in the silence. I don't have to look back to know who it is.

"A word," he insists in his gruff voice.

I crane my head to catch a glimpse of my longtime companion, my bodyguard since we were kids and the man who would offer his life for mine on a platter.

Viktor.

He's built like a giant, has more muscles than he needs, and he's been my right hand both before and in the army.

Needless to say, he enlisted just because I did. In fact, most of the men in my unit are the same as Viktor and have a similar level of infuriatingly persistent loyalty.

Part of their annoying behavior is cutting in without reading the atmosphere. The live example is how Viktor interrupted whatever Lipovsky was about to confess.

He slides back on the ground and then pushes to a standing

position and watches Viktor peculiarly. As if he's seen him before.

If discomfort could be observed on someone's face, Lipovsky's is emanating it in waves.

The view is worth watching, but not enough to have Viktor take interest in him, or worse, put him on some sort of shit list.

"Remember what I told you," I say, then turn around and head toward my guard.

Viktor throws one last glance at the private before he falls in step beside me.

"Who was that?" he asks with a note of doubt, suspicion, and every other synonym in the thesaurus.

Being distrustful is both his strongest and his weakest point.

"No one you should worry about." I glance at him. "What are you doing in camp? Shouldn't you be drinking or making sure the others aren't drinking too much?"

"Too late. The fools are wasted."

"No surprise there. They're celebrating being out of your dictatorial reign, Vitök."

"Are you sure that shouldn't be reversed to you, Captain?"

He's staring ahead, having not a care in the world after he threw out the statement as if it's a given.

"You must be tired of living." I speak in my usual somber tone, but that doesn't affect Viktor one bit.

"Speaking of living." He moves in front of me and stops, forcing me to do the same. "Your father is demanding your immediate return to the States. Apparently, things aren't the best."

"When have they ever been?"

"He said it's an order."

My jaw clenches.

The reminder of my so-called home and my father always brings a bitter fucking taste to my mouth.

It's too early to go back to that blood pit.

Not that there isn't blood here, but here, it's on my terms and with my methods.

"Let me guess, you're going to ignore him again," Viktor says, his brows drawn and that usual calculation passing through his gaze.

"You guessed correctly. Give yourself a pat on the back."

"Kirill, no. He will not let this slide."

"He can't do shit to me here."

"But—"

"This discussion is over, Viktor." I brush past him. "Let's bring the men back before someone gets in trouble."

They're the only people who matter. Everyone else, my family included, doesn't.

FOUR

Sasha

FOUR WEEKS PASS IN A BLUR.

At first, the rhythm was unbearably exhausting and drove me to the edge of my physical abilities. I nearly threw up and fainted multiple times. I considered quitting, but leaving the military institution was out of the question.

As my uncle insisted, if I'm out of here, it'll be a matter of time before I'm found and killed. Worse, I might even lead them to the rest of my family so that they can finish the massacre they started.

On the bright side, my endurance has improved with time, and I can go for hours without feeling the need to collapse.

When the captain caught me and started this challenge, I thought I would never get this far, but as he told me, it's only a mind game; once I learn the rules, everything will be easier.

Kirill Morozov. That's the captain's name.

I learned it during the time I've spent physically torturing myself to build my muscle strength.

It's been a steep hill to climb with lots of leg, arm, and abdominal work. He has no intention of making me buff since, according to his observations, my main advantage is speed and a 'decent' aim.

He still has every intention of pushing me beyond my limits, though.

A long time ago, I used to pride myself in being a strong, determined girl. I used to wrestle with Papa, my uncles, my brother, and my cousins. Running, sparring with wooden swords, and climbing trees were everyday occurrences.

I about gave my poor mama a heart attack every time I went home with my torn and grimy dresses, a dirty face, and disheveled hair. She used to give me the longest lecture as she bathed and dolled me up again.

Back then, I'd stare in the mirror and love how I looked. I adored the lacy dresses and my long blonde hair that reflected the sun. I used to play with my strands and reign as a princess over my cousins.

Despite my tomboyish activities, I loved how pretty Mama made me look. I just couldn't resist joining my brother and cousins whenever they went on a mischievous adventure.

If they were to see me struggling with training right now, they'd taunt, "Is that the best you can do, Sashenka?"

My shoulders droop as I hop down from the metal bar and stand on the ground. I continue staring at my feet, my hands balling into fists. The reminder that they're no longer here to tease or call me Sashenka anymore fills my heart with a cloud of suffocating smoke.

I tap my chest, resisting the urge to cry.

The more I tap, the more claustrophobic it gets. Gruesome images sneak into my subconscious.

I can almost feel the weight of my cousins' bodies covering mine. The *pop, pop, pop* sounds echoing in the air. The terrified shrieking, the pungent metallic smell of blood, and, eventually, how they became heavy.

They were so heavy, they crushed me. I couldn't breathe or speak. I couldn't—

A pair of big boots stop in front of me, and I straighten, thankful for the distraction.

No idea why those memories are hitting me now more than before. They were dormant for some time, but they've come back with a vengeance lately.

"It's time for the morning meeting," the newcomer announces in a gruff, unwelcoming voice.

He's Lieutenant Viktor. Captain Kirill's right-hand man. Or more like a persistent shadow. Whenever the captain isn't here to observe my progress, Viktor shows up, acting as unwelcoming as he looks.

I prefer the captain's company. No, not company. It's not like he's here to be my friend. It's that, if I had to choose, I'd pick his presence, supervision, and attention to detail.

Sometimes, it feels as if he knows my progress and my weaknesses and strengths more than I do.

Viktor is just harsh with no rhyme or reason, and I don't think he's liked me since our first meeting that night.

"Yes, sir," I say instead of asking why the captain isn't here.

Viktor would just glare, make me feel lower than the dirt beneath his shoes for even asking, and then he'd eventually dismiss me or flat out ignore me.

He starts down the hall, and I follow behind. The boots are no longer heavy, and they don't weigh me down, despite the exhaustion in my muscles. That's because I've gotten used to training in the morning and at night in addition to the official training.

Ordinarily, I wouldn't be allowed to do that by my direct superiors, but I think Captain Kirill has found a way around that regulation, because no one has bothered me since I started this marathon-like pace.

I wait for Viktor to go into the hall before I step inside. I grab a tray of food and sit in the only available spot, which, unfortunately, happens to be on Matvey and his gang's side.

Five pairs of eyes glare at me, but that's the limit of what they can do in public. After that time, Captain Kirill got them punished by our captain. I have no doubt that Matvey would finish what he started and avenge his wounded pride if he got the chance. Which is why I've made sure to avoid being in a position like the one from back then.

I'm stronger, but not strong enough to take on the five of them. Hell, even Matvey alone would be hard to defeat.

I stuff my face with the bland food. I used to eat way less than these men, but now, I'm a beast just like them. On the bright side, this means I'm improving my stamina.

It's all thanks to...

I crane my head to get a glimpse of the special ops table. Viktor sits at its head, and despite his gloomy nature, a general cheerful atmosphere radiates from the rest of the guys. They're all dressed in black, so they stand out against our green uniforms.

Some faces are as harsh as Viktor's, some are young, and others appear welcoming, serious, and, well...loyal.

I've heard so much about them. Most of those men followed Kirill from the United States. They're Russian, and most are Russian-born, but many, including the captain himself, are American-born. They still hold their Russian citizenship and have the right to serve in the Russian army if they choose to.

He recruited the rest from the professionally trained infantry he thought were worthy of joining his ranks.

One of them, a younger boy, probably about my age, laughs loudly, and Matvey clicks his tongue, then whispers, "Bunch of entitled fuckers thinking they're all that."

I narrow my eyes at him, but I tactfully choose to focus on my food.

"They're not even real Russians," goon number one agrees.

"How they think some Americanized motherfuckers are

worthy of Special Forces is beyond me," says goon number two before he chokes on his food.

Good. Hope he dies.

"Ever thought it could be something like, I don't know, skill?" I ask with a raised brow. "Besides, how are they less Russian than you, when they flawlessly speak the language?"

"You shut it, Lipovsky," Matvey snarls at me. "You get saved by the captain once, and you're suddenly a convert?"

I snort but say nothing. His jealousy of the special ops is showing, and anyone, his goons included, can see it.

"You have something to say, sodomite?" His tone hardens, and my temper flares.

Still, I regain my control as I say, "Oh, nothing. I was thinking maybe this animosity stems from the fact that you applied to the special ops and were rejected twice in a row."

"You damn—" He reaches out to me, but I duck and pretend that the food has all of my focus.

One of his goons brings him back down, whispering something about how we're being watched.

I smile at Matvey sweetly even as he turns a deep shade of red that's likely to explode any second.

"They're going back to their camp soon," goon number three says, trying to change the subject. "Good riddance."

My body goes still.

They're…leaving?

I cast a glance at the table, and, as if knowing I'd look at them, Viktor meets my gaze with his unwelcoming one.

Neither he nor the captain told me that they were leaving.

A weird sensation tightens in my chest, and I want to tap it, but I don't do that in public. I place my spoon on the table, suddenly losing my appetite.

It's not that I can't continue this pace on my own. With time, I can be strong enough to challenge Matvey and beat him.

But something's different when the captain's not around.

Yes, he's harsh, unforgiving, and has a mysterious way of destabilizing me, but all of that pales in comparison to how he's pushed me to grow into my strength.

He invested his time and teaching abilities in me—something no one but my family has ever done.

And now that he's leaving, I have no clue what to do.

If only I could be at that black table. They're so lucky to have him as a captain. Ours doesn't give a fuck about us on an individual level. All he cares about is collective results. Whenever I fall behind, he looks at me as if I'm a thorn in his side.

The chatter dies down and everyone stands and salutes. I follow suit as our and the special ops captains stride inside, following the major and lieutenant general.

I can't help being drawn to Kirill. He's the tallest of the bunch. He also has this mystic aura that's impossible to miss.

His purposeful strides eat up the distance even as he remains behind the other higher-ups. But for some reason, he feels like the most authoritarian figure here.

The most commanding, too.

"At ease," our captain says once they're all at the podium overlooking the entire hall.

A collective lowering of hands echoes in the room, followed by deafening silence.

"As you all know, the special operations unit was with us for collaborative training, but that has presently come to an end," our captain announces in a semi-bored tone. "The known information is that the unit will be leaving our camp in two days' time. But what isn't public knowledge is that Captain Morozov was here on a scouting mission. He has watched each and every one of you closely, studied your files, patterns, strengths, weaknesses, and mental abilities. He's picked the best five soldiers, who will leave with his unit. If he calls your name, step forward." He casts a glance to his side. "Captain."

I feel like I'm breathing through a straw. My heart beats hard and fast, in sync with every step he takes to the front.

If I'm selected to be part of the special ops, I'll have better security than the basic military institution. Hell, being closer to the higher-ups is a surefire way to get information about the massacre of my family.

Maybe if my uncle and I can locate the people behind this, we'll be able to get our revenge sooner and start a new life.

Maybe, just maybe, we won't be stuck in this life forever.

Captain Kirill calls the first name, a big man who's the best in our unit. He's so good at hand-to-hand combat that even Matvey doesn't go near him.

I understand the choice, but I can't help the slight drooping in my shoulders.

The second name is called. The third and the fourth follow. All are the best members of their units.

With each name that isn't mine, my heart falls to my feet. But I don't lose hope. Captain Kirill wouldn't have given me so much individual attention if he wasn't already thinking of having me join his unit.

I bet he didn't give the ones he already picked the same attention he gave me.

Unless…he did? Maybe that's why he sent Viktor sometimes. Maybe he preferred to use his time for better candidates like these men.

Captain Kirill's eyes study the crowd in an emotionless manner before they fall on me. It's a second, or merely a fraction of one, but it's enough to stifle my breathing.

Then he addresses the soldiers again. "Vasily Korosov."

The man in question steps forward and my heart shrivels and dies in a slow, painful death.

"Thank you, Captain…" The lieutenant general is about to take the reins, but I've completely zoned out.

I failed.

Again.

No matter what lengths I've gone to, I haven't been able to succeed. All I do is lose, unable to protect anyone. Not even myself.

This loss hits me stronger than I expected, because I genuinely worked harder than I ever have before. I challenged my physical, mental, and emotional limits. I went so hard on myself that I started getting cramps.

Last week, on our day off, I removed my chest bandages and went to see a doctor about it.

She said it's because the testosterone levels in my body are too high and it's messing up my hormonal cycle. She told me it might be better to switch from the shot to pills, but that would mean having my period back, so I refused.

And yet I've continued at the pace that I've become accustomed to and go beyond the mental cage my mind designed for me.

That hypocrite Kirill even said my shooting skills are a natural talent. He also nodded when he saw my improved physical chart.

Despite all of those reassurances, I still don't have a place in his unit.

I want to strangle him.

He could've just walked away. Why did he give me hope and then chose not to follow up on it?

"One more thing," Captain Kirill says, catching the other higher-ups by surprise. "I know I picked only five, but there's another member who has shown the most improvement since I got here and proved in action that he has the right mentality to join the special operations team. Aleksander Lipovsky, step forward."

The first thing I see is Matvey's open-mouthed expression that resembles a fish out of water.

The next thing I see is the blurriness in my vision, but I hold back the tears of immense gratefulness and triumph.

I don't know how I manage to do it, but I take a step forward and salute. I'm thankful my hand doesn't tremble and I don't start bawling my eyes out.

Captain Kirill meets my gaze, but there's no approval behind his icy eyes. He's really a cold man with a stone instead of his heart.

The lieutenant general congratulates us and blah blah blah, but I can't stop looking at the captain.

My new captain.

I know he's harsh and unforgiving. I know he has a tendency to make people uncomfortable in their own skin.

He's rumored to come from a family that deals in shady business. Hell, even his enlistment in the military is shrouded in mystery and reeks of unusual circumstances.

But I'm ready to forget all of that as long as he helps me improve my strength.

I have no clue what the future holds for me, but one thing's for sure.

I'll become strong enough to be able to spill the blood of those who massacred my family.

FIVE

Sasha

"YOU MADE IT TO SPECIAL OPS?"

I nod, kicking at a few pebbles, then slowly, almost sheepishly, raise my head to stare at Uncle Albert.

He's older than my late father, has bushy brows and a round face and a big nose, as well as pointy ears. My cousins and I used to call him the fat elf in our ignorant younger years.

Uncle Albert just laughed it off and even asked Papa and my other uncle not to reprimand us.

He was the mediator of the family, the account keeper, and the peace that maintained the bridge between my third volatile uncle and my hotheaded Papa.

Now, there's only he and I to protect the other two remaining members of our family. And, hopefully, find my brother one day.

Small hands reach out for my face, grabbing at air. "Sasha… Sasha…"

I scoop my youngest cousin, Mike, from Uncle's clutches. He's four years old and the only survivor of Uncle Albert's children. In fact, he's my only cousin who stayed alive.

Mike was lucky enough to be hidden away by his mother in the cupboard at the time of the massacre. The cost of that sacrifice was her life, but he, at least, didn't witness all the blood. He doesn't remember her, either, since he was only a few months old at the time.

I'd give my life to protect the innocence that shines in his light eyes. They translate everything beautiful and pure. Whenever I look at him, I'm reminded of the laughter, adventures, and mischievousness his elder siblings and I used to take for granted.

It wasn't until I lost them about four years ago that I realized just how privileged we were.

Mike's fair hair has grown, becoming longer and wilder, nearly eating up his small face. "You need a haircut, Mishka."

He giggles and then pats my cheek. "Man, Sasha."

"Am I?" I use my manly voice, and he breaks into a fit of giggles as he hugs me tighter.

"You are!"

"My little bear is so old now, he can even tell what I sound like."

"Yup! Babushka says I'm gonna be a big boy and help ya."

"You will?"

He rolls his eyes with so much attitude for a four-year-old. "Of course! You can't do it on your own, Sasha. You're no Superman."

"And you are?"

"I'm gonna be. And I'm also gonna stop Babushka from crying every night."

My heart squeezes, and I raise my head to gauge Uncle Albert's reaction. He's leaning against the wall of the old, deserted warehouse we agreed to meet in.

It took me a few hours of hitchhiking to get here, but it's located far enough from the heart of Saint Petersburg that no one could follow or locate me.

Our communications are done strictly through an encrypted

phone from my uncle's end and a burner from mine. I could've gotten one like his, but the chances of it being confiscated in the military are a lot higher than I'm willing to risk.

Gloomy silence creeps through the air of the small shed as the icy merciless winter air slips in from the cracks in the walls. The strong wind blows and whistles in a violent symphony.

Four years ago, we lost our family, our social standing, and our business. We had to stay in hiding and constantly moved from one nook of Russia to the next. Two years ago, we were found by mercenaries sent by our enemies, and once they heard I was still alive, they nearly managed to kill me if it weren't for Uncle.

Since my father was the head of the family, I'm the only heir alive. The only one who's able to gather his contacts and rebuild our business from scratch. Uncle and Babushka said it'll be dangerous if they learned I'm still alive, so they faked my death and I had to live as a man since. With a fake name and background.

A few months after that incident, I joined the army to find out who ordered the hit.

Uncle still has some contacts in there and he's also trying to rebuild our network, but it's hard when our last name is blacklisted in Russia.

"Is it true about Babushka?" I ask my uncle.

He throws up a dismissive hand. "That's not important right now. The fact that you leveled up does."

"Didn't you say the higher I climb in rank, the better?"

He nods solemnly as he pushes off the wall with difficulty and squeezes my shoulder the way my father used to do to my older brother. The memory makes my stomach coil, and my breathing deepens and hardens.

"I'm proud of you, Sasha." Uncle Albert's voice rings in the hollowness of my rib cage. "I knew you had the spirit of a warrior."

"I will do anything for our family." And I mean every word. I was too young and weak to stop the previous attack that robbed us of everything.

This time, it'll be different.

This time, I have the chance to accomplish something else.

"I know." He pats my shoulder once more before he releases me. "Promise me you'll be careful and not reveal your gender or identity. You're only safe when you're someone else, Sasha."

I nod.

"Don't get close to anyone who's prone to uncovering your real gender."

Another nod.

"I know you must feel lonely, but if you make any friends and they figure out who you actually are, none of us will be safe. I can disappear easily, but not with your grandmother and Mike. They'd slow me down and we'd eventually be in danger."

"That won't happen. I promise."

The stress of the past couple of years, ever since we fell from grace, covers his features. I stop and stare at the lines in the corners of his eyes and notice that he appears to have aged a decade or more since everything went down.

Ever since I enlisted, I've avoided visiting in order to prevent being followed. Uncle, however, is shackled by family matters—Babushka's health and temper, Mike's needs and livelihood, and all other measures he has to take to keep them well hidden and looked after.

I have no clue what I would've done without him.

Letting Mike play with the zipper of my coat, I lean in farther to whisper, "Have you found out anything about Anton?"

A sheen of sadness covers his features before he shakes his head. "I'm sorry, Sasha."

My heart squeezes, but I force a smile. "I'm sure we'll find him. Maybe he left the country or the continent. Or maybe he's laying low, knowing that we're being searched for."

"I suggest you take the worst into account, too."

I shake my head vehemently. "No. We didn't find his body, which means he's alive somewhere. I just know it."

My brother wouldn't abandon me. If he were dead, we would've found his corpse, but we didn't. I'm sure he escaped and is biding his time for revenge like Uncle Albert and I.

Maybe he was badly injured and has to undergo medical care. Whatever the reason is, I'm sure Anton is out there. Somewhere.

He's five years older than me, so he's twenty-five now. Probably doing everything in his power to survive like the four of us.

Sometimes, I hurt, wondering how he could've abandoned us. It's been almost four years, and my uncle's top-notch contacts haven't been able to find a trace of him.

Even if Anton was injured, it wouldn't have taken him years to get better, right?

Short of Mike's idle chattering and cheerful sounds, another cloud of gloomy silence overtakes the warehouse

I stroke his hair, greedily feeding off his bright energy. It's hard to believe that I was once like him—carefree, cheerful, and utterly unaware of the disaster that was brewing in the background. Those times feel like forever ago.

"We'll have to limit these meetings now that you're in special ops," Uncle Albert announces.

My fingers come to a halt in Mike's hair, and his father must pick up on the change in my demeanor since he elaborates, "It's not safe."

"But I can at least see you and Mike once in a while, right?"

"No, Sasha. Leaving the base to meet your supposedly dead family members will only warrant attention. That's the last thing we need."

My chin trembles, and I hate having the sudden urge to cry. The wound that's been pulsing beneath my flesh for four years gnaws and rips at the surface.

It's like I'm in the middle of that blood all over again. I'm losing the remnants of my family, and there's nothing I can do about it.

"Maybe once every few months?" I try in a voice so weak, I'm surprised he hears it.

My uncle shakes his head again. "Not while you're in the Special Forces. They have stricter rules and stronger intelligence. I'm just glad we can still bribe the medical examiner and give you some privileges, but everything else is dark waters we shouldn't tread near."

"Then when can I see you guys?"

"A year, or a few. Depends on whether or not you can find the one who ordered the hit within the army."

The pain in my chest grows and inflates. "He was a commandant, no? I won't be able to get close to him unless I'm promoted several times. That will take years, if not decades."

"Is that time not worth it?"

"It's not about time, it's about not seeing you again."

"A small sacrifice to make."

"Does…Babushka know about my future estrangement from the family?"

"She suggested this."

"Oh." My feet falter, and it takes everything in me to remain standing. I've never been my grandmother's favorite grandchild, but she loves me. In her own strict, somewhat patriarchal way.

It's no secret that she prefers boys. Girls are a liability—a means that could bring disaster and dishonor to their family—as my estranged aunt did when she eloped.

I've always felt like Babushka dislikes me for being saved by four of my male cousins, who all died. Her eyes tell me she wishes we'd traded places. But when I spoke to Uncle Albert about this, he said I was thinking too much.

However, he's an expert conflict avoider. Of course he'd try to build a bridge between her and me. As he did with Papa and my third uncle.

"You're still one of us. Even if the world knows you by a different name, gender, and appearance, I'll always remember you as my Sashenka."

"Uncle…"

"Say your name out loud, so you'll never forget it."

My lips tremble. It's been so long that it feels foreign on my tongue. "Aleksandra Ivanova."

"Sasha…Sasha…" Mike chants in my arms, and I smile.

When Uncle Albert attempts to take him away, he throws a fit and refuses to leave. He even announces that he's not on speaking terms with his father.

I kiss his forehead and smooth his golden mane of hair. "We'll meet again, Mishka."

"But when?"

"When you're older and stronger and you become Superman."

"Okay!" He grins, his eyes dripping with an endearing innocence.

The thought that I won't witness him growing up or hear his adorable laughter in the near future fills me with heavy desperation.

He goes to his father's arms without much protest this time, and I grab onto his coat for a bit too long before I kiss his cheek and finally let go.

"If there's anything urgent, send me the usual code," Uncle Albert tells me.

"And how will you reach me if there's something urgent from your side?"

"I have enough friends to get to you. Don't worry."

I release a resigned breath as he pulls on his and Mike's hoods, then they step out into the freezing air. My cousin continues waving and throwing kisses at me for as long as he can see me.

The moment they disappear into the distance, I slide to the ground, pull my knees to my chest, and finally let the tears loose.

After I've bid my uncle and cousin farewell, a crippling sense of loneliness grabs hold of me. It gets so bad that I find it hard to breathe or think.

To avoid being questioned, I don't go back to base right away.

I'm on the edge right now and I might crack too easily under pressure.

Usually, I'd be doing muscle-strengthening exercises during my day off, but today, I took a break and was so excited to see my uncle and Mike. I feel even more accomplished since I rose in rank.

Turns out, this promotion is more of a curse than a blessing.

It's been a week since I joined the Special Forces, and while it's more intense than in my previous unit, I've learned to push myself and gradually remove my mental cage.

The moment I get comfortable at a certain pace, Captain Kirill completely overthrows it. Not only that, but he also has Viktor as the supervisor in charge, and he's nothing short of a stoic, unbendable rock.

The other soldiers are used to him and his ways, so I'm the only one who has to adapt. Even the new recruits have integrated better than I have.

Absentmindedly, I roam the snowy streets for a few hours. The cold freezes my tears, but I still walk and walk. My feet come to a halt in front of a beautiful lace dress at the front of a shop. The creamy color gives it an elegant edge and the lace adds a beautiful feminine touch.

My heart swells. Will there ever be a day where I'll wear a dress again?

I internally shake my head. Even if I do get the chance, would I know how to move in a dress anymore?

It's been years since I wore one.

I begrudgingly step away from the shop and disappear in the herd of people. Once I'm calmer and have better control of my emotions, I head back to base.

I walk in with my back straight and my strides wide. It weirdly gives me confidence that I so desperately need in my current state.

The moment I step foot into the dormitory, large boots appear in front of me. I know who they belong to before looking up, and I straighten further before saluting.

"Where were you off to, Lipovsky?" Viktor's gruff voice sounds heightened in the silence.

"I went out for a stroll." I technically did, so it's not a lie.

"Is a stroll more important than training, soldier?"

"No, but it's my day off."

"What did you just say?"

My spine jerks, and I realize that maybe I fucked up and shouldn't have answered that way. Not that I'm lying, and I shouldn't be expected to be available for training on my days off, but someone as rigid as Viktor wouldn't understand. He has his set views and opinions, and he's like an unmovable mountain.

He reminds me of Babushka in some ways.

"Leave the newbie alone, Viktor." A different voice comes from behind me before its owner stops beside me.

The newcomer is another member of the unit. He looks a few years older than me, is built like a wall, and has angular yet weirdly welcoming features.

"You." Viktor points at him. "Stay out of it, Maksim."

"No can do. You're bullying the poor man." Maksim grabs me by the shoulder and basically drags me out back.

I don't resist, not even when I feel the murderous energy radiating from Viktor.

"Are you sure that was a good idea?" I whisper as we go outside. Instantly, my nose starts running and needles of cold penetrate my skin.

I'd rather stay in the semblance of warmth inside, but I doubt Maksim would hear that request. He seems like the type who sweeps you off your feet for some sort of adventure.

"Never mind! You don't know this, but Viktor is like a mountain you occasionally have to climb or simply jump over so that he stops being a pain in the ass, especially when we have an excuse such as a day off... Jesus, you feel so small, newbie."

I go rigid, but then I force myself to relax again. "My name is Aleksander."

"I'm Maksim. I noticed you being all stiff and alone this past week, and we don't do that shit in this unit." He tilts his chin forward. "How about some fun?"

We come to halt in front of a field for…football.

The soldiers are divided into two teams of eleven players. Concentration and contempt shine on their faces as if they're on the battlefield.

A flat-out war is taking place. Not only do they tackle and hit each other, but they basically step on one another on the artificial turf.

Maksim, showing little to no care about the brutal play, strolls into the middle of an attack and steals the ball. Then he tactfully slips from the clutches of a few angry players.

"You and you. Out." He points at two soldiers. "Lipovsky and I will be subbing in."

At the mention of my name, almost everyone's attention turns to me. I might not get as much shit from these guys as I did with Matvey and his goons, but they haven't warmed up to me either. They keep me at arm's length and barely address me at the meal table.

In fact, Maksim is the first one who's ever talked to me.

"It's okay," I say, conscious of the unpleasant energy. "I can watch."

"Nonsense." Still holding the ball, Maksim comes to fetch me by dragging me in a half chokehold that kind of cuts off my air, but I've come to know that guys generally handle each other with roughness.

In theory, I can fight the dragging, but in reality, I can't. And maybe, just maybe, I don't want to.

Despite my mother's protests, I played football with my cousins and my brother all the time when we were growing up. It's one of those games that holds a special place in my heart.

"Give back the ball, motherfucker!" someone shouts from the distance.

"That's Yuri," Maksim tells me. "The true motherfucker in this unit. Don't sleep near him, Aleksander, or you'll suffer a slow death. He snores like a dying pig."

Some soldiers laugh and point at Yuri, who glares at each and every one of them.

"Ready, bitches?" Maksim stands in the middle of the field, then—no surprise here—throws the ball in our team's direction instead of the middle.

Apparently, there's no formation in this thing. I'm not sure if I'm supposed to play defense, midfield, or offense. Turns out, everyone plays all spots at once.

All twenty-two soldiers are wherever the ball is.

No fouls are counted, no matter how many hits are exchanged. Cards? Forget about that. Fair play? No way in hell. In fact, the referee is egging the teams on and calling them names for not scoring.

To say it's chaos is an understatement.

This should be labeled combat football instead of the regular type.

Still, we keep losing the ball to the more aggressive players of the other team. They're also bulkier, which makes it unnerving to even look at them, let alone try to fight them for the ball.

At one of our aimless attacks, I stay back and tell Maksim to do the same. He raises his hands and shouts, "But we're missing all the fun!"

"Trust me," I mouth, not taking my eye off the ball. "I'll be right-wing, and you take the left. Whoever has the ball, the other runs forward, got it?"

"Well, all right. This plan better be worth missing the action for."

"It will be," I say with confidence.

As expected, a player from the other team steals possession of the ball, and he comes running in our direction.

Naturally, everyone else follows him like a herd. Maksim takes the one with the ball by surprise and steals it.

"Lipovsky!" he shouts, but I'm already running toward the goal. When he passes the ball, I'm there to catch it.

The other team runs at a frightening speed toward me. I don't wait to have the best shot and, instead, go in blind.

A couple of bodies slam into me, and I'm about to be knocked off my feet, but then I'm not.

The ones who attacked me are my teammates, and they're holding me up, cheering at the top of their lungs.

I scored.

Holy shit. I *scored*.

Maksim shakes me by the shoulders, then headlocks me. "I knew you'd fit right in, Aleksander."

I smile for the first time since I said goodbye to Uncle Albert and Mike.

"You can call me Sasha," I tell him.

"Call me Maks." He grabs me by the shoulder and faces the others. "I accept sacrifices for bringing in a scorer for the team."

They give him shit about that statement, and he just calls them names, then they're all flipping each other off.

Some soldiers slap me on the back, others welcome me aboard, and even the members of the other team give me a thumbs-up.

Does this mean I broke the ice with them?

Do I...finally belong here?

My smile falters when my gaze clashes with an icy one. Sometimes, it's like I'm staring at a piece of the Arctic Ocean.

Captain Kirill.

For the past week, he's mostly ignored my existence. Viktor was the one who oversaw my individual training while he gave the orders from afar.

For a second, I think maybe he's watching the game, but his arms are crossed, and his glare falls on me.

Frighteningly so.

My heart nearly beats out of my rib cage. I think there's a

problem with me. Otherwise, why would I feel like he's peeling my skin apart and revealing each and every one of my secrets?

And for some reason, I think he might be well capable of that.

The reality of the situation hits me then. Captain Kirill may be what makes me stronger, but he's also dangerous.

The type of danger that will swallow me alive if I don't keep my cards close to my chest.

SIX

Kirill

I READ THE REPORTS MY INTELLIGENCE SERGEANT SENT OVER and study every detail with keen interest.

The reason my unit is the most successful isn't because I have the best men—though I do consider them incomparable. It's also not due to strength or weaponry.

Every success we've had thus far is solely based on strategy. Numbers, offense, and danger level mean nothing if I devise the right plan to keep us one step ahead.

It's one of the reasons my father didn't want me to leave the States. My family depended so much on my plans from the time I was a kid. Everything my father did was low-key instructed or inspired by my tactics.

Needless to say, he's been feeling bitter since I left for the army a couple of years ago and took away his goose that lays the golden eggs.

Viktor likes to give me reports about the state of affairs back home, despite my explicit instructions not to. His excuse is that I need to be in the loop because knowledge is power, and, apparently, according to Viktor's spies, my dickhead of a brother is subtly confiscating that power after having crowned himself the head of the family once my father retires.

Of course, the process is taking place with the help of my mother. Or, more accurately, Yulia. Yes, she is the woman who gave birth to me, just like my father was the one who donated the sperm, but neither of them should've been anyone's parents.

But I digress. Only slightly.

My focus homes back in on the intelligence report in front of me and I reread it one more time.

Tomorrow's mission has to be perfect. I'll accept no failure or losses.

In fact, my plan is so bulletproof that my men and I should be able to complete it in half the time given to us.

All we have to do is land near the insurgents' nest by the mountains. Divide into two teams to clear them out from both sides. My snipers will take care of the loose ends and then, it's all history.

No matter what angle I look at it, the mission is so easy, it's insulting. But I don't underestimate the possibility of something going wrong.

A knock sounds on the door before it opens, and Viktor appears like a wall at the threshold. I've known him all my life, but that doesn't change the fact that he's a grim, stoic, and an absolute dull sight to look at.

"They're ready," he announces.

"Have you divided their roles?"

He nods.

"Very well." I push off my chair and burn the intelligence report. I already learned it by heart, so there's no need for a physical copy.

Viktor and I stride down the hall in silence. I can tell he has things to say—he always does and has played the role of a thorn in my side for decades—but he, thankfully, chooses to keep his thoughts to himself tonight.

Which is all the better since I'm a million percent sure whatever he has to say will be about returning home, taking back the power, and putting my brother and mother in their places.

What Viktor doesn't know, however, is that everything needs to happen in its own time.

My men are having dinner after a long training day. I gave them so much shit to do, I wouldn't be surprised if they're too tired to eat or sit properly. But then again, I can't have any mistakes tomorrow.

They had to learn the path we'll take by heart. If someone makes a mistake, he'll risk not only his life, but also the life of his teammates.

I'm ready to give them some leeway tonight—

I come to a halt at the entrance.

Instead of the gloomy, somewhat careful atmosphere I've come to expect before every mission, the hall bubbles with the exact opposite.

Utensils have been thrown around, drinks have been spilled everywhere, and some sort of an eating competition is going on in the corner. Laughter, cursing, and idle teasing fill the space to the brim.

But most of all, the mood is laid-back.

Maksim and Rulan are singing in their god-awful voices that I wouldn't wish on an enemy. Then in the midst of the human rights violation, a softer voice slips through.

My eyes narrow on the slim, frail soldier between my men, and it's none other than Lipovsky.

Of course.

Why am I not surprised that he's in the middle of all of this?

The others clap, shout, or bang their cups on the table in rhythm with the singing. Yuri yells for Maksim and Rulan to shut

the fuck up because they're overshadowing Lipovsky's more pleas-
ant voice, to which they sing louder.

My attention remains on Lipovsky.

Bringing him to the unit wasn't a well-studied decision. Yes,
he showed improvement, and I could see the potential in him, but
he's too much work that's not worth it.

No matter how much he strengthens his muscles, he's still
the weakest physically. He's also the one with the most glares and
subtle avoiding techniques.

He's been part of my unit for a month, and he's tactfully managed to avoid alone time with me for just as long.

It's subtle things, such as always remaining in a group and
joining Maksim's foolish antics and Yuri's physical routine.

Ever since the day he helped Team B win the football game
for the first time in months, they've all switched to his side. He has
effortlessly blended into the group and gotten used to the unit. Not
only as a soldier, but also as an actual member of a community.

Although we have a paramedic, he personally cleans the
wound of whoever gets injured and even has a small medical kit
on standby. The fuckers actually prefer him over the medic because
he's apparently more gentle.

The fuck they care about gentleness when they're soldiers?

Needless to say, he's a bad fucking influence. I could've avoided
this annoying shift in my men if I'd simply left him to rot in his
previous unit.

"Is it too late to ship him back to the infantry?" Viktor whispers my thoughts.

Or what he thinks are my thoughts.

Taking Lipovsky in was a moment of chaos that I would repeat again in a heartbeat. Yes, he's an infuriating little fucker, but
he's disciplined and plays well with the team. He's also an excellent
sniper, who's only missing some field action.

He's neither antagonistic nor individualistic. Bonus point, he
actually cares about his colleagues' well-being.

The moment Yuri became friends with him, I learned just how influential Lipovsky could be. Maksim knows everyone and is friends with the whole army.

Yuri, on the other hand, has never felt at ease, except in Maksim's company and, now, with the newcomer. After a certain incident a few years ago, he had to have reparative surgery and drew further into himself. Until Maksim took it upon himself to get him out of his funk. Unknowingly, Lipovsky has been helping with that, too.

And Yuri is an influential strategist in my arsenal. So whenever he's in a good mood, I can count on getting the best results from him.

"He's useful," I tell Viktor.

He looks at me as if I'm the fruit of Satan and an unruly hooker, not bothering to hide the map of disgust covering his face. "He's a fucking weakling who spends twice as much time to do the same activities the others do."

"It's one point five now. Not twice."

"Still more than needed."

"You weren't born a mountain, Viktor. Improvement takes time."

He narrows his eyes. "If I didn't know better, I would say you're defending the slimy fucker."

"Like fuck I am. But someone has to play devil's advocate."

The truth remains, as much as I dislike the change to plots and strategies, I prefer the unit when he's around, which is a weird confession that took me some time to come to terms with.

I step forward, and Viktor follows suit. Upon seeing us, all the noise dies down as the soldiers straighten and salute.

Viktor gives them the 'at ease' motion, and they comply at once. My gaze strays to Lipovsky, who's still between Maksim and Rulan, face red and so soft, it should be a crime for him to be in the military.

You're getting distracted again.

I let my eyes wander to the rest of my men. "As you all know, we're departing tomorrow for the mission. Viktor already divided the roles, and we practiced the path we'll take enough times that you should be able to recognize it in your sleep. Starting tonight, I want you to forget everything, including your names, and only remember the plan. As usual, I'm going to need you all to come back in one piece. If you die, I will kill you."

Some snicker, others nod while hiding laughter, but one stern look from Viktor is enough to throw them back into the serious mood.

He's an asshole. No doubt about it. A useful asshole, but an asshole all the same.

"We'll go through the plan again tomorrow morning," I continue. "You're dismissed."

They salute again, and I turn to leave. Viktor stays behind, probably to nag them like an old hag for daring to have fun.

When I'm in the hall, I notice I'm not alone. I can also figure out who it is without looking back. Only one in my unit has light footfalls without trying to conceal them.

"What do you want, Lipovsky?" I ask as I turn around.

He comes to an abrupt halt and swallows thickly. His shirt is crumpled at the top, revealing the hair-thin veins peeking from beneath his fair skin.

Lipovsky, obviously caught off guard, shifts on his feet, studies his surroundings, and breathes heavily before he finally looks at me.

"I don't have all day," I say when he remains statuesque without saying anything.

"You...Viktor gave me the role of backup."

"So?"

"Why can't I be on the front lines?"

"Because you're too volatile and I can't trust you in a precise and sensitive spot."

"I score among the top five in sniping."

"That means nothing when you lack on-field experience."

His eyes shine with that infuriating challenge that both made me notice and want to squash him beneath my shoes that first time. "How would I get that experience if you don't give it to me...sir?"

The little fuck has the audacity to act all proper and according to protocol. It'd be so easy to destroy him and break his spirit enough that he'd willingly leave.

But that's neither necessary nor fun.

I step forward. "I might give you a chance if you answer a question."

He straightens and, curiously, his colorful eyes become a bright green. "Yes, sir."

"Why have you been avoiding me?"

His shoulders hunch so fast, it would be comical under any other circumstance. "I...have not."

"Night, soldier."

"No, wait." He jumps in front of me so that his chest nearly slams against mine.

I stare down at him, and I can smell the soft tones of his skin. The little fucking tease.

"Are you blocking my way, Lipovsky?"

He jumps back, his chest heaving. "No, sir. I just...can I be honest?"

"When have you ever not?"

His eyes meet mine for one second, two, before he shifts them downward and murmurs, "You make me uncomfortable, that's why."

Well, well, would you look at that?

It takes everything in me not to grab him by the throat and throw him against the nearest wall.

But then again, all the scenarios I'm picturing in my head are frowned upon, especially with someone who's supposed to be under my care.

So I step past him.

"I answered you. Are you going to give me a chance?"

"No."

"But you said—"

"I might consider it. I did that and decided against it." I disappear down the hall and catch a glimpse of the insolent soldier glaring at my back.

Good. Because I'm going to make him even more uncomfortable going forward.

To the point where he'll hate his own skin and regret ever crossing my path.

⌐

On the day of the mission, everyone is on high alert.

However, it's not the suffocating type where it feels like a mistake is waiting to happen.

My team is focused and have the level of training to keep their heads in the game.

The sooner this is done, the faster we'll get to leave.

I'm about to head out of my office when someone barges through the door. Before I contemplate smashing their head in and using the corpse as my new mattress, the man in question comes into view.

His round belly precedes him in presence and has more character than the man himself. At least that belly has been consistent, which can't be said about him.

An air of confident smugness coats each and every one of his beady features. His darker eyes shine with pure evil. His nose is straight, high, and makes him look as arrogant as a god.

That's about the only physical feature I inherited from the man. I mostly take after my mother—something he and I share a mutual disregard for.

Viktor appears at the threshold behind him, wearing a rare apologetic expression.

He of all people knows that Roman Morozov and I shouldn't share the same continent, universe, or time—period. In fact, seeing him on the day of my mission is no different than dreaming about ravens, crows, and serpents eating from my skull.

And I'm not even superstitious.

There's no need to ask how he got here. My father has the type of power that enables him to stuff some politicians in his pockets and some military leaders in his service.

The only thing he's pissed about is that he doesn't have enough power to have me discharged yet.

I glance at Viktor and he nods, then steps outside.

Not wanting to look at my old man's putrid face, and not having the option to pray for his disappearance, I busy myself with checking my weapons.

I dismantle my rifle slowly, taking my time in doing the task. "To what do I owe this unpleasant visit?"

"You were always an insolent little fucker," he heaves, probably due to the effort he exerted to carry his belly here.

"Kind of learned from the best."

I don't look at him, but I can feel the heat of his glare hitting the back of my neck. He surely doesn't waste time in letting his true colors show through.

Having obviously lost the battle of remaining in a standing position, he all but marches over and throws his weight on my chair. Right opposite to where I'm perching on the desk.

His face is too big for his neck, his hands are too fat, his veins are about to pop, and he's sweating profusely, not even saved by Russia's winter.

"I haven't seen you in a year and this is the welcome I get?" He stresses his words in that holier-than-thou tone. The one he uses whenever he decides to 'punish' me.

Teach me the way.

Make me learn how to become his suitable 'heir.'

"You haven't seen me in a year, but I'm curious how you still expect some form of a welcoming ceremony." I lift my head. "Have you earned some royal title I'm not aware of?"

"You fucking—" He lifts his hand off the desk. It's a habit at this point that the old fuck has had trouble getting rid of.

I stare right at that hand, daring him to hit me.

Just touch me, Roman. I fucking dare you.

He lowers it back down, knowing full well I'd shoot him between the eyes.

I told him as much the last time he hit me—when I was fifteen. I said if he does it again, I'll kill him, butcher his corpse, and bury it where the sun doesn't shine.

He's been taking it seriously. That and I'm way stronger than him. I can take ten of him combined.

Roman Morozov was once the strongest man I knew. Now, he's nothing but a shadow of his former self. A clown of a fat old man whose body is riddled with enough diseases to put an entire hospital to shame.

He smooths his ugly gray tie that looks like it was stolen from a nineties B movie. "You haven't been replying to my calls or letters. Why?"

"I told you why." I click the magazine in place. "In fact, I told you the reason four years ago when I left."

"I will not be accepting that nonsense. As my eldest son, it's your duty to inherit the empire and lead the Morozov family."

"That's such an honor," I say with the most sarcasm I can muster. "But I'm going to have to pass. Let Konstantin do it."

"Konstantin is a reckless motherfucker that I wouldn't trust with the safety of a goldfish, let alone my family."

"You made him; you deal with him. Not my problem, not my talk to have."

"Kirill." He bangs both hands on the desk and rises to his full height. The motion is supposed to be some form of intimidation, but it looks more like a dying man's last plea for help.

"Yes?"

"The situation has changed in the Bratva since you left. My

position is no longer secure and there are even hints that I might be replaced by some new blood."

"Thanks for the info. I'll call when I find any fucks to give."

A dark shadow falls over his features, mingled with a putrid sense of desperation.

A long time ago, when I painted his world black and he did the same to mine, I would've given my left ball to see him like this.

Hopeless, desperate, and on the verge of spilling his beloved pride at my feet, just so I would benefit him and his empire with my services.

Now, it brings nothing but the knowledge that he's pathetic.

"What should I do so you'll quit this fucking madness and come back home?"

"The time for you to do anything has long passed. And you, dear Papa, have no say in my life anymore."

"Or maybe that's what you think."

I stare him in the eye, refusing to let him get into my head. He's done it enough for a lifetime. Even if his threat is valid, I won't let him have the power anymore.

"Are you done? Because if you are…" I point a thumb behind me. "The door is right there."

"One last chance. Are you going to come back willingly?"

"Sure. Hit me up for your funeral."

His face turns a deep shade of red, but my expression doesn't change and neither does my demeanor.

My father leans forward and snarls. "You'll regret this. I might have tolerated this stupidity, but my patience has limits, Kirill. You're not suited for leading men on the battlefield, fighting other people's wars and getting nothing but fuck all as a reward. You're my heir and were always meant to lead and grow the Morozov Empire. Fight it all you want, but you'll always be my son. You will always be like *me*."

My upper lip lifts in a snarl and I realize I almost let him into my head again. A blasphemy that shouldn't happen in this lifetime.

"See you at home, son." He pats my shoulder, then squeezes it before he's out the door.

I grab the nearest object but stop myself before I haul it against the wall.

He will not get to me.

I already won my freedom and nothing will be able to take it away.

Nothing.

"Is everything okay?" Viktor asks after my father leaves.

I fling the rifle over my shoulder. "It will be. Let's get this over with."

SEVEN

Sasha

I CAN'T BREATHE.

My feet refuse to move, and my heart thunders in a rhythm so intense, I'm surprised it hasn't ripped its way out of my rib cage and spilled at my feet.

Invisible hands claw harder at my throat the longer I stare at the man's face.

I wouldn't have missed it if I'd tried. I couldn't. The sight of his round face, thick build, and half-bald head is engraved in my memories as if I saw him yesterday.

He was at our house a few days before the massacre. My brother and cousins didn't know, because they were forbidden from the office area, but I snuck about with Mama when she was bringing them drinks.

I hid by the wall and saw this same man sitting on the chair with a nonchalant coldness while Papa and my uncles spoke heatedly.

The reason I could never forget his face is because of the psychopathic-like disinterest he held for the whole conversation. I didn't hear much because Mama quickly shut the door and shooed me away, but I heard Uncle Albert ask in a supplicating tone, "Just one more chance…"

I remember thinking a man like that wouldn't give whatever chance Uncle Albert was asking for, and I was right. I have no clue how involved he was in the annihilation of my family, but I know for certain that he played a role in it.

A major one.

It's no coincidence that he was at our house only a few days before it was transformed into a bloodbath.

It's also not a coincidence that I've seen him here, in the Special Forces camp, of all places, now of all times. Civilians aren't allowed inside training military institutions, so he must have some sort of link to the higher-ups. This is probably fate giving me a chance to avenge my family by so fittingly putting him in my path.

A red haze covers my eyes, and my muscles home in for action. I forget why I wandered here in the first place. My physical being slowly detaches from my mental being until only one thought beats beneath the surface of my skin.

Kill.

Shoot.

Revenge.

The man moves lethargically, walking with the speed of a turtle, probably due to his large build. A disapproving look covers his features, turning his face blue. There's nothing of the nonchalant coldness he regarded Papa and my uncles with that day.

No aristocratic haughtiness that made me want to punch him in the face even back then.

I study my surroundings, forcing my bloodstream and breathing back to normal. In fact, they're so low, I'm slipping into the category of camouflaging my existence. A technique I've learned since I joined the special ops.

Viktor, who's standing by the door the man came out of, slips inside and conveniently disappears from view.

Since he was followed by an army of guards the other time, I'm sure they're waiting for him outside. I only have this chance to get rid of the man.

My steps are inaudible, and my movements turn fluid as I slip forward in pursuit. Once I'm close enough to perceive the glistening sweat on the back of his neck, I lean down and retrieve the knife stashed in my boot.

The closer I get, the more I suppress my breathing, mentally preparing myself for the strike.

But the moment I'm about to stab him, a shadow appears from the opposite end of the hall.

In a second, I jump back behind a wall and glue my body to it.

The shadow is his guards. Not one, but three. Burly, tall, and with mean expressions written all over their features. If I'd killed him, I'd be in shreds about now.

My breathing heightens, coming out heavy and irregular. A tear clings to my lid as I stare at him being escorted out of reach.

There's no worse frustration than lacking power.

If I were stronger, those three guards wouldn't have fazed me, and I would've finally started getting revenge for my family.

But I'm not stronger and, therefore, will be stuck in this position of thinking 'almost' and 'could've.'

"Here you are."

I hide the knife in the belt of my pants and dab at my eyes as a body crashes into me from behind and wraps an arm around my shoulder.

Maksim has that usual joyful gleam on his face, but there's the general wariness everyone brims with today. "Why are you here, Sasha?"

My mouth goes dry, but no answer comes out. Why the hell did I come here in the first place...?

Seeing that man turned my head entirely blank, and I forgot

why I wandered here alone instead of being part of what the guys call a 'mission ritual,' which is basically meditating and worshipping their weapons.

Maksim stares down the hall, then narrows his eyes on me.

He has a boyish charm and an easygoing presence that I've gotten used to ever since he 'took me under his wing.'

Now, however, he looks suspicious. "Have you come to see the captain?"

Oh. I remember now.

"Yeah, the captain! I wanted to ask him one more time to give me a chance."

I swear I lost a few years of my life when I made the decision to stand face-to-face with Captain Kirill. Since our last encounter, I've been dreading looking him in the eye, let alone having any alone time with him.

Hell, I was ready to bribe Viktor to go with me, even though his company isn't that enjoyable. It's still less intimidating than the captain's, though.

But then I saw the man from the past, and all my plans went to hell.

"Either you're too naïve or too foolish if you think Captain would change his mind after making a decision." Maksim ruffles my hair. "You'll learn, though."

"You said you've known him since you were born?"

"Yeah, my father works for his father." He grins. "But I was too cute for my own good, so the family doted on me, in a way. Everyone except for Captain, that is."

"Why?"

He releases me, then glares in a perfect imitation of the captain's usual expression. "He was born looking exactly like this and being Mister I Hate the World, and I'm Going to Keep Viktor Close So We Can Hate the World Some More."

I smile. "Was it always that bad?"

"I'm kidding." He lets his hands drop. "Viktor had a mutation and has actually become way worse."

I hit his shoulder jokingly. "You're an asshole."

"I'm a funny asshole. There's a difference." His expression sobers. "In all seriousness, Captain is a product of his father's rigid upbringing. You know how they say some monsters are born and others are made? He falls right in-between."

"Rigid upbringing how?"

"Nothing you should worry about." He subtly ignores my question and points down the hall. "Let's get out of here before Viktor hears and comes up with creative methods for our punishment."

"But I haven't said anything."

"You listened and laughed. That counts."

I follow after, begrudgingly giving up on convincing the captain, even if a part of me is glad that I don't have to face him.

"Hey, Maks?"

"Yeah?"

"You said the other day that most of you grew up together," I circle back to the previous topic. "Does that mean everyone has come here at the order of the captain?"

"Not everyone—about seventy percent. And there was no order. Boss, Captain Kirill, decided to leave the family and enlist, so many of us followed."

"Just like that?"

"Just like that." Maksim lifts his shoulder. "Some do it for the action, but most of us are just loyal to him. Not to the level of Viktor's stoic loyalty, but those who came to Russia prefer him over any other member of the family. Besides, it doesn't hurt to gain experience in the meantime."

He speaks the words with so much affinity and sure determination. For some reason, I'm jealous of the captain. I wonder what he did that these guys would follow him blindly to the pits of death, just because he decided to leave his privileged life and enlist.

"No one in the family approves of his choice to come here," Maksim continues. "More accurately, the old boss doesn't approve. He comes around once a year or so to personally try to drag him back."

"The old boss?"

"Captain's father. You just saw him leave. That old, round man?"

My lips part, and I fall a step behind him. "That's…the captain's father?"

"Sure is. His name is Roman Morozov. We all paid our respects to him just now when you disappeared since he's our boss's father. He's always bitching about how we should go back to New York, and although we nod absentmindedly, we mean nothing of it. Where Captain goes, we go."

My hand trembles, and it takes effort to stop it from giving away my state.

The man who definitely played a role in my family's demise is the captain's father.

Why did he have to be his father?

But most importantly, what am I supposed to do with this information now?

⟳

At the start of the mission, everyone is on high alert.

Since I'm backup, I remain where the captain ordered us to—near him. We're all the new additions to the unit, and even though some have more combat experience than me, I'm consoled by the fact that they're also kept on backup.

Our mission today is to infiltrate a warehouse where illegal weapons are stored, apprehend or kill the terrorists, and then report our findings back to base.

We've landed near the warehouse that's strategically located

in a cave under a dome of snow. As per the training we've been re-
peating for weeks, we have successfully crawled to the warehouse.

Captain raises his fist, stopping all of us in our tracks behind
some large trees. He motions at the snipers to take their positions.
Three soldiers crawl away to find the preapproved locations that
offer a clean shot.

The rest are divided into Team A, led by Rulan; Team B, led
by Viktor; and Team C, aka the stupid backup, led by the captain
himself.

Captain Kirill motions at us to stand, using the trees as
camouflage.

According to the mission map, Rulan and company should've
been out already. It's not wise to delay these types of encounters
any longer than needed, considering their volatile nature.

However, the captain has been looking at the barely visible
windows of the warehouse for the past five minutes, unmoving,
like a wall of muscles.

He's wearing his helmet and is turned away from me, so I can't
see his expression, but I can see the stiffness that mounts from his
legs to his back.

If it were any other time, I'd probably be attuned to the
changes in him, but after finding out the identity of his father, I'm
not sure how to act around the captain anymore.

I can't use him to get to his father since Maksim mentioned
they have a muddied relationship. But at the same time, I can't just
forget that he's a product of that man.

Maybe my initial apprehension about the captain was correct, after all.

He's bad news and dangerous.

Rulan cuts off my hyperfocus on him when he advances forward. "Permission to go in, Captain?"

"Not yet." He stares up, then down, as if searching for an invisible needle in the snow.

"Is something the matter?" Viktor whispers so low, I wouldn't have been able to hear him if I were in the back.

"Something's off." Kirill tilts his head to the side. "No one is around."

"It was snowing just now. They're probably hiding," Rulan says, to which Kirill shakes his head once.

"Storms and snow don't scare these people. They'd have patrols to secure the premises and watch out for intruders. Unless... they knew we were coming."

"That's impossible," Viktor interjects. "Only the base knows about this mission. Our intelligence has no leaks to warrant this suspicion."

"Yeah, Captain. We trained so hard for this mission that we can do it with our eyes closed," Rulan says, and the others nod in agreement.

Heavy silence falls over the team. No one talks as we wait for Captain's decision.

He doesn't look convinced. If anything, he's surveying the premises harder than before.

But since he's the leader of this operation, he has to make a decision.

He slides his gloved fingers up and down his rifle in a methodical, controlled rhythm. Everything he does oozes authoritativeness. I've been in the army long enough to meet men who idolize control, but they soon revert back to their old selves once no one is there.

Not Kirill.

It's part of who he is. A personality trait that can't be separated from his essence.

His movements come to a halt before he announces in a clear voice, "Only Team A will proceed. Team B will be backup."

Viktor gives him a look, probably feeling left out of all the fun.

"It'd be faster if we go at the same time," someone from Team B, none other than Maksim, says, not giving a damn about the glare his team captain gives him.

"Only Team A," Captain repeats. "And, Rulan, I want you to follow your gut. If there's anything amiss, don't wait for my signal. Retreat to the pickup point, got it?"

"Yes, sir." He salutes, then motions at his team members to follow him.

Viktor and his men slip between nearby trees to their positions. They strategically crawl away to avoid triggering any of the mines that we already know the locations of due to the intelligence.

It looks easy, but it takes a lot of concentration and memory to avoid all of them while going unnoticed.

"You three." Captain motions at the guys with me. "Go back up the other snipers. Any suspicious movement, you shoot to kill."

"Yes, sir." They scatter as well so that it's only me and the captain.

I inch closer to him, my hand tightening on my rifle. "What about me, Captain?"

"You stay still." He's speaking to me, but his attention is on where Rulan and the others have disappeared to.

"Maybe you should've done everyone a favor and left me at the base then," I mutter under my breath.

The captain faces me with frightening slowness. Only his eyes are visible from beneath the helmet and they're narrowed with obvious disapproval.

"Are you talking back to me, soldier?"

"No, sir." It takes everything in me not to click my tongue.

"You obviously have dissatisfactions. Voice them."

"Those three guys score lower than me. Why do they get to be backup and I do nothing?"

"Because I said so. Do you need another reason?"

I think I glare at him. No, I'm sure I do, but I catch myself quickly and lower my head.

The dictatorial asshole.

He steps forward, unapologetically barging into my space. I

have to remind myself that I'm a 'man' and men don't cower, especially if they want to be taken seriously as a soldier.

I have to remind myself that the captain is only trying to intimidate me, but the pep talk does nothing to slow the rhythm of my heart.

Just why the hell does he affect me this way?

It doesn't help that I'm inhaling him with every intake of air. It's impossible to ignore his presence that dwarfs mine or his height that makes me feel like he's a giant.

Breathing near him is no different than sucking air through a straw.

And this isn't normal.

"Lift your head, Lipovsky. I want you to look at me again the same way you did just now."

There's a dropping quality to his voice, like it's become deeper and lower than his normal speaking tone.

And now, I'm downright scared about looking at him. Maksim told me Captain is always a wild card.

It takes a man of a certain caliber to leave a family of the Morozov's standing, just to play a game of death.

I'm slowly starting to see what type of man Captain Kirill is, and I certainly don't want to be on his shit list.

Not now. Not ever.

But he's being unreasonable by banning me from the action, so I do glare when I look up.

His eyes are ice cold, but there's a hint of fire brewing beneath the surface. It's subtle and discreet, but it's right there.

Captain reaches a hand out for me, palm open, and a prickling sensation of danger tingles down my spine.

It's like I'm facing the paw of a lion on the brink of an attack.

My first thought is to run.

But before I can do that, a loud *boom* echoes in the air.

EIGHT

Sasha

FOR A MOMENT, I DON'T MOVE.

Time stops, and my surroundings plunge into an unnerving sea of silence.

Then everything comes crashing down. Something of inhuman strength grabs my shoulder, pushes me forward, and shoves me down. My knees hit the snow-covered soil, and my chest follows, knocking the breath out of my lungs.

At first, I think the explosion was so big that it blew me away and I'm currently dying. All my goals, hopes, and little-girl dreams start flashing before my eyes.

However, the cold hits my bones and I taste it on my tongue. The savage grip is still on the back of my head, shoving me into the snow and forbidding me from moving an inch.

The residual shock wave of the explosion buzzes in my ears. It's impossible to make out my surroundings, but I can hear gunshots and a distorted "Go, go, go!"

I try to lift my head, and the firm grip slowly loosens but doesn't disappear.

"Stay down." The harsh command rises above the warped noise in my ears.

I don't have to look to know it's the captain. He has a distinctive voice and presence that's impossible to mistake.

The loosening of his grip allows me a glimpse at the situation. We're both crammed behind a tree opposite the warehouse where the sound of the bomb came from.

My lips part as the gruesome image comes into view.

The warehouse is on fire.

Shreds and tendrils from the blown-up building and blood smudge the whiteness of the snow. Some pieces sink into it, and others form a pool of water around them.

But that's not the sight that chills me to my bones. It's the human limbs scattered everywhere. They fill up the field of snow like props.

Those…those clothes are…ours.

Those men are from my unit.

A shrill sound of panic screeches in my ears. Images of blood and corpses with holes in them invade my head.

Screams. Wails. Tears.

Pop.

Pop.

Pop—

Just like back then, I'm helpless, and so broken, I can't even stop the bleeding, let alone save anyone.

They're dead.

I'm not.

They're—

"Breathe, Lipovsky." The authoritative voice sounds so close to my ear, I flinch. "Fucking breathe, Aleksander."

His command has a firm roughness, and I look down to find

that my fingers are curled around the rifle's trigger, and my shoulders are shaking so hard that I can't control them.

"Look at me." It's that voice again. There's nothing gentle about his tone, not even an attempt to sound nice, but maybe that's precisely what I need, because my head slowly turns to the side.

My chaotic breathing evens out as I'm caught off guard by the icy depths of the captain's blue eyes. Staring into them is no different than being trapped at the North Pole.

"That's it. Breathe." His voice lowers further, and it's almost welcoming but still commanding. "I'm going to need you to snap the fuck out of it, or you'll die. Do you hear me?"

Slowly but surely, I regain control of my breathing. The shaking stops, and I nod sharply.

"Use your voice, soldier."

"Yes, sir."

"Team A was hit, and Team B went in as backup, so we'll need to cover for them. Are you able to take a shot?"

Adrenaline rushes into my limbs, and I instinctively tighten my hold on my rifle. "Yes, sir."

"If you don't have the mental capacity, stay out of it. I will not have you endanger my men's lives with your indecisiveness."

"Those men are my friends." I lift my chin. "I will do whatever it takes to get them out of this alive."

There's a short pause before he nods and motions at one of the nearby trees. "Go there."

"Why not one of the previously designated spots?"

"Those are compromised. We lost all our snipers." He says it without a hint of emotion, as if he didn't just announce that many of the people I've started to consider my second family are gone.

A slight tremor rushes through me, but before it can disperse and grow, I briefly close my eyes, inhale deeply, and then crawl to the tree.

I'll think about this later. For now, I'm on a mission.

The moment I push myself into that mindset, my head clears.

Little by little, my movements become instinctive, robotic, and drip with purpose.

I don't even pay attention to the persistent sound of gunshots or the mines that go off all around us.

Boom.

Boom.

Boom.

In a swift movement, I let my rifle hang at my back and climb the tree in record time. Instead of stopping at the first solid branch, I continue up until I have the best view of the warehouse and balance on a branch.

The downside is that this branch isn't as strong. But then again, I don't weigh as much as my male colleagues, so where they'd likely break this one and fall off, I won't.

I lie flat on my stomach, rifle in position, and stare through my lenses. The first thing I do is take in the whole scene.

My mouth fills with saliva, and my body shakes at the sight of dismembered bodies—mostly our soldiers. A crippling fear grabs hold of me at the prospect of seeing either Maksim's or Yuri's body. Or even Viktor's. I've somehow gotten used to the stoic grump, and I know for a fact that his loss would hit Captain the most.

Static sounds in my ear, and I startle for a second, thinking it's another bomb. But then, the distinctive command comes, "Focus, Lipovsky."

"Yes, sir." I inhale deeply and close my eyes. When I open them, I'm filled with an unearthly calm.

I don't wait for orders or think twice as I aim and shoot an insurgent who's engaged with one of our own. The shot hits him in the head, and he falls to the ground like dead meat.

The soldier stares up for a moment. Like Captain, Team B must've figured out that we lost our snipers and, therefore, thought that no one had their backs.

Captain and I do now.

"You better stay alive," I mouth to myself as the soldier disappears behind a shed.

The moment he's gone, I aim at another insurgent, half hidden by the bomb's waste, and take him down with a clean shot to the heart.

My adrenaline level spikes.

Click.

Aim.

Shoot.

The rhythm becomes natural as I lay them to rest one after the other.

"Eleven o'clock," Captain's voice sounds in my ear. "You take right. I'll take left."

"Copy that."

I shift in the direction he ordered me to and pause when I see about five insurgents lying on the ground. With shots to the head.

Well, damn. Seems that I've underestimated the captain's shooting abilities. I always thought he was merely the strategist. I didn't know he was an essential operational force, too.

I shoot two on the right, then pause when I realize I only killed one and got the other in his shoulder. He escapes, holding his injured arm. I follow his movements and aim.

"Don't!" the captain commands in my ear, but I've already taken the shot.

And I miss again. *Fuck.*

The insurgent disappears behind the chaos of the destroyed warehouse.

"Why did you stop me…?" I ask with a note of frustration.

"Leave position. Now!" he shouts, and I catch a glimpse of someone dressed in all black at the top of the opposite hill before I slip. The shot hits the already fragile branch, and it cracks, taking me down with it.

I loop the rifle around my neck and hold on to another branch. But the sniper takes aim at that one, too. In my frantic movements to escape his aim, I choke myself with the strap of my rifle. With little oxygen reaching my brain and the chest bandages compressing my lungs, my escape attempts become sluggish.

Shit.

I loosen the sling around my neck and continue my way down.

The moment my feet touch the ground, I hide behind the tree, breathing heavily. I start to remove the sling from around my neck—

"Stay still."

The captain's somber voice keeps me rooted in place, my hands at either side of me and my heart beating so loud, I can hear it in my ears.

I search around to try getting a glimpse of him, but he's not in any of the nearby trees. He must be close enough to see me, though.

"He's watching your every move. If he gets a clear shot, he'll finish you."

"How was my position exposed?"

"He used the shots you took as a parameter to find out where you were. He's probably the one who took out our snipers."

"Fuck."

"Fuck, indeed, Lipovsky. Your life is on the line now. If you move, you die. If you stay there, you'll also die, because he likely sent the infantry in your direction."

I gulp, feeling the strap itch against my neck. Despite the fact that I'm fully covered with combat gear, ice hardens my brain.

"What do I do?" I murmur. "Should I just go for it?"

"If you're in the mood to die, then sure, Lipovsky, *go* for it."

I narrow my eyes. Was that sarcasm just now? I turn my head to the side to search for him. A shot hits the tree trunk, missing my nose by an inch.

Holy shit. This asshole has a beef with me.

"I told you to stay fucking still." The captain's command nearly pierces my eardrums. I resist the urge to massage my ears since that would surely cost me my arm.

But I can't stay still. If I do, I'll be ambushed and killed. If not by whoever the sniper sent, then by a distant shot. I'm a sitting duck at this point.

"Listen to me carefully, Lipovsky. I'm going to need you to distract him."

"How…?"

"Any way that doesn't put you in danger. But I do need him to take another shot at you."

"Uh…how can I accomplish that and not be in danger?"

"Throw a stick or your rifle."

"No way in hell. Losing my weapon is no different from losing my life."

"That's your inferiority complex speaking, and watch the tone. Now, think of something at the count of five, four…"

"Wait!" I can't think this fast.

"Three, two…"

Shit.

Shit.

"One."

It all happens in slow motion. I lunge forward, not to be a martyr, but because I honestly think the other sniper is too smart to be fooled by a stick or even a rifle.

He probably won't take aim unless he sees me in his sights. Which is why I have no choice but to go this route.

I hear the shot and the thud in my upper back before I feel the burn beneath my skin.

Pain explodes in my shoulder, and gravity pulls me down, but I manage to use the remainder of my strength to push myself back against the tree trunk.

I even tuck my legs and arms so that I'm entirely hidden and not in his range of sight anymore.

But in doing so, I scrape the fresh wound against the tree. A scream bubbles in my throat, but I bite my lip to suppress it.

"Lipovsky, you fucking—"

"Did you get him, Captain?" I ask in a drowsy voice, definitely cutting him off, and that would've gotten me in deep shit any other time, but these are special circumstances. "Tell me you got the asshole…"

My breathing slows and so does my pulse, but when my body starts to lean sideways, I forcibly shake my head and remain in the safe position.

"Of course I did, but he's not alone."

"Sorry, Captain. I don't think I can distract the other ones."

"No shit." There's a dark intonation in his voice. "How hurt are you?"

"Shot to the upper back, the shoulder, I think, but it's manageable."

"Like fuck it is. You're barely conscious."

"Ha… Guess that means my attempts to sound strong failed…"

"Don't you dare lose consciousness, Lipovsky. That's an order."

"You…called me Aleksander earlier…" My eyes droop. "I like that better…" *than the fake last name.*

No idea why I told him that, but it seemed imperative for some reason.

At least Aleksander is the male version of my real name, and Sasha is the diminutive form for both.

"Lipovsky!"

Aleksandra. My name is Aleksandra, damn it.

But I don't have the strength to say that as my head lolls to the side. Some shots sound around me, continuing the symphony of war.

I try to lift my rifle even when I can't open my eyes. It's instinct, I think. The need to remain alive no matter what.

But my fingers barely move.

I don't know how much time passes or if it passes at all before I strong arms surround me.

They feel big and cage-like, but instead of trapping me, they're holding me up.

And then his voice, one made of a strange mix of nightmares and lullabies, rings in my ear. "What the fuck am I going to do with you?"

NINE

Kirill

THE FUCKING FUCKER.

I swear to everything that's unholy, I'm going to murder the fuck out of him if he's alive.

It takes me more time than I have to spare to reach the slimy bastard. First, I had to eliminate the sniper who seemed to have a personal grudge against him—probably because he killed one of his friends or some fucking shit.

The way he was aiming at Lipovsky was an act of pure vengeance. He wouldn't have stopped until he deemed that he'd paid.

Then I had to kill the three insurgents who came rushing for his life while he was slumbering under the tree like some sort of Sleeping Beauty.

The truth remains, Lipovsky is injured due to either sheer stupidity or a grandiose sense of bravery. I can't tell which, but I digress. Only slightly.

I should leave the fucker to die, for all I care, but then again, he did expose himself because he knew that was the surest way to allow me to shoot the sniper right between his fucking eyes.

Crouching, I remove his helmet and the balaclava. His sweaty brown hair sticks to his forehead. It's obviously dyed, because sometimes he goes longer between dye jobs and his lighter roots start growing.

The rifle's sling, which has been strangling him since he was in the tree, has created stripes of red on the pale skin of his throat.

I start to pull it away, but I'm met with resistance.

His eyes are shut, and his lips are blue, which is a bad fucking sign, but the little shit actually tightens his fingers on his weapon.

Losing my weapon is no different from losing my life.

I yank the rifle out of his hold and strap it on my shoulder. Then I mechanically pull him against me. Once again, I'm struck by the sheer softness of the fucker, especially when he's not being rigid and going through all the motions to appear tougher than he actually is.

I don't have to search long for the wound. The ugly hole isn't big, but it's soaking his entire back with blood. The bullet must've hit an artery, considering the hemorrhage, and the hole with no exit on the flesh, right beside the protective vest.

It's not near any vital organs, but the blue lips aren't a good sign.

We need to get him out of here now.

Just when I'm about to lift him, a prickling sensation stabs me in the back of my neck, and I grab my rifle before I abruptly turn around.

No one is in sight, but I feel them lurking in the surrounding area. I remain in place, unmoving, then I slowly focus on Lipovsky.

The moment they do attack, I'm ready for them. I shoot the first in the heart, but when I turn to the other, he's already jumping on me and punches me in the side of my head.

My ears ring, but I grab my knife and stab him in the eye. He howls, trying to jump back, but it's already too late.

I shoot him with Lipovsky's rifle and he falls to the ground.

Motherfucker. My ear still rings from the blow, despite the helmet.

I click on my earpiece. "Alpha One to Wolf One. We have a man down, over."

Nothing comes through, not even static.

Fucking fuck.

I remove it from my ear, and sure enough, it's all crumpled.

So I switch to my portable one. "Alpha One to Wolf One, we have a man down. I repeat, one man down. Over."

This time, there's static, but no reply. Seeing how the operation was fucked sideways, I wouldn't be surprised if our communication was messed with.

I barely managed to have a small info exchange with Viktor earlier. At least he's alive. Which can't be said about everyone else.

We lost our snipers and our medic.

The helicopter isn't here yet, and there are no more sounds of gunfire. I don't know where the rest of my team fucked off to, and I can't afford to stay here any longer, or this little shit is as good as dead.

"Alpha One to base. I'm taking the man down to safety, over." Then I click again. "Wolf One, you better bring your team back alive, over."

If Viktor also loses men like Rulan did—

I promptly remove that idea from my head and start to lift Lipovsky on my back. He's so light, it's easy to carry him. But since he's unconscious, he starts tilting to the side, so I use the sling of his rifle to attach his hands to my neck.

He moans when I put pressure against his wound.

No fucking kidding, he actually moans. The sound is soft, too, like...

I narrow my eyes on his unconscious face, but I let it go.

After making sure the path is clear, I use the trees as camouflage and inch closer to the pickup location. I expect to find the others there since it's almost time for the helicopter to pick us up, but there's no sign of anyone.

I recheck my watch while I remain hidden by the trees.

The sound of a helicopter approaching reaches my ears, but I still don't leave my spot. Something's fishy about the whole operation, and since Viktor is more suspicious than me, he also won't trust the pickup.

The helicopter slowly makes its careful descent, as if the pilot himself feels the gloom the mission has cast on the premises.

I don't start toward it, waiting for it to hit the snow first. Then just when it's close enough to touch down—*boom*.

I throw Lipovsky on the ground and cover him with my body as fire eats the helicopter and whoever was in it.

Fuck. Fuck!

Some shards hit my back and leg. The first lodges itself into my vest, but the second one cuts my flesh.

I groan, but I don't wait. My wound is minor and I can walk without a problem.

I practically drag Lipovsky, then carry him on my back and run the length of the snowy forest.

Viktor will find a way out for himself and the others. That's what he does best, and I trust him to bring the rest of my men back alive.

No matter what happens, it's a survival game for all of us. And while I prefer to lead my team to safety myself, the circumstances don't allow it.

In order to save the team, I'd have to leave a man behind, and that's simply not the way I do things.

After twenty minutes of running, I'm far enough from the operation site to stop and think about a possible plan.

My options are few, considering that I have no transportation, the intercom still doesn't work, despite my numerous attempts, and the nearest hospital is no less than a nonstop eight-hour run.

BLOOD OF MY MONSTER | 85

Lipovsky won't be able to hold on that long. Hell, even these twenty minutes on top of the time he's been unconscious are a stretch.

He's getting hotter, his lips are bluer, and he needs emergency care soon.

In our initial scouting of the area, we found a few villages near the warehouse that the insurgents have used for their supplies. It's how we managed to locate them in the first place.

Thirty minutes by car equals an hour-and-a-half walk. Or an hour run. Considering I'm carrying extra weight and moving through heavy snow, it could be more.

An hour is too long for him, but I have no other choice. Either that or I leave him to die.

I put him on the ground and remove my vest, then his and bury them in the snow. Not the safest choice, but it's the smartest. If we're lighter, I can run faster.

It takes me exactly one hour and three minutes to see signs of a village. I had to turn off my and Lipovsky's GPS to avoid being tracked by whoever sabotaged my mission.

Now, the trickiest part is entering a somewhat peaceful village full of old people while carrying a wounded soldier.

They'll never let us through or help us. Village people, in general, are wary of any military forces, especially those who demand their help.

So I remove my helmet and balaclava, then place Lipovsky under a tree on the outskirts. It's freezing, but his skin is hot to the touch. Sweat covers it, and his lips have turned a pale blue.

"I'll be right back." I push his hair away from his face, and he grumbles some gibberish.

I leave his rifle in his hand, which he surprisingly tightens his hold around, though it's a weak grip.

Then I bury my weapon in the snow.

It's early morning, so there aren't a lot of people around. However, I'll likely draw attention. Despite getting rid of my helmet and weapon, I still look like a soldier.

I sneak around a few houses before I finally choose one that has a vast yard and a shed in which clothes are hanging.

After studying my surroundings, I jump over the wall and sneak to the shed. I steal two changes of clothes and even find a pair of fur-lined winter boots.

I roll them all into the oversized coat, attach them to my back, and leave the house right as the front door opens.

A small shriek sounds, but I'm already out of there.

I'll repay you for these one day, lady.

I rush back to where I left Lipovsky.

He's curled beneath the tree, his face pasty white and his rifle in his hand.

This is bad. He's at his physical limits at this point.

In no time, I remove my clothes and lay them on the snow, then put on the pants and cardigan I stole, plus the coat.

After I'm done, I lay Lipovsky down. He moans again, the sound weaker and barely audible.

I hesitate, but only for a second before I rip off his shirt, exposing his—or should I say *her* pale skin to the cold.

As I suspected, her chest is bound with a bandage, and she has the figure of a woman.

Now, I don't know why she goes by a male name or why she went through all the trouble to join the military, but I do know it's important enough that she sacrificed her gender identity for it.

Or maybe she wants to be a he, which does make sense, considering how much she loathes being weak.

At any rate, she's more comfortable being addressed as a he, but she really needs to be a she right now. The only way these villagers will help is if we approach them as ordinary people.

I remove the bandages, stopping when her breasts bounce free. They're neither big nor small. They're just the right size to grab onto while—

Focus.

I put the dress on her, then make a hole where her wound is

and soak it with blood. After I'm satisfied with the way it looks, I remove her pants, cover her with the coat, and slip the boots on her feet. They're a size too big, but they'll do. Mine will stay since they fit the clothes I got for me.

Once I'm finished, I pause, staring at her. It's weird that a mere change of clothes can make such a difference in the way she looks.

After I bury our belongings, including her rifle, in the snow, I carry her bridal style and start toward the village.

She's light, barely noticeable in my arms. Her head leans against my chest and she has a limp, bloodied arm around my neck.

"Lipovsky," I call in an attempt to keep her conscious.

"Aleksandra…" she whispers, her voice low and brittle.

So that's her real name.

Aleksandra.

I've got to say, I'm disappointed in the lack of effort in picking a male name.

A man who's pushing a carriage full of vegetables stops upon seeing me, his old face creasing in surprise.

"What is this…what is going on?" He speaks in a very regional dialect that I barely understand.

"My wife…" I soften my voice and inject it with sorrow, acting the part to perfection. "She was shot by a soldier. Please help us."

TEN

Sasha

BLOOD DRIPS ALL AROUND ME.

In the silence, the sound heightens to a terrifying crescendo.

Darkness expands for as far as my vision can see. Fog condenses and floats in a seamless motion, mixing with the blood and flowing beneath and above me.

A droplet of hot liquid falls on my cheek, then another follows, and another…

I cautiously lift my head, despite the claustrophobic sensation expanding in my chest.

There's something wrong with this situation, but that doesn't stop me from trying to gauge what's going on.

Sure enough, in the midst of the smoky darkness, bodies hang from the sky, their eyes bulging, tongues grotesquely hanging out of their mouths, and their clothes soaked with blood.

I'd recognize each and every one of their faces, even if I were old and gray and on my deathbed.

My family.

Tears fill my eyes, and I jump up, desperately trying to reach out and free their corpses, but a strong gust of wind interrupts me.

"You're a failure, Aleksandra!" The booming voice comes from overhead as if they're all speaking at the same time.

"A failure."

"Nothing but trouble."

"You shouldn't have been spared."

"Why do you get to live and we don't?"

They mix, mash, and turn into a puddle of terrifying shrieks. Their blood soaks my shirt and clings to my skin, my eyelids, and my mouth. Everywhere.

I swallow the metallic taste, nearly drowning in all the blood and yelling.

I put my hands to my ears and scream.

My eyes snap open and clash with an old ceiling. No bodies hang from there, and no blood soaks me.

My concentration is groggy, and my head pulses with pain, but I focus on my surroundings. I'm on a bed in a small room. An old fireplace stocked with wood gives the place a vintage, cozy vibe.

What am I doing here...?

I rack my brain for the last thing I did, but I still can't put my finger on it.

We were on a mission and—

Damn. The mission!

I lunge forward and pain explodes through my upper shoulder. Holy shit.

Just when I think I'll die from the sizzling burn, the door opens. I back up against the headboard, my senses on high alert, and reach for my calf knife. Only, I'm not wearing a boot, and... did my breasts just bounce with my movement?

I look down and...what the...? I'm dressed in a cotton

nightgown with spaghetti straps and a deep V-neck that reveals half of my breasts. There's no sign of my chest bandage.

Please tell me this is a continuation of my nightmare.

"You're finally awake."

I startle at the welcoming female sound and lift the blanket to cover myself. An old woman with a kind face and white hair gathered in a bun approaches me.

She's holding a tray with thin, wrinkly hands on which some blue veins peek through.

My eyes track her every movement while simultaneously searching my surroundings for a weapon I can use to escape.

She seems oblivious to my hyperaware mode as she continues her serene approach. "My name is Nadia, and I'm the nurse who's been taking care of you."

A thick accent coats her words—something more rural and different from the city's accents. She sounds like the villagers Papa and my uncles used to take us to visit during the summer.

Nadia stops by my bed, places her tray on the nightstand, and gives zero shits about my attempts to resist. Easily, she flings my good arm from beneath the sheet and hooks the blood pressure cuff to it. Then she shoves a thermometer under my armpit.

Her expression remains kind through the whole ordeal, like a patient mother who's dealing with a petulant child. "You're lucky the villagers led you to our house in time. My husband and I are a retired doctor and nurse, but that didn't last too long once you showed up at our doorstep."

"Sorry," I whisper, feeling a sense of guilt at disturbing their peace.

Nadia merely ignores my lame attempt at an apology and removes the cuff. "Normal blood pressure, good. And instead of being sorry, focus on getting better. Scars don't look so good on young ladies." She fetches the thermometer from my armpit and stares at it with efficient calm. "You're still a tad hotter than normal. I'll inject you with another dose of antibiotics."

"Uh, can we not do that? I'm sure it'll be fine in a bit."

She narrows her eyes. "When you reached our doorstep, you were dying. My husband and I didn't go through all the trouble to save you so you'd have complications now. Besides, are you seriously afraid of a needle when you were shot by a gun?"

My shoulders hunch. It's an irrational fear that I've been trying to overcome, but it's simply not going away. And yes, I do prefer a gunshot wound over a needle.

While I'm thinking of what to tell her, Nadia has already prepared the injection.

"Wait, wait!" I slide back in the bed and wince when pain explodes in my upper shoulder. "Aren't there any pills?"

"Injections are faster and more efficient." She holds the needle that glistens with a transparent liquid high. "I'll give you a painkiller after this."

"I'm really fine. I don't need both." She touches my forearm and pulls. The motion isn't even harsh, but I scream with pain.

"You were saying?" Her tone and face remain the same except for the raising of her brows.

The door bangs open, and the pain dulls to the background when I'm met with familiar icy blue eyes.

Captain Kirill.

He's dressed in casual pants, his black army boots, and a heavy coat that's covered with snow. He removes the hat, revealing the entirety of his face, and he's wearing...glasses.

My heart thuds behind my rib cage as this unusual image of him sinks in.

He looks regal, all muscle and destructive energy tucked neatly behind the casualwear. The glasses give him the appearance of an intelligent accountant who might or might not be hiding some dangerous tendencies.

"Oh, you came back," Nadia says after inspecting the newcomer. "Your wife is apparently scared of needles, so how about you help me keep her in place before she opens her stitches?"

He starts to walk inside, and I'm too stunned to talk or think, so I keep staring, dumbfounded.

"Did you buy what I asked for?" Nadia asks him.

Captain Kirill opens his coat and gives her a bag of medicine, then removes the piece of clothing and throws it on a chair opposite the fire.

He's dressed in a black button-down and a sweater that fails to leash the intensity dripping off him.

"Good, good. I thought you were going to be killed by the storm." Nadia nods. "Now, get over here."

I can't believe my ears or my eyes, because the captain actually follows her instructions and allows himself to be ordered around.

Something niggles at the back of my head, and I can't figure out what, no matter how much I think about it.

As he approaches me, looking bigger than a god and just as deadly, the reason behind my frozen state rushes back to me.

Did Nadia just call me his...*wife?*

There must be some sort of misunderstanding, because what the fuck?

My thoughts whither and vanish as he sits beside me on the mattress and wraps his arm around my waist.

The heavy weight of his hand settles on my hip, large and imposing, and effectively steals my breath.

His fingers splay out on the fabric, and even though our skin is separated by the nightgown, he might as well be touching me naked. He's never touched me this way, and the novelty of it throws me off.

"Capt..."

I trail off when my eyes clash with the warning in his harsh ones. The intensity behind them rivals the pain in my shoulder.

"It's only a needle." His voice carries like warmth in the harsh winter. Deep and firm, but not as authoritative as I'm used to. Jesus. Is this an imposter or something?

"That's what I've been telling her," Nadia supplies from beside me, but I'm too focused on the captain's face to pay attention to her.

His free hand strokes my cheek so gently and lovingly, I think I'm going to melt. "You can do this, Solnyshko."

No.

Nope.

I must be dreaming or else...or else...Captain Kirill just called me his sun. A term of endearment that's only used between lovers.

My jaw is about to hit the ground when he strokes my chin, subtly closing my parted lips.

The motion is fast and straightforward, but he might as well have provoked a war in my chest. The place where he touched me tingles and heats, leaving me gasping due to something a lot different than pain.

A prick swerves my attention to my arm that Nadia has successfully gotten a needle into. The sight fills my throat with nausea.

"Look at me, Solnyshko."

As if hypnotized, I turn my head in his direction. For some reason, his icy eyes aren't so savage anymore, but they're still dangerous. He's successfully hidden his nature behind the black-framed glasses, but not enough to fool me.

"It's going to be okay," he says in that fake softness that wrenches a shiver out of me.

What...is this? How am I supposed to stare at the captain and not think of him as my captain?

The space between my legs warms and tingles. It's uncomfortable enough that I want to push him away and go hide somewhere.

"We're all done." Nadia interrupts the moment, and I blink once as I break contact with his hypnotizing eyes.

Nadia hands over my painkillers and a glass of water. "These will dull the pain. If you're tired, sleep. My husband will be here to see you shortly."

"Thank you, Nadia, and not only for this, but also for taking us in when we had nowhere to go," the captain says in that weird tone. He sounds like the most eloquent gentleman, who's impossible to resist.

"At least one of you has manners," she says without changing her expression.

"T-thank you," I blurt.

"Excuse my wife." The captain tightens his hold on my waist. "She's not usually this way, but the gunshot has flipped our world upside down."

"I understand." Her gaze softens before she directs it at me. "You're lucky to have such a devoted husband, young lady. Not many would carry another person all that distance during a snowstorm."

My lips are parted again because they said those words. *Again.* *Wife. Husband.*

What the hell is going on? Have I perhaps woken up in an alternate reality where the captain is my husband?

"Dinner will be ready in an hour," Nadia announces, then leaves the room.

The moment the door closes, I feel the shift in energy and the intense scrutiny someone's keeping on me.

I don't dare look up at him as if I've done something wrong. The fact that he still has his arm around my waist doesn't help, though.

He lifts my chin with an index finger and leans forward, so I have no choice but to be trapped in those punishing eyes.

My lips are a breath away from his, and I can't help staring at his mouth. It's clamped in a line, the lower lip fuller than the upper one, and his strong jaw is set.

If he inches closer, the tiny space that separates us will be gone, and I'll get to taste those lips—

What the...

No.

"What are you doing, Captain?" I whisper so low, I wouldn't be surprised if he can't hear me, and for a moment, I think he doesn't.

Or I wish he doesn't.

Just then, his thumb and forefinger squeeze my chin until I wince.

"That's what I'd like to ask, Lipovsky. What the fuck did you think you were doing back there? Did I or did I not tell you not to put yourself in danger?"

"I…had no other choice. He was smart enough not to have fallen for a stick or a rifle. It smelled like a trap, even to me."

"This fucking—" He cuts himself off and breathes evenly. "You defied direct orders, and you'll be punished for it."

"Come on! I got us the guy…"

I trail off when he glares at me with his scrutinizing eyes. Jeez. It's impossible to keep staring at him and not suffer an injury of some sort.

"I'm sorry," I murmur. "And it's not like I wanted to get shot on purpose. It hurts, you know."

He releases a long breath, and I'm not sure if it's in frustration or resignation, but considering that he releases my chin and waist, I'd go with the second.

The loss of his touch leaves me inexplicably empty as he stands up and walks to the window. His movements are light and inaudible, despite his massive build. At first glance, he's no different than a giant cat lurking in the middle of the night, waiting for prey to pounce on.

For some reason, I feel like that prey.

When he opens the curtains, I'm blinded by a white fog.

I can't see anything beyond the heavy snow that's blazing outside.

In a moment, this small room feels like a haven against the exterior world.

My hurt shoulder is less tense, and the pain dulls to a throbbing ache. I grab the blanket and pull it up to my chest, my heart beating loudly.

Even my ears feel like they're on fire as I stare at the rippling muscles of his back.

"Captain…"

"Call me Kirill. The old couple will find it weird that you address your supposed husband as Captain. They're too old-fashioned and need clear labels."

I try to speak, but the words get stuck in the back of my throat, so I breathe deeply first. "Did you… Why did you dress me as a woman?"

"We wouldn't have been able to fool them if you were in your man look. You scream soldier, even now." He glances at me, and I swallow. "If you prefer being a man, you'll have to wait until we're out of here."

"You…aren't going to ask why I did this?"

"It's none of my business."

"But it's against the military rules."

"Right. That." He seems to be deep in thought. "I don't give a fuck. People should be allowed to be whoever they want to be, so if you prefer being a man, be a man."

"It's not that I don't want to be a woman, it's that I can't. I…"

"You don't have to explain yourself to me, Aleksander."

"It's Aleksandra." My face and neck heat as I say the words.

I never thought I would be introducing myself, and to Captain Kirill, no less.

Kirill.

That's what he told me to call him. Just Kirill.

A small twitch lifts his lips. It's not exactly a smile but something close. "I know."

"You do?"

"You said that when you were almost unconscious. It's Aleksandra, not Aleksander."

"Oh." I bite my lower lip, and his attention follows the motion, slowly raising my temperature.

I release my lip in a jerk and clear my throat. "I-is that when you found out I was a woman?"

"No."

"Then...when did you?"

"When I first saw you being assaulted by your ex-teammates."

"What?"

"What?" he repeats coolly with unbelievable calm.

"You...knew from the beginning?"

"Was I not supposed to?"

"No. And, seriously, can you stop talking as if this is a trivial matter?"

He turns around and faces me while crossing his arms. "I'm all ears."

It's kind of hard to look him in the eye for too long, let alone talk to his face, but I manage to control my abnormal reaction. "I...have to look like a man despite myself, so...uh, can you please keep it a secret?"

"As I said, it's none of my business."

A heavy weight lifts off my chest, but the relief is short-lived. I'm hit by all the times I was trying to toughen up, speak and act like a man.

The captain must've thought me laughable.

Still, I murmur, "Thank you."

He lifts a shoulder as if there isn't anything to be thankful for. But for me, there is. Plenty.

"When can we leave this place?" I ask.

"Not in the near future." He points a thumb behind him. "There's a snowstorm that will last for a few days. It's dangerous to even go into town in this weather."

"How about the base? Have you been able to get in touch?"

"Negative. There's no reception due to the storm. Until we find an opportunity to leave, the couple outside needs to believe our husband and wife story. They don't trust soldiers around here, and Nadia already asked me why we don't have rings."

"What did you tell her?"

"We were robbed, and then when we struggled and ran away, we were shot at. Thankfully, we got far enough to escape capture."

"They must've picked up that we don't have a rural accent. Did they ask you why we were so far out from the city?"

He raises a brow. "They did. I told them we were lovers of nature and were celebrating our second anniversary."

I can feel the heat rising in my cheeks.

"That's good acting." He motions at my face. "Looking horrified when I gave you a pet name wasn't."

Shit.

"It's just that... I'm not used to that."

He walks toward me, his purposeful strides eating the distance in no time. When he stops in front of me, I cease breathing, utterly taken aback by how close he is.

Kirill lifts my chin with his forefinger and says in a low tone, "Then get used to it, Solnyshko."

ELEVEN

Kirill

THERE'S NOTHING MORE IRRITATING THAN BEING STUCK. My annoyance level has been building in the background despite my futile attempts to remain fucking calm.

Ever since we arrived at the old couple's house yesterday, I've been trying, and failing, to reach Viktor. To avoid suspicion, I had to call him from the village's public phone, thinking maybe he had gotten back to base, but there was no reply.

He and I found out about this village during our initial scouting of the area prior to the mission. I told him that if things went south, this place would be our emergency hideout.

The fact that he hasn't come here yet is unlike him. Even with the snowstorm.

I have a firm belief that he's stronger than a boar and would be able to defeat a whole army on his own. But then there's the pesky reminder that he's only human.

Not to mention that someone targeted us with the intention of annihilating my men.

No matter which angle I look at the events from, it screams a setup, and I'm ninety percent sure I've figured out the reason for it.

That aside, if Viktor were to meet Rulan's fate—

"Captain."

I lift my head from the book I'm supposed to be reading but am only seeing a replay of the battlefield on its pages.

Lipovsky—Aleksandra—stares at me from her position on the bed. She's been uncharacteristically quiet since I grabbed her chin and called her by a pet name a few hours ago.

Her cheeks curiously flushed with a soft pink hue in the span of seconds. A fact that makes me want to repeat the gesture just for the reaction alone.

But I won't.

For now.

Nicholas, Nadia's husband and the doctor who saved her life and treated my minor leg injury, came to check on her earlier and said she's healing properly, but she can't strain herself.

It's a miracle that she managed to survive after losing so much blood. The color has been gradually returning to her face, too.

I plant my elbow on the armrest and lean my chin against my fist. "It's Kirill."

That unusual blush creeps up her neck and cheeks again. Despite her short brown hair, she looks more feminine than most women.

The strap of her nightgown slips off her uninjured shoulder and settles on her arm. The small motion teases the creamy skin of her naked breasts, which are tipped with dark pink nipples. I know because I saw them when I changed her clothes yesterday.

A sight that's engraved in my memories in spite of my futile attempts to erase it.

I must stare for longer than socially acceptable, because Aleksandra clears her throat. She appears oblivious to what I was hyperfocused on, though. Either she's too naïve or too good at this game.

"It's hard for me to call you by your first name." Her voice is softer, but it has that husky undertone that made it easier for her to pretend to be a man.

"Then you need to get used to it. Say it. Kirill. It's a very simple name."

"K-Kirill."

My lips twitch at the stutter, finding it surprisingly adorable on someone who couldn't be accused of lacking a backbone.

"Say it again but more naturally this time. That didn't sound like a wife who's been married to me for two years."

She purses her lips, obviously uncomfortable with the scenario I came up with, which is probably why I keep referring to her as my wife every chance I get.

Is this shit entertaining? Absolutely.

"Go ahead," I nudge when she remains silent.

"Kirill," she says with more force than needed.

"Again. Naturally."

"Kirill," she murmurs in a gentle tone that vibrates through my chest, then shoots straight to my dick, and my heart jolts.

Maybe I need to have Nadia and her husband look at it in case I have an internal injury. Or maybe I should stop having a front-row seat to Aleksandra's side tit.

I flip a page as if I've been reading this classical book all along. "Don't be a flirt."

"You're the one who told me to do it more naturally." She crosses her arms and then winces when she probably triggers the pain in her injury. "Make up your mind."

"If we were at camp, you'd be punished for that."

"But we aren't."

"Watch it."

"Pretty sure a husband doesn't talk to his wife in that tone."

"I do."

"You…are you married?"

"I am."

Her lips part, and she slowly lets her hands fall to either side of her. I can almost taste the dramatic shift of her mood in the air. Interesting.

"To you, remember?" I add in the same casual manner I've been speaking with.

I'm almost sure I spot some form of relief, but it vanishes when she starts to get up. "I should probably go help Nadia with something."

She stumbles in her attempts to stand, and I reach her in a few steps and then support her from behind, one hand on her arm and the other grabbing her wrist.

Aleksandra starts to push me away. "I can stand on my own."

"You don't even have the strength to breathe properly."

"I'm fine." She attempts to wiggle free of my hold, but I tighten my grip on her.

"Quit being stubborn."

Her body's still rigid, but she doesn't fight anymore. Once she's calmed down a little, I release her and reach for the velvet robe Nadia placed on the foot of the bed.

I gently pull it over her injured side, and she groans but quickly mutes the sound. I'm starting to realize that she hates showing weakness more than anything. That's probably why she didn't want me to help just now.

That's also why she looked horrified when Nadia told her I carried her all the way here. Or maybe that had to do with how she called me her husband a couple of times.

"Now, put in the other hand."

She begrudgingly complies. "I can do it on my own."

"I know."

"Then why are you insisting on helping?"

I pull up the strap of the nightgown that's been subtly teasing me for the past twenty minutes.

Goosebumps erupt on her skin, and she goes still. She even stops breathing for a second too long.

A devilish thought sparks my mind. I wonder if she'll tremble if my hand *innocently* touches her breast.

I only have a side view of her face, but the more my hand lingers on her skin, the longer she holds her breath.

After a quick thought, I remove my hand.

While it's fun to toy with her, the way she's holding her breath may cause complications.

Slowly, her chest rises and falls in a harsh rhythm as she snatches the belt of the robe and ties it around her waist.

"Are you mad about something, Sasha?"

She whirls around and stares at me with that stupefied expression. "Why are you calling me that?"

"Everyone in the unit does. I assume it's your way of relating to your true name more, yes?"

"I never said you could use it."

"Never said I couldn't."

She narrows her eyes as if I'm next on her shit list, which wouldn't be a surprise, considering all the whiplash I must've been giving her.

Sasha hasn't been with me long enough to know that my actions turn unpredictable when I'm in a situation that I haven't anticipated.

"You might want to control your expression. Our hosts are already suspicious of you, and we don't want them to kick us out in the middle of a storm, now, do we?"

She opens her mouth to say something, but she quickly thinks better of it and clamps it shut.

When she slowly walks to the door, I block her way. She subtly pushes back, but I can see the slight jerk in her shoulders before she schools the movement.

"Now what?" she asks in a careful tone.

"Now, I need you to be natural. No jerking or acting

uncomfortable. Remember your favorite married couple and act like them."

She pauses for a moment, then nods once.

"I mean it, Sasha. If we're kicked out of here, I might be able to get through the storm on my own, but you won't survive."

"Got it. Natural."

It's far from a good sign that she even needs to say it out loud, but if there's anything I trust about her, it's her strong determination to survive.

Someone else would've lost the battle during the time it took me to get here.

She didn't.

Despite the fever, she held on to life with everything in her.

We leave the room side by side, and although she attempts to seem strong, Sasha walks slowly.

I grab her by the elbow for support, and she starts to wiggle free, but I shake my head.

Her struggle wanes, but she breaks eye contact. Almost as if she's avoiding me.

Well, well, well.

Once we arrive in the living room, Sasha stops to inspect our surroundings.

The space is small but has character. A vintage green sofa and matching chairs form a circle. A plant with small white flowers sits in the middle of a glass coffee table. There's also a dark green antique teapot and two cups.

The couple obviously loves green, because their carpets and wallpaper also have green in them. Even the mantle over the fireplace that's blazing with the wood I chopped for Nicholas yesterday has Russian dolls dressed in green sitting on it.

Upon seeing us, Doctor Nicholas abandons watching a rerun of an old show.

He's older than Nadia and has a wrinkled face but a

surprisingly straight posture for someone his age. He's not over-weight like my father, who wheezes and turns blue after walking a few steps.

"Do you feel better, child?" he asks Sasha.

Her expression softens as she nods. "I do. Once again, thank you so much. I'll make sure to repay you one day."

He throws up a dismissive hand. "There's a saying I believe in. It's about doing good and forgetting about it."

"We're still thankful, Doctor," I say.

"It's Nicholas, I tell you. Come, come, sit by the fire."

"I'm going to see if Nadia needs any help." Sasha starts to walk, but the woman in question appears in the kitchen doorway.

"Nonsense. I need no help. And what are you doing out of bed?" She fixates Sasha with a stern motherly expression.

"I can move." Sasha pulls from me and does a small turn. "It's good to walk around instead of staying in bed all day, right?"

"Not if you strain yourself."

Sasha completely ignores her and steps toward the kitchen, a small smile painted on her lips.

This girl obviously knows no fear, or maybe it was purged out of her.

It's not that I don't want to be a woman, it's that I can't. Those are the words she said, and even though I already categorized the situation to be none of my business, I find myself thinking about it.

In the beginning, I assumed she went through all the trou-ble of disguising herself because she wanted to be a man, which is why I respected her wishes and even addressed her as a man. Turns out, she has to be a man because being a woman is danger-ous. She has a natural feminine aura, so does that mean she hasn't been pretending to be a man for very long?

Besides, as much as she tries to hide it, she has a very posh, educated way of using words. I know because it resembles Yulia's manner of speech that somehow affected my own Russian. One doesn't talk like that unless they were brought up a certain way that includes private tutors and a high standing in Russian society.

There's also a finesse to her movements, despite the manly image she tries to project. It's mixed with a naïve softness of someone who has been both sheltered and taught nothing of the world. At times, when Maksim blabbers on about mundane things, she listens with keen curiosity as if it's the first time she's heard of it.

It doesn't take a genius to figure out she was a princess before the military and the gender change.

How someone like her ended up in the lowest rank of the army is a mystery.

"Don't worry. Nadia will take care of her."

Nicholas's voice alerts me to the fact that I've continued staring at the entrance of the kitchen long after the two women have disappeared inside.

I internally shake my head and take the seat opposite him. He pours me a cup of tea, and I thank him for it, then take a sip, even though I'm not a fan.

"She's a strong young lady." Nicholas's voice rises over the TV, whose volume is already low. Unlike his wife, he speaks in a serene tone, soothing and welcoming.

"Strong?" I ask.

"Yes. She's out of danger now, but when I first saw her, I thought she wouldn't make it through the night."

I actually thought that, too. She's still a bit pale, but it doesn't compare to the pasty complexion and blue lips she had when we arrived.

"It takes a lot of willpower to hang on to life like that." Nicholas fingers the rim of his cup. "It could be due to either a strong love or a strong hate."

"Why do you think it would be one of the two?"

"An intuition." He smiles. "I assume it's the love part that kept her going."

Nah. It's definitely hate.

From the first day I met her, Sasha has been fighting and try-ing to be strong, and that's only because she's needed that strength to fight whoever poses a danger to the female version of her.

It took me some time, but I'm starting to put the pieces of the puzzle that is Sasha into place.

"You're lucky to be the subject of such love, son," Nicholas says. "Take it from me, it's a blessing to come across, and if you don't protect it, using your life if needed, you might regret it for the rest of your days."

I smile politely, nodding in agreement. Then he goes on to tell me about his wife and how he nearly lost her once and how they eloped, lost one son, married off another, and sent the third abroad.

It's an interesting tale that keeps my head occupied from the niggling doubt about the operation from fucking hell.

Thirty-eight hours now.

Viktor still hasn't gotten in touch.

It could be because of the storm. It *has* to be.

Nicholas is interrupted when Nadia tells us to set the table. Sasha tries to help, but the stern nurse literally swats her hand, so she stays still.

She also bluntly informs her that redoing her stitches would be bothersome.

We sit down for dinner, and although I didn't expect much, Nadia actually went all out with traditional dishes I haven't had in ages.

My mother never cooked—at least, not for me. And the woman who raised me isn't Russian.

Sasha stares at the food as Nicholas says a little prayer before we dig in. Nadia tells her to eat specific dishes, something about nutritional value and amount of salt.

Sasha slowly lifts a spoonful of soup to her lips. The moment she tastes the food, a tear slides down her cheek.

I lean over and whisper, "What's wrong?"

It's then she realizes she's crying and wipes at her eyes with her sleeve. "Nothing…it's just…this reminds me of home and Mama's cooking."

"Do you like it?" Nadia asks in a softer tone.

"I love it. Thank you for letting me relive this feeling." Sasha drinks her soup, stopping now and again as if needing to catch her breath.

I place a hand on her back, stroking it, but she shows no reaction. She's either gotten into the role, or she's too engrossed in the food to notice.

The rest of the evening has a homey feel and Nadia scolds Sasha whenever she tries to move or exert herself.

Nicholas takes another look at her, and Nadia gives her painkillers before we all bid each other goodnight.

As soon as we reach the room, Sasha lies on the bed, obviously exhausted. But since she's a stubborn being, she did everything she could to hide her condition from the old couple.

I go to wash up in the adjoining bathroom, then remove the old reading glasses I borrowed from Nicholas under the pretext that I'm nearsighted. Thing is, glasses make me look less threatening, so I always have them on while off duty.

When I return to the room, I find Sasha lying on her back, the robe scattered at her side and her eyes are closed.

Looks like she gave up the battle and fell asleep. I sit on the bed and start to pull the covers from her hold.

The bright color of her eyes meet mine as she grips them tightly. "W-what are you doing?"

"What does it look like I'm doing? I'm going to sleep."

"Aren't you supposed to sleep on the floor or something?"

"Why would I do that when there's a bed?" I forcibly pull the covers back and lie down, palm under my head, then I close my eyes.

"Then…" She inches to the edge of the mattress. "I'll sleep on the floor."

Without opening my eyes, I roll onto my side and throw my

arm over her middle. "You'll do no such thing. It's cold and uncomfortable on the floor."

Her body goes still beneath mine, but it's a careful type. A behavior like injured animals would exhibit when they're under stress.

"Kirill…"

"Yes?" I ask nonchalantly, pretending not to feel the squeeze in my chest at hearing her call my name.

"Nadia said you seemed to have taken a long journey to get me here. It must've been so hard in the middle of all the snow and with the enemy at your back. I was as good as dead, so why didn't you leave me behind?"

I open my eyes to be greeted by her molten ones. They're more green than brown now, bright, innocent, and…breakable. "You were still breathing."

"But I was unresponsive and bleeding—"

"As long as you were still breathing, I wouldn't leave you behind. That's not how I operate."

"Even if you were in danger because of me?"

"Even then."

She gulps, the delicate veins in her throat bobbing up and down. "Thank you. I think I stayed alive because I knew I had you."

Her face shines with that bright innocence again. This isn't only a display of gratefulness—it's something much *more*.

TWELVE

Sasha

THE SOUND OF THE HOWLING WIND REVERBERATES around me, but it doesn't feel cold.

In fact, it's warm.

So warm that I bury my face in the pillow and moan softly at the welcoming embrace. In an instant, it feels as if I'm back to happier times in my life.

Times when Mama would hug me to sleep, Papa would kiss my forehead, and Anton would tease me about being a baby.

Times I took for granted, oblivious to the bleak reality fate had prepared for me.

So I burrow further into the warmness of the pillow, inhaling deeply and engraving every detail to memory.

Then I pause when I notice something hard against my head. In fact, the firm surface is glued to my whole body. A pillow isn't supposed to feel like steel.

Slowly, I open my eyes. The moment I understand the situation, a wordless gasp spills from my lips.

Turns out, the pillow isn't a pillow, after all, and I am, in fact, cocooned in Kirill's arms.

I tilt my chin up to catch a glimpse of his sleeping face. The hard lines of his jaw are shadowed by the early morning light slipping through the window.

The storm is still blazing outside, but it's not dark, or maybe not as dark as anyone would expect.

His lashes are quite thick, and so are his brows. I have an undeniable compulsion pushing me to touch them, just to see how they feel.

As I lift my hand, he tightens his arm on my middle. It's the same arm he threw over me last night, and he hasn't changed his position, not even an inch. I'm the one who turned in his direction and practically hugged him back.

My hand pauses near his face.

What am I doing?

Kirill is my captain and benefactor. He saved my life because, as he said, he's not the type who'd leave any of his men behind. Not only that, but he also agreed to keep my identity a secret and didn't probe for the actual reason I assumed another gender.

Am I in awe of him due to gratefulness? I can't even look away from his face or attempt to pull away from him.

No. It's not really gratefulness, but more like an intense version of that feeling of uneasiness I have whenever he's around. Only, now, it's accompanied by a dangerous impulse. Maybe it wouldn't be a bad idea to stay in this position for a bit longer.

Without touching him, my hand hovers in the air as I trace my fingers over his brows, the straight line of his nose, the contour of his cheekbones, and the dark shadow forming on his hard jawline.

My forefinger pauses when I reach his mouth. These lips were so close to mine that I couldn't breathe properly.

That feeling has come back again, and I find myself constricted, hot, and abnormally bothered. Even the dull pain in my shoulder throbs and stings.

I shift and accidentally, or not really, inch closer to him, but then I come to a jolting halt.

Something hard and massive stabs the bottom of my belly. At first, I think there's an object between us, so I move my stomach up and down, but the 'object' grows in size.

Holy shit.

It's his…dick.

And it's erect and *huge*.

My ears heat, and my fingers that are hovering in the air tremble. Tracing his face is the last thing on my mind now that I'm being poked by his boner.

This is highly inappropriate and has the potential to screw over any professional relationship we might have had. No, it wasn't the best, and we had our differences, but it was always 'proper.' Strained but right.

It didn't help that I was more often than not uncomfortable and wary around him.

But this…this…is an entirely different beast.

The right thing to do would be to leave the bed before he wakes up and save us each from the awkwardness.

That's what my brain tells me, anyway. But do I listen? Not really.

I'm more fascinated and interested in the current display of the male anatomy. I know it's natural and by no means due to my presence, but it did get harder when I moved, so maybe I had some effect, after all?

Just to make sure, I lean closer, subtly rubbing my stomach up and down. Once again, his cock thickens against me.

I don't stop.

I *can't*.

I keep wondering how big it can get, and I'm rewarded by the twitchiness against my skin.

Yes, we're clothed, but it doesn't feel that way right now.

My belly flutters, and a sudden zap of pleasure shoots between my legs. I have to place a hand on my mouth to stop whatever sound from coming out.

"You better be aware of what you're doing or I swear to fuck..."

I come to a halt, my breath catching, and a cold sweat breaks out all over my skin.

Icy blue eyes clash with mine, and I have nowhere to go or hide. All I can do is remain here, motionless and feeling every beat of my heart thundering against my rib cage.

The scenario I dreaded earlier comes crashing down with more of an impact than I anticipated.

I can't breathe or think as he fixates me with those eyes that could be mistaken for weapons of mass destruction.

"So you *are* awake." The husky timbre of his sleepy voice carries in the air and gets stuck between us.

His large hand flexes on my hip, and I can almost feel his skin sinking so deeply into me that I couldn't shake it off even if I wanted to.

"And here I thought you were moving in your sleep." There's a slight amusement in his voice, and if I weren't so mortified, I'd swear it sounds sadistic in nature.

"I...I was." I lie through my teeth and don't sound convincing in the least.

"Is that so? I'm almost sure you were doing it on purpose."

My cheeks heat, and I start to lower my head. In a flash, he lifts my chin with his index and middle fingers.

This time, I have no escape from the cold depths of his punishing gaze. It strikes me then that the reason behind my unease has always been these eyes.

They hide more than they show. They're secretive, cruel, and hold not an ounce of empathy or mercy.

It's impossible to know what he's thinking about or plotting, let alone try to evade him.

"*Were* you doing it on purpose, Sasha?" The edge beneath his words leaves me breathless. It's almost as if he knows the exact corner he's driven me to and is now coming for the knockout.

It doesn't help that a jolt travels through me whenever he calls me Sasha. It's new and sounds intimate whenever he says it.

"No." My voice is barely a whisper, but it's calm and collected—nothing of the nervousness from earlier, as if I actually believe my words.

"Are you sure?"

My heart lunges, reacting to the insistence in his voice. I'm so close to divulging my intention for no other reason than to see the reaction he'll have. I stop at the knowledge that I wouldn't be able to handle it if I demolished the wall between us.

I can't afford to be stuck in Kirill's web with everything that's resting on my shoulders.

I simply can't afford to be distracted.

So I nod.

The moment I do, it's like I've removed a spell.

Kirill releases my jaw and lifts his hand off my waist. I can see the closing off of his face as he says, "Very well."

He rolls to the other side of the bed and gets up in one swift movement. I try to catch a glimpse of his face, but he's completely sealed himself off as the strict, unapproachable captain.

A knock on the door startles me, then Nadia's voice follows, "Are you up?"

"Yes, one moment." I start to stumble out of bed.

"No need to hurry. Just come out for breakfast and your shot whenever you're ready."

"Will do, thanks!"

As Nadia's voice and presence disappear, so has Kirill. He vanished into the en-suite bathroom while I was talking to her.

My feet itch to follow after and try to clear the air, but what's the point? It's better this way.

I did the right thing.

At least, I hope so.

After I put on the dress and tights Nadia left on the chair for me, I wash my face in the guest bathroom down the hall. It takes me more time than necessary since I have to stop every now and then due to the pain in my shoulder.

Once I deem myself presentable enough, I go to meet the old couple.

Like last night, Nadia doesn't allow me to help and, instead, gives me some medication. The shot, too, of course. I nearly cry waiting for the ordeal to be over.

"You've improved so fast," Nicholas comments as he begrudgingly lets me help him in setting the table.

"She's young and strong," Nadia replies while bringing some toast.

"I think the will is everything." He smiles at me as my uncle would. "You definitely have a strong will, young lady. Protect it with everything you have."

"My father told me to stay alive. Everything else can be fixed as long as I'm alive," I say and resist the tears that well in my eyes.

"Those are wise words," Nicholas says.

I wish he'd been wise enough to stay alive.

"Oh, you're here. Let's sit down for breakfast." Nadia ushers Kirill to the seat beside me, and for some reason, I hold my breath for a moment too long.

He's in black pants and a light blue button-down that molds against his pecs and biceps. And he's wearing those glasses again that make him look tamer than he actually is.

He thanks Nadia for the food and compliments Nicholas on a chair he made himself.

But he doesn't look at me or address me. Not even once. He's subtle about it, too. It's not that he's glaring at me or treating me differently.

Maybe I'm imagining things. After all, this is just him being himself. He's the same Kirill I've come to know during the past couple of months.

I may have gotten a glimpse of a change in him during this ordeal, but that might simply be me trying to see a human side of him.

And failing.

❧

"Do you even know how to use that?"

I lift my head at Nadia's voice. I've been kind of acting like her inexperienced apprentice in the kitchen, and she's been letting me.

Despite her stern appearance and her merciless needles, Nadia is a kind woman with a natural talent as a caregiver, which makes her the best type of nurse.

I put the knife down and smile awkwardly. I do know how to use it, but only in combat, not in the kitchen.

Nadia, who's dressed in a lively green apron, shakes her head and takes over the task.

We've been staying with the old couple for six days now. The storm ended last night, and today, Nicholas and Kirill went to the local market to stock up.

I wanted to go out, too, but my personal nurse told me that would only happen over her dead body.

The pain in my shoulder has lessened to a dramatic degree, and I can even move it freely now, but if I do it too fast, there's a dull ache.

Nadia steals a glance at me. "You don't usually cook, do you?"

I get another knife and peel the potato to mimic what she's doing. "Not really."

"How do you keep that husband of yours fed, then?"

My chest jolts, as is the case every time I'm reminded of the roles Kirill and I are playing. I've come to the realization that it's impossible to get used to this fake marriage. Sometimes, I just want to blurt out that we're not actually a couple.

But then again, I don't want to hurt their feelings after everything they've done for me. As Kirill mentioned, they're traditionalists with set values and might have trouble accepting us if we're not 'married.'

"We just get by," I answer with a smile.

"That won't do." She chops the carrots in perfect squares and stares at me. "You need to eat healthy food, not just anything to stop the hunger."

"But I don't know how to cook."

"Learn to, then. It's not that hard."

Easier said than done.

The kitchen has never appealed to me, and it's not particularly because I was spoiled by my parents or due to the fact that I was a wild tomboy.

Though I do want to learn so I can stop surviving on army food alone.

"Would you...teach me?" I ask in a small voice.

Nadia all but beams. "Why, of course! What do you think I've been trying to do all this time?"

I smile back, and she sighs, a nostalgic look covering her eyes. "A long time ago, I also didn't know how to cook well, but Nicholas was so patient. He even taught me how. See, he's the oldest in his household, and since he lost his parents when he was young, he had to make sure his younger siblings were fed and taken care of. In his teenage years, he worked a lot of jobs while studying."

"Wow, that must've been hard."

"It was." She doesn't stop chopping, but her gaze becomes brighter and reminiscent. "I watched him all the time. Ever since I was a little girl. He's ten years older than me, but I knew when I was five that we'd end up together. I bugged him, of course, and he initially had no interest in me, but after I went to college and came back, we became inseparable."

"That's beautiful." It's probably been decades since they got together, but that shine in her eyes is still blazing strong.

Something tugs at my heart at the thought of what must've been an epic love story. I think their type of connection happens once in a lifetime. We only have one chance to seize it before it's gone forever.

"How did you meet your husband?"

My pulse hikes again, and I shift on my feet as I carefully peel the skin of the potato. "He...saved me."

"How so?"

"I was surrounded by some guys in a secluded place, and he happened to walk by. He lacks empathy, so he didn't have to intervene, but he did. Not only did he manage to effectively stop them, but he also punished them for it."

That incident feels like forever ago, but the events and details are crystal clear in my mind.

A sense of ease falls over me at not having to lie to Nadia. At least, not about this.

She hums knowingly. "He seems like the responsible type."

"He is."

"Those are very hard to come by. Appreciate him while you can." She pauses and her face brightens again. "Oh, here they are."

Through the kitchen window, I catch a glimpse of Nicholas and Kirill coming through the front door, carrying grocery bags.

Nadia wipes her hand on her apron and goes to welcome her husband. Kirill brings the grocery bags inside the house, but he soon reappears in the front yard, which faces the kitchen window.

The heavy winter coat does nothing to conceal his solid build. Sometimes, he looks no different than a beast with his harsh features and unwelcome aura.

Other times, when he's wearing the glasses, he looks like a sophisticated gentleman.

At least, from the outside looking in.

He heads to the shed, then reemerges with an axe and several large pieces of wood. Then he proceeds to split them.

Despite the storm ending, it's still cold and continues to snow.

However, Kirill doesn't seem to care about that since he's removed his coat and wears only his woolen cardigan.

He continues to chop the wood in sharp, precise movements that tug on my attention.

I can't look away from him.

Ever since the morning I shamelessly rubbed myself against his erection, it hasn't been the same between us.

Yes, he holds my hand whenever Nadia brings out her needle of horror, but he doesn't sleep on the bed anymore.

In fact, I don't think he sleeps much at all, and if he does, it's on the chair, where he spends most of the night reading some book Nicholas gave him.

He's been making it a point to engage in physical contact only when necessary. And for some reason, that's been making me frustrated for no apparent reason.

I place the knife on the chopping board and rub my fingers against each other. If I want to breathe properly, I have to do something about this situation.

After a moment of contemplation, I pour a cup of tea, put on my coat, and head to the front door. I smile at the distant voices of Nadia and Nicholas coming from their bedroom. She's nagging him about not wearing enough clothes and how he needs to look out for his health.

By the time I cross the threshold, my smile disappears, and it has less to do with the freezing cold and more to do with the man outside.

My pores fill with dread, which is a familiar feeling whenever I'm around Kirill.

"I brought some tea." My voice is surprisingly welcoming and calm.

He lifts his head from his task, and I'm once again trapped in his freezing eyes that put winter and all its snow to shame.

His punishing gaze studies me from head to toe, and it takes everything in me not to squirm.

"What?" I say in a less sure tone than earlier.

"You're able to move comfortably without putting strain on your injury, yes?"

I nod.

He abandons the axe and dons his coat. "Come with me."

"Where?"

"Somewhere private, where they can't hear us."

Oh.

Not sure what to do with the cup of tea, I place it on the chopping block and follow after him. Kirill's strides eat up the distance in no time, and I have to jog so that I can catch up with him.

We wander into the small forest surrounding the village before he stops under a giant tree, leans against it, and crosses his arms and ankles.

For a moment, he remains like that, not saying anything, and I resist the urge to ask, but I've come to learn that Kirill isn't the type to be pushed into anything.

"We're going back," he finally announces.

"Have you gotten hold of the others?"

"Only Viktor, yes. He's at the base and will come to pick us up tonight."

"Thank God he's all right. How about Maksim? Yuri? The others?"

"No clue. I had to end the call because Nicholas found me."

"Oh, okay."

Something's wrong, though. I didn't pay much attention to it earlier, but the expression on Kirill's face has been hardening since he came back from the market with Nicholas.

"We'll need to leave now," he continues.

"I thought it was tonight?"

"The pickup is tonight, but we need to leave the couple's house immediately. I had a nagging feeling that I was being watched in the market today, and Viktor confirmed that our position might have been compromised."

"Okay, we'll just say goodbye and leave."

He shakes his head. "We don't have time for that. If we linger any longer around them, we'll be putting their lives in danger."

"We can't just leave without saying anything."

"We will. That's an order."

My muscles tense, but like the apathetic monster he is, Kirill simply turns and takes a few steps, then starts digging in the snow.

I watch from afar, my blood boiling, not only at the turn of events but at him. How could he envision leaving without even saying goodbye to the people who took us in and asked for nothing in return?

Soon after, he retrieves our weapons and combat gear that he wrapped in the waterproof backpack. He throws mine near me and I pick them up.

"Get dressed."

My fingers tighten around the material, and I want to punch him in the face, but I can't. One, Kirill has zero appreciation for emotional outbursts, so it would backfire.

Two, he disappeared behind a tree.

My movements are jerky and mad as I remove the coat and start to dress in the surprisingly dry clothes. Because he was smart about hiding them. Kirill is always thinking ahead, never wavering or taking a shortcut from his original path.

As I wrap the bandages around my chest, I'm fuming while nearly freezing to death, which isn't a fun combination.

With every wrap, I feel like I'm locking myself inside again. It's only been a few days, but I easily got used to being a woman and also feeling like one.

Going back to my 'man' look leaves a weird taste at the back of my mouth. Despite living like this for so long. Will I ever go back to being a woman?

"You done?"

A chill sneaks over me as Kirill comes into view. Gone are the glasses and the somewhat tamed look. He's now back to being the unforgiving captain with nerves of steel.

"Almost." I lower my head to focus on tying my combat boots.

My shoulder strains with the angle, and I wince.

Kirill lifts up my shoulders so that I'm standing. "I'll do it."

"There's no need—"

"If you rip your stitches before we even leave, I'll be the one who's burdened. Stay still."

I bite my lower lip to stop myself from hurling curses at him. It's like he's making it his mission to sound like an asshole. Though, it probably comes naturally.

Efficiently and in record time, he finishes tying the laces and rises to his full height.

"I'm going back," I announce.

"You're *what?*" I don't miss the annoyance in his tone.

"I have to bid Nadia and Nicholas goodbye."

"What part of 'that's an order' do you not understand, soldier? We are not going back, and that's final."

"I won't see them. I can't, anyway, when I'm looking like this, but I can at least slip them a note of thanks." I step closer, keeping my head up. "Not only did they help me, but they also helped you and offered you warmth and shelter from a deadly storm. How are you supposed to protect your soldiers if you can't display gratitude to your benefactors?"

Kirill lifts his hand. "You little—"

I close my eyes, waiting for him to punch me for the insolence.

I wait and wait.

And wait…

But the impact doesn't come.

When I open them again, he's staring at me as if he wants to slash my throat open, but his hands are at either side of him.

"Five minutes, and then we leave."

"Okay!" I jump, smiling, but it soon disappears when it's faced with his complete apathy.

Damn tyrant.

I pick up my rifle and run in the direction of the house, thinking about the words I'll scribble on the note.

Thank you for everything (minus the needles). If I have a chance, I'll come again for those cooking lessons and—

My feet come to a halt when I arrive at the backyard. Silence.

Long, overbearing silence. No chopping of wood. No sound of Nadia's voice.

It's an eerie type of silence.

Something is wrong.

"Get down!" Kirill shouts as someone opens fire in our direction.

THIRTEEN

Kirill

M Y INSTINCTS HAVE NEVER FAILED ME.
So when I made the decision to get the fuck out
of here, I wasn't doing it arbitrarily. This is an emergency situation—escaping is a necessity, not an option.

However, Sasha didn't listen to reason and insisted on going back to the old couple. A decision that landed us straight in the middle of this fuckery.

Three armed men in gas masks open fire, then disperse as soon as we approach the house.

The critical part is that they came from inside the house.

The worst part, however, is that they're wearing gas masks, which means some sort of chemical weapon is involved.

At my shout, Sasha drops to the ground behind a tree, but her eyes are shifty and her hold on her rifle is unsteady.

She must be mulling over everything that I just thought of in her own mind and coming up with the worst possible scenario.

BLOOD OF MY MONSTER | 125

Two elderly people have no chance when faced with terrorists with firearms and chemical weapons.

When I was with Nicholas in the market earlier and felt eyes on me, this is precisely the turn of events that I dreaded the most. I promptly cut the trip short and insisted we go back to the house, but maybe that wasn't the right decision either.

"Lipovsky," I call with an authoritative tone, but that barely gets her attention.

"Sasha!"

She jerks, her eyes growing in size as they fly back to me.

I stop behind her, taking note of her chaotic reaction. "Are you there?"

She nods once. "Nadia and Nicholas, they...they..."

"We have to get rid of these men to be able to find them. I'm going to need you to cover for me so I can go inside. Can you do that?"

"Yes, sir."

"I need your head in the game, soldier."

Her chin lifts slowly, subtly, before she nods with tangible determination. "Sir, yes, sir."

She leans against the tree trunk, and I slip around the house, using the wall as camouflage. I shouldn't trust her to cover me under the circumstances, but I do.

Because here's the thing about Sasha. She works best under pressure, and even though she's worried about the old couple, she won't make a mistake that will cost them their lives.

Sure enough, as I steadily move in the direction of the house, she takes one of the men down.

My movements are easy, confident, and without an ounce of second thoughts. She's an excellent shot and won't allow any miscalculations. At least, not when it comes to this.

When I reach the entrance, I kill a man in black on the spot. One thing nags at me, though. I can't locate the other one. Considering Sasha's lack of action, she probably can't either.

Still, I continue to use the wall as cover and advance toward the house. The moment I step inside, I hold my breath. I can take it for five minutes, which should be long enough to find Nadia and Nicholas—

My movements jerk to a halt in the middle of the green living room that's fogged up with gas.

Two bodies sleep over each other on the floor, a pool of blood forming beneath them.

I rush to their sides and check their pulses. As the seconds tick by, the finality of the situation hits me upside the head like a motherfucker.

Even in their last moments, they're holding hands and leaning against one another.

Nadia's eyes are rolled back, showing more white than the irises. Her husband's eyes, however, stare at nothing, completely devoid of the life I was witness to not an hour ago.

I close their eyes, lost for words. They believed in a divine being and kindness, so hopefully, that being is now taking care of them.

A rustle comes from behind me before a haunted whisper follows, "No…"

I whirl around to find Sasha standing on the threshold, wearing a gas mask and holding another that she probably removed from our victims.

Directly behind her appears a shadow of movement, and I don't hesitate as I lift my rifle and shoot him between the eyes.

She doesn't look back, doesn't even think about her carelessness that almost killed her just now.

Instead, she runs inside and falls to the ground, in the middle of all the blood, not caring that her clothes are soaked with it.

"Nadia…Nicholas…wake up…" Her voice shakes, and so do her hands as she grabs the nurse's wrist. "No…no…"

I pull the free mask from her hand and strap it around my face, then suck in a generous inhale. "They're dead. We need to go."

Her head jerks up in my direction, and I could swear she's

about to point her rifle at me. "That's it? They're dead and we need to go? What type...what type of an unfeeling monster are you? These people saved our lives when they didn't have to and they're now dead because of it. They're dead, Kirill!"

"If you don't move, you'll also be dead, and all their efforts will be for nothing. Get up. *Now*."

"No." She shakes her head, voice filled with a brittleness I've never heard before.

It's not so much weakness as it is rage against that weakness, mixed with a hint of self-destruction.

"They're...they're like this because of us. Those men, they're here for us, not them, and we...we..."

I grab her by her good arm and haul her to me so fast and hard that she's stunned into silence. She crashes against my chest, and I shake her for good measure. "Listen to me and listen good, Sasha. If we don't leave right now, we might be ambushed. There's no telling how many men were on this mission or if they have backup. We need to leave this town before we get anyone else killed. So either you follow me, or I'll knock you out and take you by force."

Through the glass binoculars of the mask, I can see the tears clinging to her eyes and the red-hot anger flaring to the surface.

But I don't wait for her. I don't give her another chance, and I certainly do not offer her pity.

I release her with a shove and turn around to leave. At first, I think she's chosen to stay, but when I glance back, she places a blanket over the old couple's bodies and clasps her hands together in what seems like a prayer.

The moment I'm out of the house, I remove my mask and throw it down. That's when Sasha catches up to me.

Her shoulders are drooped, and her rifle hangs loosely around her chest, lifeless, almost as if it's lost purpose.

She robotically removes her mask, showing a pale face, red eyes, and tear marks streaking down her cheeks.

I start to reach a hand out for her, but stop midway. Not only do I have no clue how to comfort people, but even if I did, it'd serve no purpose in this situation.

Sasha is a soldier and she needs to act the part before she gets us into deeper shit.

Our priority is to get the fuck out of here before we're ambushed again.

Wordlessly, I turn around and start the careful but strategic retreat into the woods. Sasha follows behind, her movements robotic but focused. She doesn't waver or trip, but she's also not paying enough attention to her surroundings.

Once we're far enough from the village, I break into a jog, and she follows suit. I keep a steady pace to avoid her feeling any discomfort from her injury.

We continue running for two hours straight until we get to the pickup point—a cottage in the mountains that's owned by Viktor's family. We could've set the meeting at one of the military safe houses, but I've completely lost faith in the institution after the planned setup during the mission.

It doesn't take a genius to figure out that it was a setup, and that fucking cost me the men I grew up with. Men who were supposed to be under my protection.

I control my breathing as I find the key under the flowerpot and push the old door open.

"We'll stay here for a few hours until Viktor comes to get us."

Sasha nods and strides inside, her movements mechanical. Her expression looks dissociated from reality.

She remains standing in the middle of the shabby cottage with old furniture and threadbare rugs for one second.

Two.

Ten.

Thirty.

In fact, she doesn't move for a whole minute before her shoulders shake and she grabs her rifle with both hands.

Then, all of a sudden, she turns around and starts heading toward the door.

I step in front of her, effectively making her come to a halt. That's when I get a close look at her face. It's hard and tinted red, even though her lips are turning blue from the cold.

"Where do you think you're going?" I ask in a collected, completely detached tone.

"I'm going back to bury Nadia and Nicholas, and if I'm ambushed, I'll kill every last one of those fuckers. I'll spill their blood and crush their hearts."

"No, you won't."

She physically jerks forward. Admittedly, she's strong, probably due to the adrenaline and the anguish that's creasing her brows. But she's not strong enough to push me away.

When that tactic doesn't work, she uses her rifle to try to hit me, but I easily grab the end of it, wrench it out of her hold, and throw it on the nearby sofa.

So she goes for my rifle like a fucking survivor with no care for her life. I remove it from around my shoulder and throw it onto a chair.

Does that stop her? Of course not.

She all but engages in hand-to-hand combat with me, knowing full well that she can't win.

Her blows are vicious, full of contempt, and focused on one mission—getting through me to the door.

I kick her in the shin, and she falls to her knees on the wooden floor, but she promptly jumps back up, fists protecting her face.

So I do it again, harder this time so that the thud resounds in the air around us. If I hit her for real, I'll definitely reopen her stitches, so this is probably the only way to make her give up without my resorting to bodily harm.

The little shit actually stands back up, though slower this time, and resumes her combat stance. Guard up, shaky legs barely holding her upright, and face red.

I give the illusion that I'll go for her legs again and she steps back, but when she does, I grab her by the throat and push her against the nearest wall.

Her whole body goes slack, whether due to the blow or my closeness, I don't know.

She doesn't even attempt to fight my grip, but she does try to kick me. I tighten my hold on her neck, giving her enough room to breathe, but not enough to encourage a fight.

"Snap the fuck out of it. If you go, you're dead."

"So be it." The resignation in her tone is final and resolute as she holds her head high. "What's the point of living if I can't even protect myself or anyone around me? If I'm supposed to live on after losing so many people, then I'd rather not!"

Angry tears stream down her cheeks and cling to her chin before hitting my hand.

"Let me go, Kirill."

"I didn't save you so I could personally send you to your death."

"Why did you save me?" Her tone weakens. "You shouldn't have. If you hadn't, Nadia and Nicholas would still be alive."

"We don't know that. No one does. But there's one thing for certain. If you go back there, all the effort they put into you will be for nothing." I release her. "If that's what you want, go right ahead."

Her lips purse, then she grinds her teeth and releases a sound of absolute desperation.

This time, she can't seem to control the tears that pour out, soaking her chin. She tries to wipe them away and miserably fails to put an end to them.

"Why am I so weak?" She dabs at her eyes with both hands even as she cries like a baby.

"You're not weak." I pat her shoulder. "You're just human."

It's only a simple gesture and a few words to make her snap the fuck out of it, but it's as if I've opened Pandora's box.

Sasha throws her whole weight against me. Her head leans on my chest, and her sniffles echo in the air.

"I can't…I just can't stop thinking about how it's all because of me… Everyone dies because I exist in their lives…"

Who's everyone?

I don't ask that, though, knowing full well that she's not in the right state of mind to answer. Or that if I do ask, she might pull away, and that option doesn't necessarily appeal to me.

She places her chin on my chest, staring up at me with eyes so wretched and full of pain, they nearly appear black. "Am I cursed?"

"Only if you believe you are. Try to think that you're not."

An ironic smile lifts the corner of her full lips. "You make it sound so easy."

"You can make it easy."

She buries her face in my chest again and nuzzles her nose in my clothes. My hand twitches, but I have no fucking clue if it's to remove her or hold her closer to me.

One thing's for certain, her closeness has become fucking unbearable ever since the day she 'unknowingly' dry humped me.

I was seconds away from pinning her down, tearing her clothes off, biting her skin, and fucking her until she cried and screamed.

Every time she's come close since, I've been having the same images. Only, they've intensified tenfold.

Like right now.

It doesn't matter that she's grieving or having a weak moment that she hates so much. All I can think about is biting, marking, and sucking on her skin. Maybe even confiscating these tears so that they belong only to me.

So no one else but me will be able to see her in this state.

My body goes rigid despite myself. The weight of the image and the need to act on it are clashing, and the only loser is my resolve.

If Sasha notices the change, she doesn't act on it and continues crying in my chest.

I close my eyes and tip my head up.

Fuck.

These are going to be the longest few hours of my life.

FOURTEEN

Sasha

NADIA'S AND NICHOLAS'S DEATHS HIT ME HARD.
It felt like the massacre all over again. Their bodies in all that blood was a cruel reminder of my parents, my cousin, and everyone who left me forever.

I'm not even close to dealing with that, but just when I thought things couldn't get worse, they dramatically have.

After Viktor picked us up from the cottage, it took us almost a day to arrive at the base since they couldn't deploy a helicopter.

That's when we were hit by one piece of devastating news after the other.

Rulan and his entire unit were wiped out.

Viktor lost two men, and a few others were wounded.

The general atmosphere at the base is so tense and thick, it could be cut with a knife.

A depressive mood worse than mine hardens the men's expressions and ages them beyond their years.

When I was out there during the mission, all I thought about was eliminating targets. I chose not to think about the scattered remains of our men in the snow.

Or the blood.

Or the pain that would cause.

Now, however, all the emotions hit me in one go. It's excruciating and surreal to think we lost people I used to eat, train, and play football with.

Most were young, ambitious, and had their entire future ahead of them.

Rulan…the man with furious loyalty and a headstrong personality, is gone. For good.

I cast a glance at Kirill, who's striding to where the wounded are with Viktor. He doesn't stop to change his clothes or to answer to the higher-ups who must be waiting for a report on the mission. He chose his men.

His expression remains neutral, collected, and absolutely undisturbed as he pats one soldier on the shoulder and nods at another.

Either he's unfeeling or a man of steel who's not familiar with the concept of emotions. It's why he could be so detached from Nadia's and Nicholas's deaths.

It's also why he could keep a cool head while receiving the news of his men's deaths.

It's precisely why he's the captain. No one else but him would be able to pull what remains of the unit together.

"Sasha!"

I whirl around just in time to be engulfed in a bro hug. I wrap my arm around Maksim's back and wince when he squeezes my bad shoulder.

He steps back. "What is it? You okay?"

"Just a little gunshot wound." I roll my arm. "I'm good as new, though."

"Jesus, man. I thought we'd lost you and the captain."

We both turn to where I think he disappeared to around the corner. My breath catches when I'm caught in his suffocating attention.

Kirill stands there for a beat, eyes cold, hooded, and full of contempt. The expression disappears as soon as it appeared, and then he rounds the corner.

My heart, however, doesn't slow or calm down. If I said it was only because of the look just now, that would be a lie.

I've been this fidgety and out of sorts ever since he let me hug him in the cottage yesterday. He didn't physically comfort me, but his presence was enough to create a sense of safety.

It's how I managed to pull myself together and abandon the suicidal thought of throwing myself into a dangerous situation.

He didn't need to say anything or to even touch me. Just the feel of his hard muscles and steady heartbeat were enough to silence the demons inside me. I was relying on myself for years and that entailed burying my emotions and struggling to survive. I got so used to that feeling until that small moment when he let me hug him. Having someone there for a change was dangerously addictive.

"Earth to Sasha." Maksim snaps his fingers in front of my face, and I blink.

"Yeah?"

"What made you zone out like that?" He steps closer and makes a tour around me. "Did you hit your head?"

I playfully smack him on the side of his arm. "Maybe *you* did."

"Nah. I'm as good as the devil." He smiles, but there isn't that usual carefree energy behind it.

If someone like Maksim is this affected, then there's no hope for the rest of us.

"I'm sorry about Rulan and the others," I whisper low, as if I'm scared he'll hear me.

"Why would you be? You didn't kill them."

"No, but I know how close you guys were… I got so used to him and I didn't even know him for long."

"He was just a clown." His shoulders droop. "To think we were singing so casually the night before his death, having no fucking clue what was waiting for us."

"Maks…"

"He went with honor." He nods as if to himself. "He saved a kid by covering him with his body because he was a responsible fucker."

I squeeze his shoulder and he inhales shakily. I wish I could tell him it's okay to cry or scream or do whatever necessary to express his grief, but these men are backward and would see it as a weakness.

"Anyway." He raises an imaginary glass. "I promise to live all the years he couldn't, singing for both of us."

I clink my imaginary glass against his. "I'll join."

"That's my man!"

"Where's Yuri?" I ask, casting a glance at my surroundings.

"He got his hand fucked up." Maksim wraps an arm around my shoulder and leads me down the hall.

Soon after, we arrive at a room where a few soldiers are lying on beds, some with bandages, others with casts. It's a gruesome view of the aftermath of violence.

Near the window, I spot Yuri's frame, facing away from us, his bandaged hand hanging limply at his side.

We slowly approach him, but the moment we're within reach, Maksim all but slaps him on the nape. "Yo, fucker, look who's back!"

Yuri turns around with every intention of smacking his friend into oblivion, but he stops upon seeing me.

"Sasha!"

I'm the one who gives him a bro hug this time and resist the urge to linger for a bit too long. I'm just so thankful they're both alive and well. I'm already fragile, and if anything had happened to them, too, I wouldn't know how to survive it. Rulan and his men's deaths are affecting me enough as it is.

While Maksim is the heart of the party, Yuri is the soul. His face is classically handsome. Dark blonde hair, a square jaw, and a set of familiar, welcoming eyes. It always feels as if we met in a previous life.

"He hurt his shoulder." Maksim points a thumb at me, then juts his chin in Yuri's direction. "You injured your hand, but I'm as good as new."

Yuri slams his whole palm into Maksim's face and pushes him away. Then he pulls out a chair for me before he sits on the bed. "Let's talk like grown-ups without this spoilsport between us."

"You damn traitor! Are you exchanging me this easily?" Maksim headlocks him and hits him teasingly.

A faint smile paints my lips and grows the more I watch them. They're a better distraction than the chaos in my head.

Yuri swats Maksim away as if he's nothing more than a fly and focuses on me. "What happened with you and Captain? How come you went missing for days?"

"When I got shot, Ki...I mean, Captain took me to a small village where we remained in hiding until I got better. We would've come sooner, but there was a storm."

"No wonder we couldn't get a signal." Maksim places both his hands on the mattress and leans against them. "Viktor was going berserk trying to locate the boss. I'm glad you're back, but Captain won't have it easy."

I lean closer in my chair. "What do you mean?"

"He's with the higher-ups now, who will, without a doubt, put the blame on him for the mission's failure, when it's clear that it was plotted all along. It doesn't matter what he might have done, he was set up for failure from the get-go. Those stupid fuckers planned all this."

"Shut it." Yuri kicks his friend in the shin, and the latter howls.

"What the fuck was that for? I'm telling the truth here. Sasha deserves to know why he took that bullet."

I stare between them, grabbing for a sliver of information. "What's going on?"

"Remember the fat man who came on the day of the mission?" Maksim asks.

"Captain's father?"

"That's the one. He's always wanted Boss back in New York and has been trying to get him to discharge from the military for years. Since he failed and most of us chose to stay with the boss, what do you think his next course of action would be?"

"Try to force him."

He snaps his fingers. "Exactly."

"We don't know for sure." Yuri lowers his voice. "But it's true that the old boss met the captain's commandants prior to leaving."

"In our line of work, we don't believe in coincidences," Maksim supplies.

"Does...could the captain share the same suspicions?" I ask.

"I'm sure he does." Yuri's brows draw together. "If we thought of this after the mission, then he must've figured it out during. It's probably why he was hesitant about sending the units to that warehouse."

Shit.

If that's the case, and he was sabotaged by his own father, then how can he stay that calm? Just what type of steel is Kirill Morozov made of?

Maksim changes the subject to focus on me, and I realize they're trying to escape the reality they find themselves in and whatever the future holds for them.

Omitting the husband and wife roles Kirill and I played, I tell them about Nadia and Nicholas while fighting tears.

"It's a miracle they accepted soldiers in their house," Yuri says. "Most villagers have a distaste toward us."

"Uh, the captain stole civilian clothes, and we pretended that we were attacked by soldiers."

"Smart." Maksim grins. "As expected of Captain."

Yuri nods in agreement. "Point is, you came back safe and sound."

I'm not so sure about that. It feels as if something has been missing since I saw the blood and the old couple's corpses. A part of me has remained in their house and refuses to return.

That part of me is so riddled with grief, it's impossible to chase away the red haze that's been turning my vision hazy.

So I choose to focus on Maksim and Yuri, still feeling grateful that they're safe. I don't know how I would've dealt with all this if something had happened to them.

Soon after, the others join in and we catch up on the mission and the aftermath.

What seems like an hour passes by before a solemn-faced Viktor appears at the threshold of the entrance.

The captain follows behind, eternally calm and unaffected. He's nothing more than a monster dressed in human clothes.

I will never forget his practical, methodical expression when he was looking at Nadia's and Nicholas's faces. Or when he received the news of his men's death.

Nothing and no one can affect him, and I'm not sure why that fills me with a sense of dread.

Everyone stands at attention, and a shuffling of beds and limbs sounds from behind us as the injured men try to stand at attention.

"At ease," Viktor says.

When everyone complies, Kirill steps to the middle of the room, naturally stealing everyone's attention. He stands tall and erect, like a charismatic performer. When he speaks, his tone carries like a cool breeze. "The mission made me realize that I can't escape my destiny and that if I attempt to, I'll keep losing loyal men who followed me without asking questions. For that reason, I'm leaving the army and going back to New York. I understand if you want to stay here. I'll personally make sure you're transferred to elite units. Those who do not wish to remain here are welcome to come along. We're leaving in three days."

And with that, he turns and exits the room with Viktor in tow, leaving us in a jumble of confused emotions.

⟨❧⟩

Not one, and I mean not one man, has decided to stay in the military. Not even those who secretly like the military lifestyle and the bursts of violence.

According to Maksim, their excuse is a simple, "We'll get plenty of violence in New York; it's just a different type of violence."

That leaves me. I always thought I'd spend a few years in the military, go up in rank, and get close to the commandants so I could find out who ordered the hit on my family.

But due to the change in the situation, I'm not so sure about the next step.

So I call for an emergency meeting with Uncle Albert at the usual warehouse. My shoulders drop when I find out he's come alone this time, without a certain little boy climbing him as if he were a tree.

My uncle has thinned, looking way unhealthier than he did the last time I saw him. It's been only a month, but it feels like a year ago.

It's strange how time functions. When I saw Nadia's and Nicholas's bodies three days ago, it felt as if I'd been thrown back in time to when my own family experienced a similar tragedy.

After we got to the base, I told Captain that I was going back to the village to make sure the couple were buried properly, but he said he'd already taken care of it. Not sure when he had the time, but he got it done.

However, the couple's deaths wasn't the only thing that affected me. The fast-paced nature of the events that followed made me more conscious about what other tragedies await me.

Uncle Albert and I break after a hug, and he studies me. "You look…different."

"It's the muscles." I flex my bicep, and he smiles, showing his straight, perfect teeth.

"No, it's something else, but I can't quite put my finger on it."
He leans against the wall beside the entrance to the warehouse.

Freezing air slips through the cracks as a charged silence falls
between us. I called him for an emergency, and he's waiting for me
to spill. But I don't know where or how to start.

"What's wrong, Sashenka?"

My chin trembles, but I don't give in to the tears. "I just came
back from…uh, a mission, and it was kind of brutal."

"Are you okay?" He studies me with new eyes, affectionate
and full of compassion like those of Papa.

I shake my head. "I'm fine, but the unit lost a lot of men. So
Kirill, the captain, decided to take what remains of the unit and
go back to New York since he thinks his father won't leave him
alone otherwise. But the thing is, his father is someone you know."

A crease appears between his brows. "Someone I know?"

"The man who came to talk to you guys in the main house
before everything went down."

"What man, Sasha?"

"The overweight man with a balding head. His last name is
Morozov."

My uncle's expression darkens, and an incomparable sense of
rage emanates from him in waves. "How do you know that man?
Have you met him? Talked to him? Did he recognize you?"

"No to all. I only saw him from afar. He's…the captain's father, but he doesn't really get along with him, so I don't think he's
involved. No, I'm sure he isn't. They're just related by blood, but
that doesn't really mean they have the same character…" I trail off.
What am I doing?

It definitely sounded as if I was defending Kirill. In front of
my own uncle.

"You'll stay away from that man and his son and their world,
Sasha."

"W-why?"

"You don't need to know. Transfer to another unit and stay in Russia where I can look after you."

"Can't you at least tell me what that man had to do with the massacre? I can go to New York and kill him. I can—"

"You'll do no such thing!" Uncle Albert's voice booms around me with the lethality of a bomb.

The only other time he's spoken to me in this harsh tone was when he told me to run while I was half dazed. When he pushed me out of danger's way so hard, he broke my arm.

Just like then, it feels as if the situation is heading in a disastrous direction.

My uncle grabs me by the shoulders and lowers his head to stare into my eyes, his gaze firm, filled with the sternness of a parent. "Listen to me, Sasha. Those people are a pack of wolves who are only out for destruction. If you see them, you walk the other way. Got it?"

I stare silently for a moment, and he repeats, louder this time, "Got it?"

I nod once. "Can't you tell me more?"

"No. It's for your own safety."

"How is it for my safety when I know nothing about the reason I had to lose my whole life? I lost my parents, my cousins, and almost everyone I know. Don't I deserve to know why they had to meet such a fate?"

"It was just a bad business transaction."

"What type of business costs a family their lives? Were we just in investment and stock exchange, Uncle? Or was there something else I don't know about?"

"We are a law-abiding family."

"Then do you mind telling me how such a law-abiding family was practically begging a mafia man like Roman Morozov for help mere days before their eventual ending?"

"Drop it, Sasha."

"But—"

"Out of all the people who've known about Morozov and his shady methods, I'm the last one alive, and that's only possible because I'm in hiding. Do you now understand why you can't know?"

No. But I nod anyway.

"Good." He reaches into his pocket and retrieves a small blue candy. "Mike sent you this. He's been hiding it under his pillow for a month."

I take it with both hands. "Is everyone okay?"

"Yeah. We're hanging in there, but don't worry about us. Just take care of yourself."

After some catching up, my uncle reminds me to stay away from all the Morozovs, then disappears through the snow.

I spend the entire way back to the base thinking about his warnings. I'm ninety-nine percent sure that Kirill's father had something to do with my family's fate.

If I remain in the army, I'll never find out the connection between that man and what's become of me.

Uncle Albert said we wouldn't meet or talk unless there's an emergency. That means we likely won't be in contact for months.

When I reach the base, I'm resolved to discover the truth. There's nothing that can stop me from seeking revenge. Not even my uncle.

Despite the low morale I've suffered from since Nadia's and Nicholas's deaths, I feel a slightly different mood as I catch glimpses of everyone packing their bags. The badly injured will also be going since, shocker, Kirill has access to his own airplane.

Very convenient.

I'm about to join Maksim and Yuri in helping the injured soldiers pack when a wall appears out of nowhere.

Sorry, I mean Viktor.

He stands in front of me in all his stoic glory. "Where have you been?"

"Outside."

"Outside where?"

"Just outside."

He narrows one of his eyes, but then he points behind him. "The captain is asking for you."

"He...is?"

I don't know why I thought Kirill would now avoid any alone time with me.

Judging by Viktor's scowl, he doesn't appreciate my unnecessary question.

I step past him and head to the office. The moment I knock, a nervous breath leaves me.

"Come in."

I try and fail not to be affected by his voice.

In the office, I find him perched on the front of his desk, studying some paperwork, and only his back is visible. The hard muscles peek from beneath the thin black shirt, appearing stiff.

"You wanted to see me?" I ask in a careful tone.

He doesn't turn around. "You'll be transferred to the sixth unit effective tomorrow."

My heart falls, but I swallow the feeling and keep my cool. "Do I get a say in this?"

"Tell me the unit you had in mind and I will see what I can do. The sixth and ninth are the best. Which one do you want?"

"I want to go with you to New York."

His hands pause on the paper, and he slowly faces me. The ice of his eyes meets mine for the first time since I stepped into the room, and, despite their coldness, they manage to warm me up from head to toe.

A few silent seconds tick by before he asks, "You want to go where?"

"New York. With you."

"No."

"Why not? You gave everyone that choice."

"Everyone who came with me from New York. You didn't."

"But I want to go."

"And be what?"

"Whatever Maksim and the others will be."

"Maksim and the others will be my guards."

"I'm...fine with that."

"You're a woman, Sasha." His voice lowers. "My home isn't the place for you."

"That's sexist. Besides, if I can handle the army, I can handle this."

While still facing me, he grabs the table. His hands tighten on the edge and his biceps bulge beneath his shirt as if he's stopping himself from doing something extreme. "There's one difference."

"Which is?" My voice lowers, and I'm breathing with difficulty again.

"I will be your boss, and I will demand complete obedience."

"I understand."

"I'm not joking, Sasha. Out of here, it's not martial law. It's *my* law. Your life will be mine."

I nod again. Yes, I might be going to a more dangerous place than where I am right now, but that's better than being stuck in the same environment and doing nothing but surviving.

If putting my life in this emotionless man's hands is what I have to do, then so be it.

FIFTEEN

Kirill

THE CONCEPT OF HOME HAS BEEN FOREIGN TO ME since...forever.

It's not a place where I feel safe or even liked. It's a mere battlefield, where only the stronger comes out alive.

My father didn't shower my siblings and me with affection. He downright pit us against each other so we'd become invincible.

My mother had only one purpose—get her favorite child to lead the family, no matter how many strings she had to pull.

That sense of internal wars and calculations has been a part of me since I was a child, and it's only continued to grow over the years.

When I was old enough to put an end to it, I took the chance and flew to the other side of the ocean.

Though I always knew I would come back, because my ambition can't be contained in the military, I didn't know it'd be this soon.

Here I am. At the doorstep of our highly secured mansion that's located on the outskirts of New York.

It's huge, old, and has the spirit of a dozen devils rolled into one building. The brick façade looks dull, unassuming of what actually lurks behind the walls of this place.

The three-story house sits on a large piece of land with huge gardens surrounding it, a pool in the front, a clinic, and two annexed houses for the staff, one on the east side and the other on the west.

It's exhausting to recount the facilities Roman made sure to include in his lion's den. Such as an indoor pool, a golf course, and even a spa.

He turned the property into a royal castle, since he likes to think of himself as some sort of king.

Upon my arrival, it's no surprise that only the staff comes to meet me. Not that I want to see anyone's face right now. I only came for one purpose and one purpose alone.

My father.

He killed my men, and that was the last mistake he'll commit in his lifetime. I'll make sure he rots in that grotesque body of his until he wishes for death.

The rest of the men went to the annex house to settle the injured in at the clinic and visit any family members they have here.

The only two who remain with me are Viktor—since he sometimes considers himself my shadow—and Sasha.

Maksim calls her name and asks her to join him and Yuri in whatever vain endeavors they're going to engage in, but she tells them, "I want to meet everyone first."

"Yikes, good luck with that." Maksim gives her a salute.

"You know where to find us," Yuri supplies needlessly.

I cast a glance behind me, and her smile drops as fast as it appeared. Instantly, she returns to her stoic expression that's a marvelous imitation of Viktor's grumpy existence.

Everyone has discarded their army uniform, but she's the

only one who looks small and thin in her black slacks and white button-down.

Or maybe I'm the only one who sees it, considering I know exactly what's hidden by the bandages.

To say I'm taken aback by her decision to come with us would be an understatement. It always felt as if she had roots buried deep in the Russian soil, and in the military specifically.

She nearly lost it when I told her to discharge in the beginning, which means she had a motive to be there.

I never thought she'd easily abandon that motive and Russia to follow me here.

But then again, maybe she did it because of Maksim and Yuri. Considering that she was always a lone wolf, she's annoyingly close to those two and might think of them as companions for a lifetime.

Whatever her reason, I don't give a fuck. She made the mistake of offering her existence to me and I'll have so much fun molding her into whatever the fuck I wish her to be.

Usually, this isn't a game I like to play, but then again, no one toys with my steel-like control the way innocent-looking Sasha does.

Viktor clears his throat from my right, and it's then I realize that she's shifting in place under my scrutiny. It's not too noticeable, but it's there.

I push my glasses up my nose with my middle and ring fingers. "Don't leave my side. Got it?"

She swallows twice before answering, "Yes, sir."

My lips twitch as I face the entrance again. I like how she calls me sir; it's different from when everyone else does it.

"Kirochka!"

I'm attacked out of nowhere by a warm hug from a small woman with dark skin.

I pat her back as she hangs on to me with all her might and only pulls back to inspect me left and right as if I'm livestock.

One might think Anna is my mother for all the care and

affection she shows me. Truth is, she's the only mother figure I've had, and I've only known her since I was a teenager.

In the years since I last saw her, she's become thinner and bonier. A few more lines surround her eyes and appear on her forehead, and some white hairs start to invade her hair.

She's dressed in an elegant brown skirt and a pressed white shirt.

"You've gotten bigger and even have more muscles. Oh my." She pats my arm. "Have you been eating right? Did you make sure of it, Viktor?"

"Yes, ma'am." Even Viktor's tone of voice changes to that of complete respect in front of Anna.

After all, she's the only mother figure he knows, too.

She faces him. "And have you been eating well? You look skinnier to me."

"I'm just fine."

"Don't fine me, young man." She swats him on the arm and then hugs him. He just remains stoically in place. He's never really known how to accept the flood of affection Anna offers.

"Welcome home, boys. I missed you."

She then pulls back and casts a narrowed glance at Sasha, who has been silently watching the exchange. "And who is this boy who looks malnourished?"

"My name is Aleksander. Everyone calls me Sasha."

Anna stares at me. "You brought someone new?"

"He wanted to come."

"You can't just bring him over because he wanted to come." She points a finger in Sasha's direction without looking at her. "He looks suspicious."

"I'm actually over here," Sasha says in a calm tone, but her ears are turning red. Also, she actually speaks with no Russian accent. It's a bit stiff, but it sounds natural.

That's hard to accomplish, even for an American-born Russian.

The accent is usually there no matter what. Viktor, Maksim, and Yuri have it.

She really did have those private tutors in her previous life.

"Hush, boy." Anna still doesn't look at her. "Why are you doing this, Kirochka? It's not like you."

She's right. It's not.

When Sasha expressed her desire to come along, the most logical solution would've been to refuse.

One problem, though. I couldn't.

Especially when she agreed to place her life in the palm of my hand to do with as I please.

Is it sadism? Probably. But even I can't recognize what the end goal behind it is.

I can sense the contempt rising in Sasha, but the moment she steps forward, probably to give Anna a piece of her mind, I ask, "Is my father inside?"

A dark shadow falls over Anna's face, and she seems to forget about Sasha and her suspicions. "Why, yes. The lady of the house and Konstantin didn't want to inform you of this, probably not wanting you to come back, but Mr. Roman is…not doing very well. He has been severely ill for a while now, and it only got worse after he went to Russia last week."

Even better.

When I step in the direction of the house, Anna takes my hand between her smaller ones. "Be tolerant of everyone inside, my boy. Everything's changed, but some things remain the same."

"You don't have to worry about me."

"Nonsense." She gets on her tiptoes to touch my hair and pat my face. "I'm going to see the others. You take care of him, Viktor."

"Yes, ma'am."

With one last unsure look, she heads to where my guards went earlier. Anna is the mother of the orphans. Whenever a child lost his parents, she took it upon herself to raise them 'right.'

I'm not an orphan, but I found more affection in that woman than in my own parents.

The moment I stroll inside my so-called home, I'm greeted by the tension-filled, unwelcome atmosphere of the living room.

The baroque style of the sofas, chairs, and ceiling gives it an elegant aura that's stained with invisible splashes of blood.

Two pairs of eyes fall on me in pure contempt. The first belongs to the woman who gave birth to me.

She hasn't changed one bit. Her golden hair falls to her shoulders in the usual stuck-up sprayed style. She's wearing one of her straight red dresses with a gold belt and matching heels, and she's sitting like a queen on her throne.

If Yulia Morozova were an actual ruler, I would've been sentenced to death the moment I was born.

The second malicious stare that could get someone accidentally killed belongs to my brother, Konstantin, who's two years my junior.

He has lighter hair than me, a more angular facial structure that could never look friendly, and my mother's eyes.

Which is the first reason to put him at the very top of my hit list.

"Look who's done playing soldier and came back."

The second thing that would land him on my hit list is the aggravating way he speaks. It's like he's begging to be shot, just so that he can be silenced forever.

"Missed you, too, little bro." I smile, matching his provocative tone with my own, then nod at Yulia. "Mother."

She rises, her posture stiff, and walks in my direction. When she stops in front of me, I'm gutted by the smell of her strong perfume that could be used like a weapon. "Why are you back, Kirill?"

"Yes, brother." Konstantin stands beside Yulia like a good little mama's boy. "You said you might give up everything here, and we wouldn't see your face again, so what brings you here?"

"Your father. He's a pesky, insistent piece of work, that one.

He even killed my men to force me back here. Seems we can't get rid of each other that easily."

"Take the plane to Russia and leave," Yulia announces as if it's a given. "You're neither wanted nor needed here."

This woman treats me as if I'm lower than the dirt beneath her shoes. A long time ago, I used to wonder why she hated me so much, why she looked at me with so much contempt that I thought she might kill me one day.

When I saw other mothers shower their kids with love and affection, I wondered why I didn't have one of them.

Now, I don't give a fuck.

"What Mom said," Konstantin supplies. "I'll be the Morozov leader as soon as the old man is gone."

"How about no?" I guard my cool façade and even smirk. "I don't know what type of plan you two have, but I'm tempted to tear it to pieces and bathe in its blood. I'll make sure to watch you flounder and die as slowly as possible."

The slap reverberates in the air before I feel it. Soon after, the burning starts where Yulia's hand connected with my cheek.

"Insolent," she spits out.

"So you keep telling me, *Mother*. I'm glad to live up to your expectations."

She raises her hand again, but this time, it's gripped tightly before it connects with my face.

By Sasha.

"Please refrain from physically abusing him, or else I'll take drastic actions."

"You…who has the audacity to touch me…" Yulia, obviously lost for words due to the volatile turn of events, stares at Sasha as if she's a demon.

Konstantin starts to push her away. "I'm going to kill this fucker—"

I grab Sasha by her free hand and push her in Viktor's direction so he'll keep the suicidal little shit in check.

"How dare he touch me?" Yulia all but shouts her head off. "I want him dead. Right this instant!"

"Yeah, no." I smirk. "Aleksander just takes his bodyguard job way too seriously. He reacts badly whenever I'm harmed, so I advise you to refrain from doing that in his presence."

"So you're out picking up stray cats now?" Konstantin's words are laced with mockery.

"Maybe. At least they're more loyal than your mercenaries." I start to turn around. "I'm off to see Father."

"You won't win in this, Kirill," he shouts from behind me. "The power has shifted since you left, and the ball is in my court now."

I glance at him over my shoulder. "You say that as if I can't just snatch it back."

"Sooner or later you will leave. I promise you that," Yulia says all confidently with her irritating aristocratic tone.

But I don't pay her any attention.

Sasha, however, doesn't move as swiftly as Viktor and I, probably glaring at Yulia or something equally useless instead.

Viktor all but drags her out with him, whispering something to her in clipped words.

Soon after, the three of us are in front of my father's office. However, his senior guard tells us he's in his bedroom.

My parents haven't shared a room for as long as I can remember.

Viktor and Sasha remain outside as I knock on the door and, without waiting for a reply, slip in.

The dark curtains are drawn, casting a pitch-black shadow on the vast room. The stench of illness reeks in the air, blending with the walls.

I hit the light switch, bathing the place in harsh yellow light.

There's a cough, and then a moan of pain reaches me from the corner of the room.

The bed creaks under the extravagant weight lying on it, and a small voice whispers, "Kirill, is that you?"

Of course, even when he's sick as fuck and battling death tooth and nail, he knows that I was on my way.

He planned it. Made it happen and gave me not one ounce of a way out. Yes, I could've forced my men to go back and insisted on staying in Russia, but then I wouldn't be able to get my revenge on this man.

I stroll to his bedside, one hand in my pants pocket and the other hanging nonchalantly at my side.

My father has always been larger than life, so to see him as a shadow of his former self is weird. Is this really the great Roman Morozov?

His face is gaunt, and he's lost weight, even though he's still large as fuck. His eyes have sunken into dark sockets that barely contain them anymore.

Lips blue, skin pasty, he looks like the real-life personification of death.

His weak hand is holding on to the oxygen mask as he stares at me. For the first time, it looks like he actually sees his son, not the heir he spent years molding into whatever he saw fit.

The heir he beat, put in solitary confinement, and forbade any contact with the outside world for weeks.

The heir he made sure is only seen as competition by his own siblings and a target to be eliminated.

"How far the mighty has fallen." I shake my head, tsking.

"You're here," he says in a weak voice that's barely audible.

"You made sure of it, no?" My lips tilt in a smirk. "I probably should be thankful since you gave me a front-row seat to see you looking this way."

"Son...you'll be the leader now. You can't...can't let Konstantin take it...that oaf is...is..."

"Just like you?"

"No. *You* are like me... When I look at you, I see a younger version of me, son."

"Lies." My voice hardens.

"You are, Kirill. You're a true Morozov. This...this ambition... this need for more and more...the not being satisfied with whatever you accomplish is in your blood. *Our* blood."

"Stop it." I lean over, and he just smiles.

"You, too, are plagued with the need to have everything you can't see...go bigger...do more and more...and have everything. But nothing is enough... No one is enough..."

"I said. *Stop* it."

"Just like me." He breaks into a fit of coughs, and blood splashes my glasses.

He tries to put the mask on again, but it falls on his chin. He's so weak that he can't even move his hands properly.

I grab it for him, staring at him through the red droplets of blood on my glasses. "You killed my men, Father. The very men who followed me and trusted me and had blind loyalty to me are dead because you are my father, and I am a Morozov. You succeeded in bringing me back, but that's your last mistake. Yes, I will lead our name, but I'll destroy everything you made all these years. I give you my fucking word."

He coughs and splutters, a dying man's breath ripping out of him in a haunting melody.

I don't look away, don't even blink as I watch through the red. I stand there as my father spits his last breath, all while holding the mask out of his reach.

When his irises stare at nothing, I snap the mask on his grotesque face and clean the blood off my glasses with his sheet.

When I slide them up my nose again, the world is much clearer and cleaner from the loss of another miserable soul.

Now. It's time for my reign.

I won't stop as a higher-up in the Bratva. Sooner or later, I'll have the whole fucking thing.

He was right about one thing, my father. I will eat the world for breakfast and that still won't be enough.

When I step out, I find Viktor and Sasha arguing about

something. Or more like, she's arguing, and he looks like he's contemplating whether to bury her dead or alive.

"So what if she's his mother? She has no right to hit him."

"As I was saying, you don't get involved in anything that's related to the boss's family."

"Says who? And I didn't know you were such a domesticated cat, Viktor. You act all tough, but it's actually all white noise."

"Watch it, you little disrespectful fucker—"

"Meh. Losing respect for you as we speak."

Finally, they notice my existence, and their bickering comes to a halt.

I face Viktor, "My father is dead. Announce it, make arrangements, and do whatever it takes to get me the will from the lawyer."

He pauses for a second before he comes to his senses. "Yes, sir."

Sasha, however, remains frozen long after Viktor disappears around the corner. Her lips are parted, her stance is stiffened, and she looks like she's seen her worst nightmare.

"What do you mean dead? He can't...?"

"He can't?" I repeat.

She opens her mouth, but it closes again, then opens, like a fish out of water.

"Dieee!" A shrill female shout fills the air as my sister attacks me with a knife.

Like they say, home sweet home.

SIXTEEN

Sasha

I THINK I DON'T LIKE THIS PLACE.

Scratch that. I'm sure I don't.

Ever since we got here, it's been one freak show after another. And that's saying something, considering all the disasters I left behind in Russia.

First, there's a woman who fawned over the unfeeling monster Kirill, but called *me* suspicious. Then, we upgraded to a strange mother who flat out tried to kick her son out the moment he walked in, and then proceeded to slap him.

I wasn't even through processing all those events when Kirill announced so coldly and emotionlessly that his father had died.

As in, the man I came all the way here for to uncover what happened to my family and the reason they were targeted is gone.

I had all these strategies in mind to get close to him, but none of them will work now for obvious reasons.

I'm still trying to think about this fallout when another crazy woman lunges at Kirill's back while holding a big kitchen knife.

Usually, people freeze up in situations like these. I certainly did a long time ago when my cousins were slaughtered in front of me.

I couldn't move and I even considered dying right there and then.

However, that's not the case right now. I don't know if it's the military training, but my reflexes have become sharper, and my response time has gone from average to lightning speed.

In a fraction of a second, I grab Kirill by the shoulder and start to flip him around. I realize too late that if I shove him out of the way, I'll be the one who's stabbed—in my still-healing shoulder.

That doesn't stop me, though. Just when I think I've successfully turned Kirill, he effortlessly pushes me away with a strength that throws me against the wall. Pain explodes in my injured shoulder, but my good one takes most of the hit.

The knife slashes the side of his arm, and blood pours out, soaking his white shirt in bright red, then drips onto the floor.

Due to the force of her lunge, the girl, who looks about my age, crashes against the wall next to me. In no time, she stands upright, a shimmering rage shining in her eyes that are a shade darker than Kirill's. Her hair is blonde, though, and long, stopping at the hem of her silk sleeping shirt and getting tangled with the buttons.

She tightens her hold on the knife that's dripping with blood and stares pointedly at Kirill.

He doesn't even pay attention to his wound or show any signs of discomfort.

Sometimes, I wonder if he's human or, in fact, a robot in the form of a person. The more I see his cold reaction to events, the surer I am that his insides are icier than those frightening eyes.

"Hi, Karina. Does this welcome mean you missed me?"

"I'm going to kill you!" she snarls from between clenched teeth, then runs in his direction again.

This time, I'm quick enough to grab her from behind. I twist her free arm, and when she starts to struggle, I use force to pin it to her back.

She waves the knife blindly in the air and nearly cuts me. Actually, she does, judging by the delayed burn in my neck.

But I manage to twist her other hand and turn it around. She loses her grip on the knife, and it clatters to the ground. The girl still kicks and thrashes against me, her full attention on Kirill.

"Fight me, you fucking coward!" she shrieks. "Fight me!"

Is this tiny girl really asking Kirill to fight her? Even those in the army never did that, knowing full well they would lose.

"Let her go," he tells me with deceptive calm.

"But she's trying to kill you."

"Take the knife away and release her."

Slowly, I loosen my hold, then instantly make for the knife and hold it behind my back to be sure.

The girl, Karina, jumps at him, face red, and starts cursing in a stream of unintelligible words.

She does sound American when speaking in English. So did his brother and mother earlier. In fact, so does Kirill sometimes. They're really Russian royalty in the States.

"You grew up, Kara," he says in a weird affectionate tone that I've never heard before.

She punches him in the chest. "No thanks to you, asshole, jerk, fucking bastard. I was praying you would die every day. Why did you come back alive?"

"Cat with nine lives?"

"Go die. I hate you, I hate you!!"

"I know," he says with superhuman understanding and strokes her shoulder. "Would you hate me any less if I told you Father died?"

"Fuck you and him!" She kicks him in the leg, then stomps in the direction she came from.

Then she turns around and points a finger at me, then at her red wrist. "You're gonna pay for this, you stupid motherfucker!"

Then she's out.

That little—

I'm about to give the psycho a piece of my mind when Kirill steps in front of me and, as if sensing my thoughts, he shakes his head. "She's mentally unwell. Don't mind her."

"Did you forget the part where she was trying to kill you? If she's mentally unwell, maybe she should be admitted to a psych ward."

"She's not violent…except for the incident just now."

"No shit."

I inspect the cut on his arm, and my hands get soaked with blood. It's a huge gash that slashes through some of his tattoos. "This will definitely need stitches. If you could remove me so easily, you could've blocked her attack, too."

"I could've, huh?"

"You totally could, but you chose not to. Why?"

"She needed to get that one in, or her anger wouldn't have subsided."

"You're really…weird."

"Makes two of us."

I clear my throat. "Is there a doctor in this place? There must be with all the houses and departments. Can't you ask him to look at this—"

My words are cut off when a warm finger traces the pale skin near the pulse point of my throat. He's stroking the injury, I realize. "Next time, when something like this happens, do not, under any circumstances, put your life in jeopardy for me."

I try to swallow, but it's stuck, just like my breathing. "Isn't that what I'm supposed to do as a bodyguard?"

"No. There are always better solutions that don't include being a martyr."

"I…wasn't trying to be one."

"Really, now?"

My lips part, and my train of thought flies out the window

because his finger has moved up. He's fully exploring my throat now, tracing, touching, and leaving an inferno of goosebumps in his wake.

I can't for the life of me focus on anything other than his sensually dark touch. The feel of his skin on mine is forbidden yet so addictive. So raw. So...wrong.

"You were ready to allow yourself to be stabbed in the same shoulder that's injured because you were playing the martyr. That business won't happen again, am I understood?"

"No."

"No?" The edge in his voice would send anyone running, including me, but I have to put my foot down about this.

"I don't understand how Viktor and the others claim to be your guards while allowing your so-called family members to attack you. Whatever the reason, I'm not like them. You hired me to be your bodyguard, and I intend to do my job to the fullest."

"Sasha..." It's a warning laced with an unspoken threat. His icy eyes shimmer with the hint of danger that's part of who he is.

He's a cold, emotionless man who doesn't seem to care about the danger he brought on himself the moment he stepped foot in his house.

No wonder he chose freezing Russia over this.

He might be emotionless, but I'm not. Kirill has saved my life more than once, and I'm simply not going to stand by when his own life is in danger.

"Yes, sir?"

"Drop the innocent tone, and don't fuck with me." His hand flexes on my throat.

I have this weird sensation that I'm caught in the web of a lethal spider. No, maybe I'm trapped in the lion's den.

"What did I tell you before I agreed to bring you with me?"

"My life is yours." I speak without difficulty, but I can feel his hand on my throat with every word.

"That's right. It's mine." He digs his thumb into my pulse point. "So when I tell you not to throw it away, you fucking listen."

"I won't. If you're not in danger."

I can see the shadow falling over his features, and I'm not sure if he'll snap my neck or squeeze it to death.

For a moment, he goes for the second. His grip tightens, and I'm robbed of oxygen in a swift movement.

But then he lets go as fast as he grabbed me. "Go."

"How about your wound?" I realize I'm speaking breathily, almost too much so.

"Are you a doctor now?"

"No, but I can get you one."

He narrows his eyes for a fraction of a second before they revert back to normal.

"Let me try to stop the bleeding first. Do you have a first aid kit somewhere?"

He nods down the hall and starts walking that way without paying me any attention. I end up following anyway because his wound is dripping on the hallway carpet and definitely ruining it.

Once we reach the last door, he pushes it open and slips inside, then switches on the light.

A large room with an en-suite bathroom comes into view. There's a black leather seating area and a king-size bed on a high platform, but otherwise, it's too sterile-looking.

Kirill sits on the bed and juts his chin to the side. "It's in the bathroom. Make it quick."

I nod and rush inside, then fetch the kit and come back. My feet falter when I find him unbuttoning his shirt, slowly revealing the hard ridges of his muscles before throwing it to the side.

There's no doubt that Kirill's physique was sculpted by a god. He's not too bulky, nor too lean, but he has a perfect eight-pack and wide shoulders that fit his height.

Various tattoos swirl around his biceps and sides, giving him a darker edge. They're different in shape and form, ranging from a skull to a gun, a knife, birds, and snakes.

It's like his body is a map for these haunting images.

He places both hands on the bed and leans against them. "Are you going to stand there all day?"

I blink twice, then jog forward and nearly drop the kit in my haste. Through it all, Kirill watches me with no change in his expression, like a damn robot.

I try not to ogle his physique and tattoos as I sit beside him and start cleaning the wound. He doesn't whine, wince, or express any discomfort, but then again, I didn't expect him to.

Silence falls between us, short of any noise I make with my extremely careful movements. Despite my best efforts to act natural, I'm in a state of hyperawareness. My skin tingles, and my ears are so sensitive that they feel hotter with each passing second.

I'm almost sure it's due to being in this setting with Kirill. Maybe I should've let him get a doctor and deal with the wound on his own, after all.

"Why do your family members hate you?" I blurt to dissolve the tension, then follow up with, "If you don't mind telling me, of course."

"Why does anyone hate? You'd probably have to ask them that."

So he won't answer. Got it.

"I'm sorry about your father," I whisper, triggering my own feeling of emptiness for losing the only lead I had.

Unless he left some evidence behind? He seemed like the type of man who documented important things.

"I'm not." Kirill stares at the ceiling, seeming lost in a world no one can reach.

I want to peek into this world. I want to witness a fraction of what a person like him thinks about. His brain must work differently from the rest of ours.

"He was old and sick and had to die one day. This is as good a day as any," he continues.

He really doesn't care, does he?

Not about the men who died because they followed him to Russia or about Nadia and Nicholas, who welcomed us into their home.

Not even about his own father.

No wonder he's hated by every member of his family. Sometimes, I hate him, too.

I also hate that I'm indebted to him. Not that he'll hold me accountable for it, but he has helped me multiple times, and I can't just take without giving something in return.

"So what happens now?" I ask after I finish cleaning the blood.

"Now"—a slow smirk tilts his lips—"I take over the world, Sasha. And you'll be right by my side."

SEVENTEEN

Sasha

MOROZOV IS A BIG NAME AROUND HERE.
When I chose to come to New York, I was fully
aware that they're an essential part of the Bratva. I just
didn't know how essential.

Turns out, they're pillars of the entire organization and hold
a prestigious position of power at the top. The demonstration of
said power manifests itself in the sheer number of people who are
attending the funeral, including the Pakhan.

It's been three days since Roman Morozov's death, and during
this time of 'grief,' Kirill has been going out to meet people and
making phone calls.

His father hadn't yet been buried and he was already rekin-
dling old relationships and basically crowning himself as the new
leader.

I've been standing in the shadows while Kirill and his family
members accept condolences. All except for Karina.

I saw her dressed in a black dress earlier, and her mother attempted to force her to come downstairs, but the girl literally ran to her room and locked the door.

No one has seen her since, and I don't think anyone here cares about her absence. Maybe they're used to this behavior from her.

Back to the current moment. I stand on the periphery of the professionally decorated garden as part of security. If it weren't for the black and white velvet tablecloths and the image of the deceased man, one would think this was a wedding reception.

The part that makes me stop and stare isn't the number of people with a dangerous aura in one place. It's also not the one-hundred-eighty-degree change in both Yulia's and Konstantin's behavior in public compared to their viciousness in private.

It's how utterly composed Kirill is through the whole thing.

Every now and then, I can't help ogling him. In my defense, I don't mean to, and I usually stop when I notice I've been looking for too long, but it's a compulsion I can't put an end to.

Maybe I am taking my bodyguard role way too seriously, and I'm watching him this frequently to be able to protect him.

At least, that's what I tell myself every time my eyes stray in his direction. On the other end of the garden, he stands with a few higher-ups from the Bratva, one hand in his pocket and the other clutching a drink.

He's in a dashing black suit, tie, and shoes, looking straight out of a fashion show. We're all wearing black suits, but he's the only one who makes it appear regal. The black-framed glasses add a sense of powerful intelligence to his sharp features.

On anyone else, those glasses would look nerdy, but on Kirill, there's something entirely sinister about them. It's his expression, I realize. There's an overpowering control lurking beneath his calm façade. A dangerous edge that's pushing him to accomplish more, no matter what price he has to pay.

He had already lost half of his men, and even that didn't stop him.

Probably nothing ever will.

A finger taps my shoulder, and when I look to the side, Maksim pokes my cheek with his forefinger and then grins, appearing proud of himself.

"Aren't you tired, Sasha? You should go rest for a bit."

"I'm fine."

"You won't be saying the that when you're deathly exhausted by the end of the day. And it's going to be a looong day."

"Because of the funeral?"

"Because of what happens after the funeral." He juts his chin in the direction of Yulia and Konstantin, who are also in their own small circle with the mafia leaders. "Those two won't stop until they have power over the Morozov family, and guess who's in their way."

"Kirill?"

"Correct. I wouldn't be surprised if they sent those snipers to the last mission we went on, just to get rid of him. His recent return that's coincided with the old boss's death is the worst disaster that could've befallen them."

"But wasn't he named the heir in his father's will?" The lawyer was ushered here the day of Roman Morozov's death, and he read the will to the family.

Kirill is to inherit ninety percent of his father's assets—that includes countless properties, cars, a plane, and a multi-billion-dollar stock fortune. Karina gets ten percent on the condition that she signs away her votes to Kirill and assigns him as her proxy. In fact, considering her 'challenged' state, Kirill is named as her guardian and that gives him the authority to not only have control over her money but also to throw her in any mental institute if he chooses to.

Konstantin and Yulia only got one thing—permission to live in the house with Kirill and only if, no surprise, they don't challenge his authority.

Needless to say, his brother threw a fit and threatened to sue.

However, Yulia, who didn't look surprised in the least, just grabbed him, and they left together.

Maksim hums thoughtfully. "On paper, yes."

"What does that mean?"

"The will means nothing if he can't prove himself in the real world. In other words, he has to snatch back the power Konstantin and Yulia have been building during all the years he was gone. Yes, Boss had his father's support, but not everyone will blindly follow his will. It's a psychological game that's a lot harder than it looks."

I inch closer to my friend. "Whose support does he need?"

"The main players', of course. First of all, the Pakhan." He points at an old man with whitening hair and a calm, wise demeanor. "Sergei Sokolov, head of the Bratva ever since his brother died. He's kind of laid-back, but he's strict and has old ways. Second of all, his similarly old-fashioned friends are the two next to him. Igor." Maksim juts his chin in the direction of the strongly-built older man. He looks like a wrestler but has a white beard, hair, and a few wrinkles around his eyes. "That's the first of the four kings. His household is self-sufficient and shrouded in mystery, but he's been close to the current and previous Pakhans. In fact, he's known them since they were young, so anything he says or recommends will have a major impact on Sergei's decision-making process."

My gaze strays to the third in the circle. He looks as old as the rest, but he's leaner and has a somewhat sleazy businessman appearance and an erect posture that looks impenetrable.

"That, my friend, is Mikhail, the second of the four kings. He's stuck in the eighties, has the worst temper of the three, and is prone to be a wild card, depending on his mood. I honestly think the only reason he's still in power is because of his closeness to the Pakhan and some decent offspring who know how to handle business. He certainly doesn't most of the time."

"So, in short, if Kirill gets the approval of Igor and Mikhail, he'll take his father's place?"

"Not really. See the ones he's standing with?" He diverts my attention back to Kirill, and a frisson goes through me just like every time I look at him.

As a matter of fact, Kirill has been with those two men more than any of the other guests. One looks as frightening as Viktor. Only, he has a beard, a massive muscular body, and tattoos swirling up his neck like snakes.

The other man more or less shares Kirill's body type, though he's not as classically handsome. He has high cheekbones and a mysterious look in his gray eyes.

"Yeah," I tell Maksim. "I suppose they're also important in the great scheme of things?"

"How did you figure that out?"

"Boss wouldn't have given them so much of his time if that weren't the case."

"That is correct. Those two hold even more importance than the four kings." Maksim grins. "The bearded one is Vladimir, who's a few years older than Boss. He's a stoic authoritarian, an absolute nightmare if you break any rules around him, and might as well be mistaken for a stone in a person's body. He's also the Pakhan's right hand. The one who goes to war and makes sure the Bratva remains strong."

"I see. How about the other one?"

"Now, he…he's the actual wild card. His name is Adrian. He's the strategist of the Bratva and knows everything about everyone—the Pakhan included. And when I say everything, I mean every single fucking thing. It's impossible to cross him and even more futile to go against him."

"So the best thing to do is get him on your side."

"In theory, yes. In reality, however, he's on no one's side but his own and only holds loyalty to the Bratva. He's strong enough to only answer to the Pakhan and be considered the strategist. He's a bit of a recluse, though, and doesn't show up as much as everyone else."

My gaze falls on the men again. While Vladimir and Kirill

talk, this Adrian, who I'm starting to think could be the key to Kirill's inauguration, remains silent, composed, and detached. He barely drinks from his flute, only offers nods occasionally, and doesn't seem to be disturbed by any presence near him.

That is a dangerous man.

Maybe on the same level as Kirill.

I focus back on Maksim, needing more information to understand the current climate. "I assume Roman Morozov was one of those leaders, and now, one of his sons will take over?"

"You assumed right. Roman was the third of four kings. Boss already lost the internal family vote. Konstantin has Yulia's vote and her family's support."

"Her family?"

"Bankers. Those suckers are richer than God and have the immorality of the devil." Maksim clicks his tongue. "She was one of the reasons her husband rose in power so tremendously in the first place. She's using that same method to support Konstantin."

"But isn't Kirill a member of their family, too?"

"Not one who brings in profit like his brother does. They don't care what the name is as long as he's profitable and is tolerated enough by Yulia to recommend him to her family, but…" He pauses. "And this is a big BUT. Boss can still rule without internal support. He just won't be able to sleep soundly at night because of how hostile the environment in the house is. Every day will be a battle for his life."

"How about…Karina? Does she get a vote?"

"Yes, she does, but she might have switched to team Konstantin. She used to be close with Boss, but that was before he left for Russia. Now, she has joined her brother and mother's anti-fan club."

I can see that. In fact, I still remember the rage and hostility in her eyes when she stabbed him. She didn't look like someone who's on Kirill's side.

Hell, she's been doing the 'I'll slice your throat' motion whenever she sees me.

But there's a weird shift in her expression whenever he's around. Maybe if I get to the root of the problem...

That thought trails off when Maksim says, "None of this matters if he somehow gets the votes at the next general meeting. Sergei, Vladimir, Adrian, and the three kings, Igor, Mikhail, and Damien, all get to decide whether they will welcome Konstantin or Boss in their midst. Someone from the business front of the Bratva might get a vote, too."

"Wait. Who's Damien?"

"No clue." My friend lifts his shoulder. "He wasn't around when we left. Rumor has it, he killed the previous king, slaughtered his family, and conveniently took his place. The guards who stayed here while we were gone describe him as a crazy, volatile motherfucker. But we have no way of checking those facts since he chose not to show up today."

"Can he do that? Miss a leader's funeral, I mean."

"Out of respect, no. But if he's as much of a dark horse as everyone describes him to be, he probably doesn't give a shit about things like that."

I see.

I'm starting to understand how this operates. In a way, it's no different than the army. There are codes of conduct, hierarchy, and goals to be attained.

The only difference is there's no military law. Just the law of nature—you keep whatever you get.

You kill whoever poses a threat.

Survival of the fittest.

I still don't know why Kirill chose to stay here instead of going back to Russia. His father is gone, so he can't interfere in his missions anymore, and he still has loyal men who will follow him anywhere.

He did say that he'll take over the world, and there was a genuine gleam in his eyes. Dark and sadistic but definitely bright.

So maybe, instead of the army, this is what he actually enjoys doing.

This danger-infested environment does seem to be more in line with his personality.

"Come on." Maksim grabs my shoulders and pushes me in the opposite direction. "At least go grab something to eat so you won't fall on your face. Even boring Yuri is on a break."

"I guess I can take some time off."

"Thank fuck. Go. Don't come back for another hour."

I salute, and he grins in such a charming way that I have no choice but to mirror it.

Once I'm out of his sight, I don't go to the kitchen. One, Anna dislikes me. Two, Viktor will be a grumpy asshole and give me some type of chore. That guy has zero understanding of the concept of resting.

Three, and most importantly, I've been thinking about something ever since Maksim started getting me familiarized with all the players in this game.

Kirill might not have asked for my help, but I have a role to play. Besides, if he stays here, I have more chances to uncover his father's involvement with my family's massacre.

The main house is buzzing with people, servants, and a general grim atmosphere, but when I go upstairs, it's the exact opposite.

The halls are silent, and a more nefarious energy reeks from the walls, growing the farther I go down the hall.

Once I arrive in front of the room I've come for, I stop and inhale a deep breath. That proves to be futile, though, since my heart rate picks up.

All of a sudden, the door opens, and I'm greeted by a hellion of a girl. Even though she looks more presentable in her black, lacy mourning dress and a veil that covers half her face, there's no other word to describe Karina except for menacing.

"What do you want?" she asks with a psychopathic grin. "Oh, have you come to have your throat slit?"

"No," I say bluntly. "But I did want to talk to you."

"Oh, fuck off. Don't you have to be that bastard Kirill's shadow or something?" She's about to slam the door in my face, but I jam a hand against it and force my way inside.

Her room is dark, all the curtains are drawn, and she has some satanic-like circle of candles in the right corner.

It smells like her, though. Something lavender-y and girly.

"What the fuck do you think you're doing, asshole? I'm gonna scream the whole house down, you fucking psycho! You're going to be dead before you blink."

"Is that so?"

She swallows, her throat moving up and down. "If you think I'm bluffing, try me. I swear to fuck I'm gonna have the guards skin you alive while I watch."

"Funny you'd say that, because I could swear you don't like it whenever people are around. That's why you only have your meals in your room and even ask the maids to leave them in front of the door so you won't have contact with them. It's also why you ran away from the funeral without even showing your face."

"That's none of your business, you stupid fuck! I'm gonna have your balls for dinner tonight. We will see if you'll continue using that tone then."

"That won't be possible, but here's what might." I pause until she starts tapping her heel on the floor, showing her lack of patience. "How about you support Kirill?"

"I'll support him in Hell when he's being burned for eternity."

"You act like you can't stand the sight of him, but really, he's the only one who thought of you today. Not only did he ask the cook to send breakfast and lunch to your room, but he also specifically told your mother to leave you out of the proceedings. She didn't listen, but his intention was there."

Her lips purse, but there's a subtle softness in the corners of her eyes.

So I was right. Karina acts like murdering Kirill is her life's mission, but I often catch glimpses of her watching him from behind the curtain of her window like a creep.

She also makes sure to barge into his room every night to threaten him, but she no longer carries weapons.

He ends up hugging her, and she runs back to her room, cursing him all the way to Hell.

It's not that she hates him. It's that she probably feels abandoned by him. Someone as reclusive and odd as she is has lost her sense of reality. She's too sheltered, too spoiled, and too rich for her own good. As a result, she keeps her distance from the world, but when she gets attached to someone, it's for life.

I'm guessing Kirill was that someone, but when he left, she didn't take it well.

"What do I care what that piece of shit does?" She lifts her chin. "Why don't you do the world a favor and drive him off a cliff so both of you can die?"

"Careful what you wish for, Miss. If Kirill doesn't succeed in his endeavors, he'll go back to Russia."

"Hmph. As if Kirill would change his mind so soon. You know nothing about him, asshole."

"I certainly know more than you do. He already left you once, do you honestly think he won't do it again? Will you be able to survive this time?"

Her smug expression falls and she stares at me in horror. "You...you..."

"Remember my words." I salute her with two fingers and walk out of the room under an onslaught of her curses.

Yes, I could've gone about this a different way, but I didn't have time. Or maybe I'm just being molded into someone of Kirill's caliber.

At any rate, Karina is the only ally he can have here, despite her antics.

At least I hope she chooses to be on his side in this internal war.

Now, I need to figure out how to help Kirill get to the top. The more I'm of use, the more he'll trust me.

The more he trusts me, the closer I'll get to revealing his father's involvement in my family's death.

EIGHTEEN

Kirill

I HAVE A PLAN.

It'll take time, effort, and, most importantly, patience, but sooner or later, it'll work.

Everyone in the organization thinks I wasted time in Russia, but it was the military that shaped my strategic mind into its current state.

While my father's brutal torture filled my mind with red, it's the military's discipline that allowed me to redirect that energy into clear focus.

My plan is dangerous and has a twenty percent margin of error, which is undeniably a lot, but I choose to focus on the eighty percent success rate.

I stroll out of my room to find Viktor at the door. His expression is solemn, but his attitude hasn't changed since we returned—something I appreciate. "The Pakhan has set a meeting for later today at which you and Konstantin have to be present."

Didn't take him long. Only a week after the old man's funeral. I adjust my glasses with my middle and ring fingers. "Is everything in place?"

"Everything's as you ordered."

"Good."

"The madam and your brother are waiting downstairs."

"Are they now?"

"Mrs. Morozova said, and I quote, *I will not take this insult. Tell him to come down at once.*"

My lips twitch and I choose to remain where I am for as long as possible. Just to fuck with Yulia's and Konstantin's heads.

I cast a look at Viktor's surroundings. "Where's the...persistent shadow?"

"Other than me?"

I raise a brow. "You know exactly who I'm talking about, Viktor."

I would swear he's about to roll his eyes, but he stops himself at the last second. "He's buggered off somewhere. Apparently, dainty Lipovsky didn't like sleeping sandwiched between Maksim, Yuri, and the others."

"*Sandwiched?*" I repeat slowly.

"Like back in camp." Viktor matches my tone and then narrows his eyes. "Is there a reason why Lipovsky is the topic of discussion?"

"I'm assigning him to be my night guard."

"That impulsive fool?"

"He's learning."

"But I am your guard at all times."

"Don't be jealous. Besides, you can't be awake at all times or you'll be inefficient."

"I don't like this, and I don't trust him. He's new, looks suspicious most of the time, and I'm seventy percent sure he's hiding something."

"Now, you're being paranoid." I teasingly push him with

my shoulder, then head to the stairs. "Tell Maksim to fetch him. Actually, no. Make that Yuri."

I don't turn around, but I can feel my guard's eyes drilling holes in the back of my head. Viktor never liked Sasha—for all the right reasons.

He thinks she's too weak to protect me, acts on impulse sometimes, doesn't think of the consequences of her actions most of the time, and she behaves suspiciously.

Not to mention she has an infuriating habit of talking back.

These are valid points that I should probably pay more attention to, but I don't.

It's not because I trust Sasha. On the contrary, I do believe that she's hiding more than her gender.

And because I have my suspicions about her, I have to keep her closer now more than ever.

"He's doing this on purpose to fuck with our heads." My brother's voice reaches me as I get to the bottom of the stairs.

Yulia, who's dressed like a queen in some dark red dress, lifts her nose higher in the air. "And you're letting him get in *your* head. You will never win against Kirill if you keep rising to his provocations."

"You're right, Mother." I stroll inside, a hand in my pocket and looking absolutely nonchalant. "He'll never win. The rest of the sentence is redundant."

My brother, who can't control his temper to save his life, pushes off his seat, eyes blazing. "You think your games could affect me?"

They already are, fool.

I ignore him and stare at a composed Yulia. If she didn't blink, one would think she was a statue.

"To what do I owe this morning's meeting?" I ask.

"While it's true that your father named you as the head of the family, that won't be possible if we vote you out." She pauses. "We're here to do just that."

"Are you sure, though? Konstantin here will only bring trouble to the family due to his *tantrums*—to put it mildly. He's not leader material. You know it, he knows it, and everyone in your family knows it, too, considering the worried phone calls I've received since I landed here."

"You fucking—" Konstantin lunges in my direction, but I swiftly grab him by the arm, turn him around, and twist it against his back.

"Down, boy."

That only makes him thrash harder, but he doesn't manage to free himself from my hold.

"As I was saying." I meet Yulia's stonelike gaze and throw her favorite son in her direction. "Not leader material."

My idiot of a brother is about to attack me again, but Yulia stands and clutches his shoulder, keeping him in place.

"We're voting you out," she says easily, with no change in her expression, as if nothing of the previous show happened.

"How about a deal instead?" I approach and then stop a small distance away from them. "I will lead this family and give you larger cuts in return. If you disagree, I'll just take everything. You have... twenty seconds to accept the offer."

"You're a fucking bastard with no code of honor whatsoever." Konstantin steps forward. "You should've stayed in Russia while you could."

"Ten seconds."

"It's two to one, Kirill. You're voted out." Yulia sounds as cold as ice.

I definitely got my tone and mannerisms from her. We're two unemotional beings who can't be perturbed by any change of events.

She hates it, though. I can always see the amount of loathing she has for the fact that I'm more like her than her darling Konstantin will ever be.

"Five."

"Fuck you," Konstantin tells me.

"Aaaand zero. Your time is up."

I'm about to turn and leave when I spot a petite girl with a mane of blonde hair running down the stairs, her fluffy robe flying behind her.

She marches straight to Yulia and Konstantin. "Don't I get a vote?"

"Why, of course." Yulia stares at her like she's a nuisance that shouldn't be here.

And by *here*, I don't mean this meeting, but the world in general.

Konstantin smiles victoriously. "It's three to one now, brother."

Karina looks out the window across the room as she says, "My vote goes for Kirill."

"As I said, three to—" Konstantin cuts himself off and swings to face Karina. "What the fuck did you just say?"

"Kirill." She looks him right in the eye. "He has my vote."

He grabs her by the arm and starts to shake her. "What the fuck is wrong with you? You know what? Your vote doesn't count."

"Mother just said it does." She glares at him even as she winces.

I step between them, effectively breaking his hold on her. "Leave her alone."

"Were you plotting this all along? Getting Karina? You didn't even care about her before, and now, you're acting all brotherly and shit? Wow. You're such a fucking asshole."

"What did he give you?" Yulia asks, barely managing to hide her irritation.

"Nothing. I just felt like it." She lifts a shoulder, crosses her arms, and stares behind her.

At the top of the stairs, I catch a glimpse of a smiling Sasha giving Karina a thumbs-up.

Something my sister lifts another shoulder to and mutters, "Whatever."

Then she climbs up the stairs.

When I glimpse back at Sasha, she's already gone.

That little fucking—

I offer a fake smile to my mother and brother, then follow after Karina.

She actually tries to run away, but I catch up to her at the top of the stairs and grab her by the elbow.

"Why did you do that? Now, you'll make an enemy out of them."

She swings around and pushes me away. "They already were, and so are you. Everyone in this godforsaken place is my fucking enemy."

"Kara..."

"Don't call me that!" Tears rim her eyes. "You lost the right to call me that the day you left me running after your car in the rain."

I purse my lips. "I couldn't take you with me. You were too young."

"Fuck you. I hate you."

"If you hate me so much, why did you vote for me to stay?"

"Well...I want you to suffer here where I can see you."

"Did Sasha, by any chance, have something to do with this?"

"That asshole couldn't affect me in any way. You should kill him, Kirill. He looks useless."

And yet he managed to get you out of your room without any form of threat.

"I'll think about it."

Her eyes bug out. "Really?"

"Yeah. You might be mad at me, but I will keep my promise to protect you, especially from my own men."

"He...is not *that* bad. I guess we can put him on probation, and if he does anything fishy, we'll slice his throat."

I ruffle her hair. "As you wish, my lady."

She pauses, chin trembling, but then she pushes me away and runs to her room shouting, "I still didn't forgive you!"

My lips pull up at the corners as I watch her flying back to her room as if her life depends on it. She'll probably remain there for a week after all the unwanted exposure she's had to the outside world.

Karina had no reason to come down just now and face the mother she's intimidated by, but she chose to help me.

I wait for Sasha to show her face, but she flat out ran away.

She can't run for long, though.

I check my watch as Viktor appears by my side like a ghost. "We're ready."

"Go."

It's one word, but he knows exactly what to do.

The game is starting.

～

Two hours later, I'm sitting in my father's office, which I took as my own the day he died.

I've been going through all of his files, records, and archives. I'm the only one who can, because he left me his passwords and keys. Yes, actual keys—he was old-fashioned like that.

The old fool trusted me to continue the Morozov legacy.

In going through his assets, files, and everything in between, I come across a nice tidbit.

There's a little black book in which my dear papa transcribed every shady transaction he did with higher-ups here, in Russia, in South America, and all over the world.

He did it in detail, too, highlighting people he'd already received a favor from and putting stars by others he hadn't.

The heinous crimes and great lengths he went to in order to achieve power are spelled out one by one in this little gem.

Something I'll certainly make use of in my future endeavors.

On the side of my desk, I'm slowly building a large house of cards. The geometrical shape and the amount of effort I put into this task helps in opening up my vision for all sorts of scenarios.

My phone vibrates on the desk, threatening to destroy my

creation. I carefully grab it and lean back in my office chair to check it.

Viktor: Operation phase one is completed.

Kirill: Remain on standby until further instructions.

Viktor: Copy that.

I'm about to place my phone in my pocket when the door barges open, and Sasha appears on the threshold. Her shirt is disheveled, and her face is sweaty.

"Don't you know how to knock?"

She breathes heavily before she blurts, "Your...your mother was kidnapped."

"Is that why you decided to stop avoiding me?"

She strides inside, her brow furrowed. "How can you be so calm? Your mom...she was taken in the middle of the road."

"Were you following my mother, Sasha?"

She swallows. "Is that important right now?"

"Maybe."

A dark shadow falls over her eyes, making them appear somber. When she stops in front of my desk, her lips roll forward in a strangely adorable pout. "I know your mother isn't the best person out there, but I'm telling you right now that her life is in danger. I saw it with my own eyes when the masked men hit her car, eliminated her bodyguards, and kidnapped her. So you have to do something. *Now*."

I slowly place two cards at the top of my house. "Why should I? She wouldn't have done anything if the roles were reversed."

"Then how are you any different from her?"

"Who says I am? She's my mother, after all."

Her expression doesn't change, neither in surprise nor in shock. Instead, she announces in a calm tone, "I don't believe that."

I stand up, and she flinches back slightly. It wouldn't have been noticeable to an outsider, but I know the exact reason behind the gesture.

She prefers to avoid me.

Interesting.

"I might take action if you tell me why you were following my mother."

"I was…trying to figure out who she was going to meet."

"Have I given you the order to do that?"

"No, but I thought—"

"Did I ask you to think?" My voice deepens, and Sasha must feel it, too.

Tension crowds her shoulders, and she looks at me like a mouse who's trapped.

"Answer the question, Sasha. Have I brought you here so you'll think?"

"No."

"That's right, *no*. So quit the habit of being a busybody and a problem solver when I haven't asked you to take action."

"Well, I'm sorry I tried to help."

"Apology declined."

"I take it back then. It wasn't sincere in the first place."

I narrow my eyes on her disobedient ones. If it were anyone else, I would've either fired or shot them for the insolence.

But something about Sasha's defiance has been stirring the ugly beast inside me.

I don't want her out of my sight. On the contrary, I want her so close that I can possess her. That her being will merge with mine.

My eyes meet her defiant ones. "You're pushing it."

"I just don't understand why I can't help. You did that for me countless times. Why can't I do the same?"

So she's considering what I've done a favor, and all this time, she's been paying me back.

Interesting.

"Karina is out of this game. If I'd wanted to get her involved, I would've, but I didn't, because her condition doesn't allow her much stress or pressure."

"I didn't pressure her."

"You want me to assume you asked nicely?"

"Well...almost. I didn't threaten her, though. In fact, she's the one who threatens me with bodily harm every time she sees me."

"Next time, don't get involved, or at least notify me when you do."

"I can agree to the second, but I can't guarantee the first...sir."

I don't miss the way she added the last word as an afterthought. I'm going to have my hands full with this one for sure.

"From tonight onward, you'll be my night guard."

She blinks, probably at the abrupt change of subject.

I've been meaning to make this decision ever since we came to New York. The idea of her sleeping 'sandwiched' between Maksim and Yuri has left a weird taste in my mouth.

In the beginning, I thought about giving her a solo room, but that would look suspicious. Not to mention that the little fucker Maksim has no sense of personal space.

So the best way to keep her from sharing a bed with my men is to assign her as my night guard.

"Okay. What do I do?" she asks.

"Stay by my bed as I sleep."

"Oh...uh, are you sure you don't prefer someone else...like Viktor?"

She's running again. I can see it in her awkward body language and backpedaling speech.

"This is not a request. It's an order."

She's about to say something else but stops when I point at my creation. "Do you know why a house of cards has a bad reputation?"

"Are we really talking about a house of cards when your mother needs help?"

"Answer the question, Sasha. Do you know why?"

She throws her hands in the air with so much attitude, I'm tempted to push her against the wall and abandon all the plans I had for today.

"Well, it takes a lot of effort and concentration to build, but it can be destroyed in no time."

"Yes, and no. See." My hand hovers over the top card. "They're made of paper, and while paper can be molded, it's still fragile."

With a flick of my finger, I tumble the creation I spent an hour assembling.

"Listen carefully, Sasha. This place is a house of cards, and I don't belong inside it. I will always be the one who puts it together or destroys it."

She furrows her brow, not seeming to understand the meaning, but that's fine. She'll get there with time.

I round the desk and she subtly pushes back, keeping a safe distance between us. I adjust my glasses with my thumb and forefinger to stop myself from choking the fuck out of her.

"Did Konstantin hear about my mother's kidnapping?"

"I think so. He was talking about the worst timing and things like that on his way to his car just now."

"Good."

"How is that good?"

She falls in step beside me as I leave the office. "Are you going to ask him for help to save her?"

"Of course not." I grin. "A hero doesn't share his cape, now, does he?"

"You'll surely lose time with this. Is it okay if you're late to the Bratva's meeting that's being held specifically for you?"

"No. But it'll all work out."

Everything, including Sasha, will go according to plan.

NINETEEN

Sasha

KIRILL ASKS ME IF I WANT TO BE THERE FOR...THE rescue operation of his mother.

He sounds so casual about it that I can't help but be a little appalled.

My reaction to his actions is more about me than him. I know that. I really, *really* do.

It's not that he's changed, but maybe I'm freaked out about the fact that he hasn't changed.

In fact, he's been being unapologetically himself in a very direct manner. He was strict and unapproachable in the army, probably due to martial law, but now, he's shed his outer skin and is letting his inner self loose.

Not that I expected him to change, but I did think maybe being around members of his family would compel him to behave differently.

Little did I know that they would bring out his apathetic side.

I sit in the passenger seat as Yuri drives the car to the location where Kirill said his mother is. I asked Yuri if the boss put a tracker on her, and he just lifted his shoulder.

He didn't have to spell it out. *Everything is possible in this family.*

I stare at Kirill through the rearview mirror. He sits with effortless charisma like a king. It's scary how natural he is at looking calm and authoritative even when he's doing a mundane task such as scrolling through a tablet.

His long, veiny fingers rest on the device with easy control. I can't stop looking at his masculine hands. The fact that they could also be used for destruction doesn't lessen the strange effect they have on me.

"Faster, Yuri," he says without lifting his head, and a small smirk tilts his lips. "We don't want to be late for saving my dear mother."

This man is a psychopath.

I'm still shaking from the scene I witnessed near the highway. It looked like something right out of a movie but also so realistic, it left me in a temporary state of shock.

Not only did a minivan tailgate her car, but then, all of a sudden, they ran her off the road.

I was sure Yulia had died in the accident, but soon after, she was shoved out of the vehicle by her bodyguards, who were knocked out and thrown to the side of the road by men in black ski masks.

Everything happened at lightning speed and ended before I could think of a solution. I considered following them, but I knew I would be as good as dead if I did. So I called Viktor, who said, "I'll take care of it," and then hung up.

Maksim was unreachable, and when I got back to the house, Kirill was lounging like a bored king on his throne. He also acted as if the news of his mother's kidnapping has no importance whatsoever.

We arrive at a warehouse that's far from the city. Only a few abandoned industrial buildings are in sight, their old yellow-gray colors clashing with the afternoon sky in a beautifully gruesome image.

I jump out of the car, but Kirill doesn't move, seemingly engrossed in whatever business he's been doing on the tablet.

I bang on the window, and he stares at me as if I'm a nuisance. I catch a glimpse at what he's watching, and my face heats.

It's...porn.

Holy shit.

Is that what he was zeroing in on during the entire ride?

He doesn't act flustered or abnormal as he turns off the iPad, throws it on the seat, and takes his time getting out of the car.

With the same nonchalant energy, he walks to the door of the warehouse. I catch up to him and blurt, "Shouldn't we have some sort of a plan first? They probably have a sniper somewhere. We really should've brought more men with us. And is Yuri really supposed to stay in the car—"

My words come to a halt when he does something that stuns me into silence.

Kirill leans down and bites my ear. It's not a lick or a nibble. It's a flat-out bite that sends both a chill and zings of pain down my spine. Then, just like that, he pulls back.

I can feel the heat rising in my cheeks as I grab my assaulted ear. "What...what was that for?"

"Your silence." He speaks casually, but there's an unusual edge beneath his words.

The fact remains, what he did has the desired effect, and I stop talking. I do grab my gun and survey our surroundings, though. My senses are on high alert as if we're back on that mission that ended it all.

I also can't help overthinking about the turn of events in the current situation. Did they call him for a ransom? Is that why he's so calm?

Kirill casually pushes the warehouse's door open without even pulling out his gun.

I freeze in the entrance when I spot Yulia strapped to a chair. Her mouth is sealed shut with duct tape. Her usually elegant hair looks disheveled, and dried blood lines her temple.

But she's not what makes me stop and stare. It's the men beside her. Viktor, Maksim, and a few of my other colleagues.

What are they doing here?

Did Kirill send them prior to our arrival?

No.

I take in my surroundings, and something definitely doesn't feel right around here.

There are no bodies, no signs of struggle, and definitely no remnants of the 'saving Yulia' mission.

As I stand there, dumbfounded, and slowly but surely play what happened in my head, Kirill approaches his mother.

She wrenches her shoulder back in a hopeless attempt to free herself from the bindings.

Kirill's back nearly hides the entirety of her, and I have to step to the side to get a better view of her expression.

"You went through a lot, Mother." He speaks with frightening neutrality. "You even got injured for it. I applaud the dedication."

Muffled sentences leave her duct-taped mouth, and Kirill nods as if understanding every word.

"You welcomed me with the utmost affection, so I have to fulfill my filial duty and return the gesture." He slowly removes the duct tape, as if intentionally wanting her to feel every second of discomfort. "The same can't be said about your dear Konstantin. He knew about your kidnapping and still went to the Pakhan's house. Some would even say your favorite son doesn't give a fuck about your life or the possibility of your death."

"You foul piece of trash! I'll tell Sergei you planned this entire thing. If you think doing this to me will get you anything—"

Kirill slams the duct tape back on her mouth, killing any words she had to speak.

"Now, don't strain yourself. It's not advised at your age. Besides, do you honestly think Sergei will believe you over me? You seem to forget that I was an asset to the organization even when my father was alive. Know your limits, Mother." He stares at Maksim. "Take her back home. Make sure she's safe and sound."

My friend nods and starts to untie her, but Kirill shakes his head. "Take her just like this. Only untie her when you reach the house. I'm sure you'll understand, Mother. Your nagging is grating, and I prefer not to expose my men to any unnecessary stress."

A muffled scream rips from her, but Kirill is already heading toward the warehouse door.

Yulia thrashes and screams behind the duct tape, eyes blazing and her whole regal demeanor ripped to shreds.

I'm frozen by the scene but only for a few seconds. I snap out of it when Viktor silently follows Kirill to the car and takes my previous spot beside Yuri.

I hide my gun, feeling like a clown. Apparently, I'm the only one who wasn't aware of this situation.

"Get in." Kirill peeks from the back seat, and I nearly stumble inside before catching myself.

Silence falls over the car as Yuri revs forward and drives at high speed.

I place both hands on my knees, gripping tightly for a moment too long. I think even Yuri was aware of the 'kidnapping Yulia' operation and everything that followed, because he wasn't given orders about our next destination, yet he's definitely driving like he knows exactly where we're going.

Turns out, I'm the only one Kirill doesn't trust enough to disclose these sensitive details to.

Of course, I understand that our few months of acquaintance doesn't mean much compared to men who literally grew up with him and were raised by Anna.

Even Maksim and Yuri, who are my closest friends, feel so distant right now. They're loyal to Kirill, not to me.

Maybe my efforts to belong to that loyalty circle are futile, after all—

My thoughts are abruptly cut off when a large, strong hand envelops mine.

Kirill's.

I've always noticed how big and veiny his hands are, but to actually have one of them crushing and dwarfing my own is entirely different.

Just like earlier when he bit my ear, he catches me completely off guard, and I'm not sure how to react.

My internal temperature hikes up, though, and my heart thunders in the confinement of my rib cage.

Kirill, however, ignores me. He's looking at the front seats with his easy expression, even as he pushes down on my hand.

It's then I realize that my knee is bouncing and I slowly force it to a halt.

Kirill strokes the back of my hand in an approving manner. I catch my breath, unable to draw in air properly.

"How long until we get there?" he asks, completely unaware of the complicated emotions he's stirring within me.

"Twenty minutes," Yuri replies.

"Make it ten."

"Yes, Boss." And then he practically turns the car into a bullet.

While I know Yuri is trained in high-speed driving, I still think we'll crash as he zigzags between cars and nearly hits a truck.

Through it all, Kirill still has his hand on my knee. Or more like, his hand engulfs mine that's on my knee.

I suspected this before, but I'm entirely sure now. I really hate how much he affects me with his mere words and presence.

And, now, his touch.

My skin tingles, and something on the inside attempts to claw its way out.

Tactfully, I grab his hand with my other one, remove it, and subtly scoot to the end of the seat.

Kirill's head tilts in my direction, a mysterious look covering his face as he slides his glasses up his nose.

I clear my throat. "Is anyone going to tell me what the plan is?"

"All the pieces will fit together soon enough," Kirill says.

"Was kidnapping your mother part of the plan?"

"A huge one, yes."

"Watch your tone, punk," Viktor warns from the passenger seat, fixating me with his signature glare.

The car comes to a stop in front of a large metal gate. Everyone stays still for a moment, probably being examined by the cameras. Then the gate creaks open, and Yuri speeds inside the enormous property.

By the time we arrive at the mansion's circular driveway, I'm about to vomit from motion sickness.

And I've never even had that before.

We step out of the car that's parked behind a dozen others. We find Konstantin's men chatting happily with other guards, probably the Pakhan's.

They stop talking upon spotting Kirill and make way for him. Only two guards are allowed to escort him inside. Since Yuri is staying by the car, I follow Viktor and Kirill to a grand hall.

This place is even more majestic than the Morozov family house, and that's saying something since that mansion looks royal.

This one, however, has a grimmer feel. In the entrance hall, there's a huge painting of a war between angels and demons. Blood splashes all over the piece, and gruesome facial expressions are drawn in spine-chilling detail. I can almost hear the horrifying screeches of the mythical creatures.

A big, burly man with a stoic expression that matches Viktor's opens the double doors to the conference room.

Kirill strides inside without so much as a nod.

Viktor and I follow, then stop when he does.

The dining room is decorated with a gold-themed table, a huge chandelier, and candelabras on the fireplace.

But the atmosphere is neither welcoming nor joyful.

The men who attended the funeral sit around the table. At the head, there's the Pakhan, the big boss, and the one who calls the shots, Sergei.

Vladimir and Adrian are sitting on the leader's right and left respectively.

Then there's Igor and Mikhail. The old-fashioned and older generations.

Beside Mikhail sits Konstantin, looking smug, with a smirk lifting his lips as if he's already a victor.

On the opposite side, sits...a woman. Blonde, serious, and with elegance dripping from her expressionless face.

I saw her with Sergei at the funeral. Maksim said she's his grandniece and the previous Pakhan's granddaughter.

She has no opinion on the on-site operations, but since she's climbing the ladder in the organization's legitimate front, V Corp, she has voting rights.

Behind every member stand two guards like Viktor and me.

"You're late," Vladimir announces in his booming voice.

"Are we a joke to you, Morozov?" Mikhail adds in an accusatory tone.

Igor nods. "That's disrespectful, not only to us, but to the Pakhan himself. It doesn't look good for your application to be part of this table."

Kirill pushes his glasses up his nose with his middle and ring fingers, not appearing affected in the least. "I apologize for the delay, but I had a legitimate reason."

He pulls out his phone and shows them a picture of Yulia bound, bleeding, and barely consciousness.

"On my way here, I received this picture of my mother, and I had to go save her. She's now safe and sound back home." He faces Sergei. "I don't believe I'm worthy of any position in the Bratva if

I betray my own. If I can't protect my family, how can I protect a bigger organization?"

Igor turns to Konstantin, whose smile has vanished. "Is this true?"

"I didn't know she was kidnapped."

"Oh, yes, you did. You received the same image, no?" Kirill shows the cc at the top of the email. "If you could confirm your attendance via email, surely you've seen this picture. The only difference is that you chose to ignore it."

"You—" He stands up and falls back down again at everyone's silent scrutiny.

"I apologize on behalf of my brother," Kirill continues in his serene tone. "He's still too young and doesn't understand the value of family yet."

"You're the one who left for Russia!" Konstantin accuses.

"At Father's orders. As I said, family."

"Roman did mention that he sent Kirill to Russia for further training," Igor says.

Kirill's expression remains neutral, despite knowing that's not the case.

I'm not surprised that his father lied to his friends. He didn't seem like the type who would've wanted to advertise his authority being challenged. So it's plausible that he made them think the Russia episode was all part of his plan.

After all, judging by the will and the sensitive material he left for Kirill, he always considered him his sole heir.

Sergei places a hand on the table, and everyone's attention flies to him. No further words are exchanged, and heavy silence clings to the tension in the room.

"I'm disappointed in your misconduct, Konstantin," he says in a slow, composed speech pattern.

When the younger of the Morozov brothers starts to speak, Sergei lifts his hand, effectively shutting him up. "Nevertheless, we promised a vote, and we'll conduct a vote. Those in favor of Kirill joining our table, raise your hand."

Igor is the first to do so, followed by Vladimir, Adrian, and the woman.

Then, finally, Sergei himself.

When he raises his hand, Mikhail does, too, although reluctantly.

Konstantin's face turns red, just like his mother's earlier. All he can do is watch as Kirill topples his carefully constructed plans that he probably spent years devising.

"We won't even need to wait for Damien," Sergei says. "Welcome aboard, Kirill. Konstantin, I expect you to support your brother going forward. You can take your leave."

"But—"

"*Now.*" There's a nonnegotiable quality to Sergei's voice that the younger Morozov has no choice but to follow.

As soon as the door closes behind him, Kirill takes his brother's seat. "I apologize for his behavior. He still has a long way to go."

"Indeed," Vladimir says. "I trust you'll keep him in check as you promised."

Kirill nods. "You have my word."

Oh, I see.

The pieces of the puzzle start to fall into place.

Kirill already had a plan A and a plan B. The first one was his mother's kidnapping and making himself appeal to Sergei's sense of loyalty and family.

But if that somehow went awry, he already had a plan B in place. Vladimir and most likely Adrian and Igor. He must've made some deals under the table, so they'd vote for him instead of his brother.

I stare at his back from my position behind him.

This man…is on another level.

And I'm genuinely glad to be on his side. I wouldn't have survived if I were his enemy.

I'm starting to believe that he truly meant what he said. This isn't simple ambition.

Kirill wants the world, not caring who he has to trample in his path.

I pay close attention to the meeting. Kirill tells them how he'll improve his father's legacy and even gives them his word about the percentage of profit they can expect from him this time next year.

One hundred percent. No shit.

By the end of the meeting, everyone looks at him through a new lens. He has a godly presence that demands both attention and weariness.

Some are apprehensive—Mikhail, Vladimir, and Rai. Others are appreciative—Sergei and Igor.

The only one who remains neutral throughout the whole meeting is Adrian.

There's no sense of victory on Kirill's face when we leave the dining room and head to the front door.

No sense of success or celebration.

He knew this would be the result all along. His level of strategizing is out of this world.

As we're about to get in the waiting car, a tall, muscular man approaches us.

His shirt is barely buttoned, and his hair looks like he just got out of bed. But despite his overall disheveled appearance, he is anything but.

A sinister edge lurks in his gray-green gaze. It's the look I've seen on the faces of soldiers who joined the army for bloodlust.

When he's within touching distance, I slip in front of Kirill, hold up a hand against his chest, and say in my deepest, manliest tone, "Step back."

The man's deadly expression falls on my hand. "Why, aren't you a tough little shit?"

He starts to twist my hand with ease, but I slip it out and manage to grab his and then twist it to his back.

Before I can pin it, though, he whirls around and punches me in the face, sending me flying against the pillar.

The breath knocks out of my lungs, and I cough several times as I feel a bruise doubling the size of my face.

In fact, I can't feel my face. And why is the earth so hazy?

"As I was saying." I hear the newcomer tell Kirill. "Are you why I was woken up so early? You don't look that special to me. You sure you're not supposed to be the accountant—"

The last thing I see is Kirill's fist connecting with the man's face before my world turns black.

TWENTY

Sasha

A LOW ACHE STARTS AT THE BACK OF MY SKULL AND THEN spreads all down my spine. However, the pain pales in comparison to the scene in front of me.

I'm in a vast white field, frozen in place, as heavy snow blows over my coat and hair.

When I look down, Mike stares at me with blood tears in his eyes. The view is gruesome in the otherwise white surroundings.

I try to reach out for his little face and wipe away the blood, but I can't move.

His small hands grab onto my coat as he whispers in a frighteningly haunting tone, "Save me, Sasha."

I startle awake, breathing heavily as sweat covers my skin.

"Mishka…" I murmur, then frantically study my surroundings. There's no indication that my baby cousin would magically appear and offer me his gummy smile that makes everything better.

Instead, I find myself in a familiar minimalistic bedroom. I look down and see that I'm in a loose T-shirt instead of the white shirt and jacket.

"You don't look like yourself, Sasha."

I slowly sit up against the headboard to be greeted by Kirill in his sharp black suit. The only difference from earlier is that he's lost the jacket and rolled the sleeves of his shirt to his elbows, revealing the striking tattoos swirling down his strong forearms and teasing over his veiny hands.

When I start to talk, a strong ache spreads all over the left side of my face, and I wince.

"Don't force it. I told you that you look different." He speaks in his signature casual tone, but I also sense a concealed edge beneath his words that I can't interpret.

"Did I lose consciousness...after being punched in the face?"

That's so lame, and here I thought I was getting stronger.

"While you were running on lack of sleep and food." He grabs a tray from the nightstand and puts it on my lap. "Besides, you didn't get punched by just anyone. That was Damien."

"The final member of the organization?"

He nods.

"And you just punched him back?"

"Like he'd just punched you, yes."

"But I was in the wrong."

"Just because you stopped him doesn't mean you were wrong."

I sit up straighter in bed, hyperaware of the shifting of the mattress beneath me. "Will that cause problems for you?"

"Considering he was laughing like a maniac after I nearly broke his nose, I would say no. But then again, who knows with a crazy bastard like him."

"Maybe if you apologize—"

"Nonsense," he cuts me off. "Eat. Anna made this for you."

"She...did? I thought she hated me?"

"She doesn't hate you."

"She just doesn't like me?"

"That dislike is currently on pause since she learned you were unconscious due to defending me."

Yikes. Now, she and everyone else must be labeling me a weakling who needs to be babied.

"Isn't this your room?" I ask carefully, once again hyperaware of my surroundings and, especially, the man standing right beside me. It doesn't help that the sheets smell like him, and I have to dig my fingers into them to stop myself from bringing them to my face and inhaling them.

"Those are some impressive deduction skills," he says with a note of amusement.

"You could've just let the guys take me to the annex house."

A shadow darkens his light eyes and his tone turns lethal. "If by that, you mean that you're fine with the *guys* finding out about your true gender, then we can do that right away."

"I...didn't mean that."

"Then be thankful and shut the fuck up."

My shoulders snap upright, and heat explodes across my skin. "You don't have to speak to me in that tone. In fact, I'd prefer it if you didn't. I only had a legitimate concern about your image. I didn't want you to look weird for taking a guard to your room, but maybe I was overthinking."

"You were. As long as I have the power, no one dares to question me about my choices. So let me worry about my image and eat, Sasha. I won't ask a third time."

I narrow my eyes. "And what do you intend to do if I somehow disagree?"

In a swift movement, he puts the plate back on the nightstand and then all but lifts me. In no time, he takes my previous place on the mattress and brings me down on his lap.

I'm speechless for a second too long as I'm crushed by the hard muscles of his thighs and chest. He wraps his arm around my back and rests it on my hip, then grabs the tray.

"I...was joking. I can eat on my own."

"You might have been joking, but I certainly wasn't. I told you I won't ask again." He takes a spoonful of the soup and jams it against my lips. "Open."

I don't mean to, but my mouth trembles. A war erupts in my core as I'm surrounded by his rare warmth and his scent.

Damn how good he smells all day. Every day.

And now that he's so close, I'm forced to breathe him instead of air.

"Let me down," I murmur, barely hearing the words myself.

"Open your mouth. I won't ask a third time."

I let my lips part, even though I don't want to. At the same time, I'd rather not find out what he'll do if I don't comply.

Kirill is a force of nature not to be reckoned with. I know because I've seen him in action, and he low-key terrifies the shit out of me.

Annoyingly, though, I also find myself weirdly fascinated by his abnormal mind.

He slips the spoon inside, but I don't taste the food. It's impossible when all my senses are being held hostage by this…enigma of a man.

The act of feeding another person should be normal, or at least, not important enough to cause such unbearable tension. However, due to who Kirill is, it's anything but.

It also has to do with the position I'm in.

Each of his movements oozes with suffocating control, and I'm hopelessly caught in his web. I stare at my hands in a desperate attempt to disperse the tension that's wrapping itself around my neck like a noose.

"Um…congratulations," I say in a small voice.

Kirill slips another spoonful of soup into my mouth. "For?"

"Getting the position as your father's replacement."

"You say that as if there was a possibility I wouldn't." He raises a brow. "Did you doubt me, Sasha?"

A frisson goes through me like every time he says my name. It's especially aggravating when he does it in that rare, amused tone.

"I did, but only until I found out you had two plans to get that position."

"Two plans?"

"The first is playing the hero for saving your mother and subtly highlighting Konstantin as non-filial. The second is buying votes in case the first plan didn't work."

"That's where you're wrong." He strokes the corner of my lips to wipe something off, but his fingers linger there for a second too long, feeling unbearably sensual. "There weren't only two plans, there were three."

"What's the third?"

"Getting rid of Konstantin."

"You...planned to kill your own brother?"

"Getting rid of him doesn't necessarily mean killing him. I'm more creative than that."

I was wrong. Kirill isn't only dangerous. He's a literal menace.

I turn slightly in his direction. "Don't you feel apprehensive about having all these enemies?"

"Nothing great was ever achieved by only having friends." He strokes my mouth again, but this time, his thumb presses on my bottom lip until it pulses beneath his touch.

My awareness of the weight of his arm around my back and over my hip feels heightened. But most importantly, I can't ignore the growing bulge against my ass.

The more he strokes and presses on my lip, the bigger his erection becomes. A chill travels down my spine and into the very marrow of my bones.

My face heats, and so does my neck, despite my attempts to keep my reaction under control.

This is the first time he's touched me this explicitly since that day during the snowstorm when I was injured. Maybe it's because

I thought this would never happen again, but now that it has, my body resurrects to life despite myself.

"Are you blushing, Sasha?"

I try to swallow, but it gets stuck at the base of my throat, so I just shake my head once.

"Your skin looks red."

"That's because...I'm hot."

"That you are."

My heart beats so hard, I'm surprised it doesn't jump from its confinements and lay itself at his feet. "W-what?"

"What?"

I can't say it. I want to, but I just *can't*.

He just called me hot. I heard it, but I'm not sure if it's real or if my head is playing tricks on me.

"What are you doing, Kirill?" I ask instead, finally voicing the thoughts that have been running through my head.

He places the tray on the nightstand. That's when I notice I'm done. Maybe I finished a while ago, but I have no memory of the food.

He spreads his large hand on my hip, eliciting a shock wave through the thin material of his shirt.

His icy eyes devour my face for one second.

Two.

Three.

"I'm trying to decide whether or not to fuck you."

I choke on my own breaths, and any logical thoughts seem to fly out the window.

"You...*what?*"

"You don't have a hearing problem, so quit acting like you do." His free hand strokes my cheek, then makes a slow path to my mouth. "I've wanted to fuck you since we were in that village. I contemplated throwing you down, opening your legs, and taking what I wanted. I fantasized about leaving my marks on this translucent skin, and not letting them fade. I imagined taking you over and over until you screamed and cried while begging for more."

My body goes slack against his as my temperature reaches its boiling point. My ears burn and tingle, begging for more.

But that's not the only place that pulsates with each calm word out of his mouth. My core throbs, and I have to clench my legs. The slight shift causes my ass to brush against his massive erection.

I go still, so scared of breathing that I only do it in small increments.

"While it's so tempting to spread your legs and fuck you, I won't. Do you know why?"

I shake my head, trying and failing to ignore the overwhelming sense of disappointment that spreads through me.

"I can't seem to figure you out...*yet*, and I don't get entangled with possible enemies."

"I'm...not your enemy." *I would be long dead if I were.*

He narrows his eyes. "You're hiding something—or possibly some *things*. I do not for one second believe you followed me all the way from Russia just to pursue a career as a bodyguard."

"Then why did you let me tag along?"

"I told you. Because I get to have you under my thumb."

"Keep your enemies closer, huh?"

"Something like that." He sinks his fingertips into my hip. "We can rectify this situation if you confess."

"You're not a priest, why would I confess to you?"

"No, I'm not. I can be your father in Heaven, though."

"I decline." I start to push at his hand, but I might as well be moving a mountain.

"Don't be stubborn. I know you want me, Solnyshko. You watch me when you think I'm not looking, and you even get hot and bothered. I can smell your arousal right now. If I reach between your legs, I'll feel it, too."

"Too bad for you, I don't get entangled with enemies either." This time when I push at his hand, he releases me.

I only manage to breathe properly when I leap out of the bed and stand at a safe distance from the monster in tailored clothes.

"If you don't need anything." I nod and turn around, barely resisting the urge to jog to the door.

"Run all you like, Sasha, but one of these days, you will confess, and I'll reward you."

I give up trying to look cool and break into a run.

If I refuse to deal with these feelings plaguing me, surely they'll disappear, right?

TWENTY-ONE

Sasha

THREE DAYS LATER, I HAVE A FADING BRUISE DUE TO Damien's punch, and the tension in the house has gone up a notch.

Yulia always looks at Kirill like she wants to strangle him—which isn't a surprise, considering he did kidnap her.

Konstantin has been sneaky and going out for multiple meetings. Yuri told me that just because he lost his father's power doesn't mean he's out of the game. He still has his mother's influence to fall back on, and he'll use it to its full capacity.

Karina has been coming out of her room to watch me or her brother like a creep before she runs back to her self-confinement and slams the door.

Me? I've been actively trying to avoid Kirill as if my life depends on it.

It takes every ounce of professional willpower I have to look him in the eye and not think about the feeling of his body beneath mine. His fingers on my lips. His hand gripping my hip. His erection beneath my ass.

His breath, his smell, his warmth. *Everything.*

It's impossible to forget. I didn't even get a proper taste, but I still want more.

And more.

And even…more.

But I can't. I *won't.*

No matter how tempted I am by Kirill, no matter how hard it is to keep this fiery, unusual attraction at bay, that's exactly what I will do.

He's dangerous to everything I've been trying to build. I lied when I said he wasn't my enemy. After all, he's Roman Morozov's son, and depending on that man's involvement in my family's murder, he might become my enemy.

I've spent the last couple of days actively memorizing the mansion's security system. While I hated using Maksim, I had to learn how everything around here worked. The cameras, the alarms, and the guards in charge of surveillance.

The interesting tidbit I came up with is that there are no cameras in any of the bedrooms or the office. If I somehow manage to get into there without looking suspicious on the hall's cameras, I'll be able to get some information.

I've been to the office before, but only when Kirill and Viktor were there.

Most drawers have keys that Kirill changed to password protection. The safe is thumbprint protected, so only Kirill can open it. That doesn't matter, though, because I don't think Roman considered his involvement with my family a sensitive enough secret to hide in the safe.

He probably thought of the whole ordeal as something trivial. Hell, I have to be prepared for the possibility that he considered it unimportant enough that he left no record behind.

I won't know until I try, though.

208 | RINA KENT

Keeping my steps nonchalant, I walk down the hall leading to the office, then knock on the door and try to open it.

Locked.

Of course it is.

Still, I remain there for a moment, contemplating the best and fastest way to pick the lock without looking suspicious.

"Do you need something?"

I startle, but I subtly compose myself and turn around to face Viktor's solemn existence. "I was searching for Boss."

The stonelike man raises a brow. "In front of a closed door?"

"I thought maybe he was inside. I knocked."

He remains expressionless, and it takes everything in me not to fidget. I swear he does it on purpose just to see me squirm.

But we're not in the army anymore, and he's not my direct superior. I lift my chin, but that does nothing to change his unwelcoming features.

"Boss is asking for you at the training grounds. Now."

The best way to make me forget about Viktor's presence? His stupid boss. There goes my attempt to avoid him for another day.

"Did he say why?"

"No." Then he starts to stride out.

I make a face at his back. He turns around abruptly, and I pretend to be touching my hair.

"Move it, Lipovsky."

"I prefer Sasha or at least, Aleksander."

"And I prefer you not talk unless absolutely necessary, but we don't always get what we want."

Asshole.

I follow him to the training ground near one of the annexed houses. It's basically a giant gym attached to an indoor pool, a sauna, and a clinic. The guards have everything here to stay in shape, day in and day out.

There's no need to ask Viktor about Kirill's whereabouts. I

spot him in the middle of the fighting rings, watching the matches with a critical gaze.

He's in his usual black pants and white button-down that's rolled to his elbows. He appears pensive with his arms crossed and his glasses sitting up on his nose, giving him a dangerous edge.

This is why I've been trying to avoid him since that night. Hell, I've been trying to minimize our time alone since he found out my actual gender.

I just can't stop looking at him the moment I see him. There's no end in sight for my strange awareness whenever he's around.

Upon noticing me, Kirill pauses, and I swallow thickly before striding toward him with mock confidence.

I take refuge in the fighting sounds of the other guards and the fact that Kirill and I aren't alone, so no funny business can happen.

He steps into one of the sectioned rings on the floor and I follow him inside it.

My feet come to a halt in front of him, and I have to look up because he's stupidly tall. "You asked for me?"

"Yes." He uncrosses his arms, letting them fall to either side of him. "This is the next step of your training."

"Next step?"

"You didn't think the training you received at camp was the end of it, did you? That was merely muscle strengthening." He runs his gaze over me in a mechanical manner that feels like fire. "You still have a long way to go."

"Is it…because Damien's punch knocked me unconscious?"

"It's because he was able to land a punch when you were supposed to be detaining him. You're a good sniper, but you won't always have a gun on you. In the case of hand-to-hand combat, you'll be greatly disadvantaged and possibly killed in the span of seconds. We need to fix that. On guard."

"What type of training is this?"

"Simple." He beckons me over with two fingers. "Punch me."

"I…can do that?"

"No, but you can try."

"What are you talking about? Of course, I can punch you."

A slight twitch lifts the corner of his lip. "Try then."

"What do I get if I manage to do it?"

"Any reward you pick."

"You're underestimating me, aren't you?"

"Maybe you're the one overestimating yourself." He beckons me again.

"One punch, right? Anywhere?"

"In the face."

"I'd hate to ruin your handsome features."

A rare smirk curves his lips. "You find me handsome?"

Shit. "It's...common sense."

"Uh-huh. Don't worry, Sasha. You'll do nothing to my *handsome* features. Now, are you going to stand there all day?"

I don't waste time and lunge at him. Not only does he duck, but he also hits me in the back, knocking me down on the mat with effortless ease.

Pain throbs along my lower belly and back, but I manage to get up again. Kirill stays put, his expression as calm as a monk.

Okay. I didn't think this would be easy, but then again, while I personally witnessed Kirill being an excellent sniper, I don't know much about his combat skills. He did throw me against the wall when I was attempting to protect him from Karina. He also hit Damien and inflicted damage, which means he does have strength.

He just chooses not to show it.

"Again." Another beckoning with two fingers.

That motion is starting to piss me off.

I summon all my strength and sprint toward him at full speed. My feet give out from underneath me, and I end up on the ground with a more painful thud than earlier.

He didn't even let me come close this time. I glare up at his neutral expression, and now, I do wish to inflict damage on those features.

"Again."

I stand up on wobbly feet and fling off my jacket, toss it out of the ring, then roll the sleeves of my shirt up.

Kirill's face remains the same. Timeless and emotionless. It doesn't change. Not when I let out a battle cry and raise my fist, not when I attempt to punch him, and certainly not when he throws me against the ground. Again and again and *again*.

One hour later, I haven't managed to touch him, let alone punch him.

My shirt sticks to my back with sweat. I'm breathing so heavily, I'm nearly wheezing, and my organs feel rearranged from the number of impacts I've taken.

He doesn't do it in a way that would inflict permanent damage, but he's so firm in his subduing methods that I feel each and every one of them.

Other guards surround us, having finished their individual training.

"You've got this, Sasha!" Maksim's voice comes from behind me.

I look in his direction and give him a thumbs-up. Yuri, who's standing by his side, doesn't have the same encouraging expression.

He shakes his head at me as if telling me to give up. That no one here can take on Kirill. But that's the thing. I just refuse to give up.

"Again." There's a harshness in Kirill's tone this time. More than usual.

When I go for him, he all but sends me flying across the ring. A collective "Ahh" comes from my colleagues as pain explodes all over my side.

Shit.

"Again."

I try to stand up on unsteady feet, but even I am aware that I can barely stay upright. Fighting and landing punches is impossible. We've been going at this for so long and my fist has never connected with any part of his body, let alone his face.

Hell, he doesn't even look tired or like he's exerted any amount of energy.

Damn it. This is so embarrassing.

"Sir, you can't go inside." Viktor's urgent voice booms through the space.

I'm not sure if I should be alarmed or thankful for the interruption. Aside from when Rulan and his men died, I haven't sensed an air of urgency like I do right now.

Even Kirill, who didn't change his expression the entire time he was beating me up for sport, grows taller, more imposing, and larger than life. I take a peek at the newcomer while catching my breath.

It's none other than Damien. All alone.

As Maksim outlined, it's virtually impossible to find any of the Bratva leaders on their own. One, assassination attempts are real.

Two, they generally don't want to die.

Three, and most importantly, having bodyguards is the most logical and secure thing to do.

I'm starting to really believe that Damien has a screw loose somewhere, because he's solo. I doubt Viktor and the others could've stopped his guards if they'd come along. Usually, bodyguards, especially the inner-circle ones, are ready to die for their bosses.

Damien spins around to face Viktor. "You. Stop following me like a fucking lost puppy before I kick you."

Viktor doesn't reply, but he looks at Kirill. "I'm sorry, Boss. I couldn't stop him."

"Blah fucking blah." Damien slides in front of Kirill, wearing a manic grin. "Hi, motherfucker."

"Care to explain the reason behind your unwanted presence?" Kirill asks point-blank.

"Now I understand who taught your guards their sense of hospitality. I must say, zero out of five, strongly fucking not recommended."

"Still doesn't answer my question."

Damien pushes me out of the way. "You, pretty boy, get out of here."

Did he just call me a pretty boy...?

Kirill doesn't move, but it's almost as if he grows more intimidating with his harsh eyes alone. When he speaks, though, he sounds absolutely collected. "Damien. You have exactly three seconds to tell me why you're here before I throw you out. One...three."

Damien grins and widens his eyes. "Why else? To fight. of course."

"What makes you think I want to waste my time fighting you?"

"You've got to be fucking kidding me. You were fighting with the useless pretty boy who can't pull a punch to save his fucking life, and you call fighting me a waste of time? What the, and I can't stress this enough, fucking fuck are you on about?"

"I refuse." Kirill pushes past him and heads toward the house.

Damien follows after him. "Come on, you know you want to."

"No, I don't."

"What if I pay you?"

"Not interested."

"What if we bet on something?"

"Still not interested."

"Even profit?"

Kirill gives him the side-eye. "How do you even know the meaning of that word?"

"Couldn't give a fuck about it, to be honest, but I'm good at it, and I know you understand its value."

Kirill continues walking without saying anything. Damien follows him inside, seeming so pleased with himself.

"You okay, Sash?" Maksim wraps his hand around my shoulder in a bro hug, forcing me to stop staring at the house.

"Uh, yeah. Sort of."

"If it's any consolation." Yuri joins my other side and hits me on the back. "None of us can win against Boss. He's just...made of stone."

"Yeah, don't sweat it, Sasha," another guard says.

"You held out pretty well in front of his alien stamina," one more says.

They all either pat me on the shoulder, ruffle my hair, or hit me on the back. The latter does more damage to my aching body, but I smile through it.

Suddenly, all the embarrassment and weakness I felt earlier gradually disappears. I haven't known these guys for a long time, but they've slowly but surely become like a family to me.

"Let's get you something to eat." Maksim and Yuri drag me in the direction of the kitchen.

"Is Damien really here just to fight?" I ask Maksim. "Or does he have an ulterior motive?"

"I was wondering the same thing," Yuri says thoughtfully. "If it were any of the other Bratva members, I'd be certain they were here to spy, but according to the data I gathered about Damien, I'm pretty sure he's really here to fight after he had a taste of Boss's strength the other day."

"Yeah," Maksim adds. "I'm gonna throw a wild guess and say he's not sophisticated enough to be a spy."

"He could do it unknowingly, though," Yuri says, his tone of voice changing. "There's absolutely no trustworthy people in the organization. They all want to be at the top, whatever it takes."

Kirill included.

He's at the top of the list of people who would use any methods to reach his goal.

Maybe he's started to rub off on me, too, because ever since he asked me to punch him and told me he'd reward me with anything, I've been thinking of an important position.

One where I would have as much access to the main office as Viktor and could finally investigate what Roman left behind.

TWENTY-TWO

Kirill

REACHING GOALS DOESN'T HAPPEN ARBITRARILY. Not only do I need to make them happen, but every path the other party takes should, without a doubt, lead back to me. I have a zero percent margin of error and no tolerance for mistakes.

A fact my men know about me, which is why they're fine with training like machines all day, every day, just like we're still in the army.

It's one of the reasons I took them to Russia in the first place. Some needed discipline, and others needed to be acquainted with a harsh lifestyle and to know what it's like to live with a sense of deprivation.

Unlike what they thought, I never planned to stay in the military all my life. It's bland, too strict, and doesn't allow any type of meaningful progress.

However, they had to believe that or else they wouldn't have put their all into it.

It's not a question of training as much as it's a change of mindset.

I did miscalculate my father's desperation to bring me back to New York, though. Despite all his clinginess and his annoying fucking existence, I never thought he'd kill my men—*his* men—just to force me back to where he thinks I belong.

After I went through his logs and papers, I found out exactly why he did it. His power was wavering, and his accounts are suffering.

The first happened because he made a few mistakes and took the side of the wrong people in other crime organizations' internal wars. As a result, he gradually lost the Pakhan's trust. Interestingly, the one who gained it for making all the right choices is none other than Adrian.

He has impeccable information-gathering skills, a secretive method of working, and keeps a low profile, even within the organization.

Most importantly—he makes the right decisions. All times. Every time.

Since I came back, I've known exactly who my ally would be, and he goes by the name of Adrian Volkov. No, he didn't agree and merely ignored me, but he's already on my side.

He just doesn't know it yet.

The second mistake my father made, on a financial scale, was apparently getting on Yulia's shit list, because she's been slowly but surely distancing him from her banking people. She made it her mission to forbid her family to give him low-interest loans and slowly cut his relationship with them.

This didn't happen when he was in his prime, no. Yulia is too smart to commit an amateur mistake that would've gotten her killed. She waited, bided her time for decades, and was very patient.

As soon as the illnesses started to gang up on him, she

slithered out of her hiding space like a snake, snatched the power that he married her for, and started to gradually funnel it to the useless Konstantin.

Unlike what other people would assume, I don't hate my brother. I just find him utterly...impulsive. If he were to get full rein, he could and would get himself, Yulia, and Karina killed sooner rather than later.

It's probably why my father didn't want him in power, no matter what.

He knew that I'm a better fit to keep his legacy alive and protect his little Karina. As much of an asshole as my father was, he did dote on my little sister. After he screwed up her life, that is.

One of the reasons why I'm a better fit is because I have solid control over my men, unlike that fool Konstantin, who lets them do whatever they wish.

It's a sense of respect as well. They were more avoidant and scared of me before Russia. But after the military and the countless missions we carried out together, they respect me as a leader, which is, again, another reason that Russia had to happen.

Is that manipulative? Maybe. But in order to be at the top, it's imperative to have the right people by your side.

I tell myself this is also why I'm basically torturing Sasha in training. It's been a month since we started, and she's still on the ground more often than not.

Someone else would've given up already. Many of my guards definitely did when I started this test back in the military. They just admitted defeat and went on with their lives.

Not Sasha.

Every day, she comes to the training ground dressed in sweatpants that majorly fail to hide the line of her hip and stomach.

Sometimes, I wonder if I'm the only one who notices her feminine traits or whether they're all completely oblivious.

She has an hourglass waist, for fuck's sake. Yes, she hides it, but still, those two fuckers, Maksim and Yuri, are touchy with her all the time.

They also had the audacity to ask Viktor if they could take over the night duty for Sasha so she could get some sleep.

I had Viktor shoo them away in his signature unwelcoming tone.

Fuck those two. Sasha will remain on night duty indefinitely.

She spends the night right outside my room. I'd prefer it if she were inside, but she refuses. Because she's carefully keeping her distance.

Except for when it's time to fight.

That's when the fire inside her blazes, and she turns into an entirely different creature.

She has the determination of a cat who has an attention span of twenty seconds. Every day, she forgets that she was defeated and jumps back into the ring for more.

Is she making progress? Yes. Will she be able to defeat me anytime soon? Probably not.

This is starting to become more routine than anything else. The highlight of my day isn't trying to form any type of alliance or slowly stripping the control Konstantin has over some of the clubs.

It's being in that ring, waiting for Sasha to appear with her defiant expression.

I'm about to head there when Viktor appears in front of the office door like a damn ghost.

"Make some noise, would you?" I start down the hall, and he falls in step beside me.

"Igor is requesting to meet with you."

"Why?"

"Didn't say. He wants you at his house tonight."

"Hmm. Tell him I'll be there."

That old man was one of the most eager to have me, instead of Konstantin, take over. I'm sure it has something to do with old-fashioned rules, where the eldest son should inherit his father's legacy.

"Copy that. Since you'll be busy tonight with the meeting, should we head to the club now?"

"No, I have a training session."

"With Lipovsky?"

"Why is that voiced as a question when you know the answer?"

"I don't trust him, Boss."

"Why not?"

"He's just…suspicious."

"What a massive argument you have there, Viktor."

"You know it, too. He's been getting close to the young lady."

I stop in the middle of the hall. "Karina?"

"Yes. She lets him into her room and asks Anna to prepare snacks for them."

"Why is that bad news? In fact, it's good that she lets anyone into her chamber of horrors. Even *I* am not allowed in there most of the time."

"Seriously?"

"What?"

"He could take advantage of her, Boss."

I laugh, and he watches me as if I'm an alien, so I stop and call forward my serious expression. "I will cut his head off if that happens."

"Doesn't mean it'll stop him. Wouldn't it be better to prevent that situation before it happens?"

"He's not going to take advantage of Karina. I promise."

"How can you be so sure?"

"He's…let's say, attracted to men."

"He does seem gay."

"Is that so?"

"Doesn't take a genius to figure it out."

"Then why did you think he'd take advantage of my sister?"

"The fact that he has a functional dick."

I suppress the need to laugh again, and Viktor narrows his eyes on me. "He was acting strange in front of your office a while ago."

"Strange?"

"He pretended that he was there to knock on the door and search for you."

"And that's strange how?"

"The fact that I caught him doing the same thing again last week. And another time this morning. I was watching the surveillance video and caught him looking at the lock for two seconds before he left."

"Are you watching him, Viktor?"

"He needs to be watched."

Interesting. This means Sasha has something in the office. Or maybe she's searching for *something*.

What could that be?

"Let me take care of him. Stay out of it and stop watching him."

"But, sir—"

"Stay out of it, Viktor. That's an order."

He purses his lips in clear disapproval, but he doesn't push it.

His words, however, definitely bring a lot of ideas to my mind. Such as Sasha's actual motives for coming to New York.

⌒

During today's training, Sasha managed to touch my chest. It wasn't a punch, and she collapsed right afterward, but she had this victorious smile on her face.

As if she'd done what she set out to do all along.

She didn't gloat, didn't attempt to even count that contact as a point, but she did look at me with those defiant eyes that get me all fucking hard.

No. It's the idea of what look I could put in those eyes that gets me hard.

"Let's go. I know just the right thing to do so you can relax."
Maksim gathers her by the shoulder, and she uses him for support
in order to walk. My eyes narrow, but I soon conceal it.

The right thing to do to help her relax.

That's what he said, unless I'm hearing things. I'm about to
follow after, when my phone rings.

I'm fully ready to ignore it, but it's rare for my sister to call me.

My attention remains on Sasha disappearing with Maksim
into the annex house as I pick up. "What can I do for you, Kara?"

"I told you to stop calling me that!"

"Fine, fine. What seems to be the problem?"

"Do I need a problem to call you?"

"No, but there must be a reason." And she hasn't threatened
to kill me in my sleep yet.

"I need a favor—no, I need you to do something for me."

"I refuse."

"What…but why? You don't even know what I was going to
ask."

"You want Sasha as your personal bodyguard, no?"

"How did you…? Anyway, yeah, and you're gonna give him
to me."

"He's not a toy, Kara."

"Don't care. I want him to be my bodyguard."

"My answer is still the same."

"But…but you have, like, a thousand of them. Why can't you
spare Sasha?"

I wish I knew the answer to that. "Still a no."

"I voted for you the other day. You owe me a favor, you fucking bastard!"

"I didn't ask for a favor, and I certainly never agreed to owe
you one."

"You fucking manipulative, Machiavellian, psychopathic asshole with no moral compass. I swear to fuck—"

"I'll ask Anna to bring you some herbal tea. Helps with the agitation." Then I hang up.

I can almost imagine her throwing the nearest object against the wall, and while I don't want her to injure herself, I also won't go check on her.

Karina's problem is being spoiled, sheltered, and out of touch with the outside world.

I might have left her to her own devices before, but there will be no more getting what she wants just because she asks for it.

After she developed her chronic anxiety due to Roman's brutal parenting methods, he spoiled her rotten, probably out of guilt. He also didn't think that she mattered in the great scheme of things because she's a girl.

I'm not making his mistake.

Although I have a thousand documents lying on my desk, waiting to be reviewed, I make the very 'logical' choice to follow Sasha and Maksim.

I've never liked how close they've gotten since the army. Yuri, too, even though that fucker is smarter and knows how and when to keep his distance.

Maksim has little to no sense of self-preservation and might—*will*—accidentally end up with a chopped-off head pretty soon.

I manage to escape Viktor's consistent shadowing since he's busy supervising the others, and slip into the house.

Not long after, I catch a glimpse of Maksim jogging down the hall, shouting, "Gonna bring some refreshments. Go on ahead of me."

Ahead of me.

I wait for a few moments after Maksim disappears in the direction of the kitchen, then head the opposite way.

Turns out, the place where Maksim wanted Sasha to go ahead of him is the sauna.

I halt and shove a hand in my pocket, then slide my glasses

up my nose. Is this woman planning on sweating in the sauna with…Maksim?

It takes me a couple of minutes to try and ease the fire that's mounting in my chest. I partially fail, because when Maksim reappears, two drinks in hand, I honestly wonder why I shouldn't snap his neck.

"Boss," he says with bewilderment. "You need anything?"

"Yes. I need you to go investigate Igor and his men. Take Yuri with you."

"Now?"

"When else?"

"Uh…let me at least take these to Sasha and tell him I have to go."

I subtly take the drinks from his hands. "I'll do it. Go."

He doesn't appear happy with the order, but he does leave, even though it takes him a moment, and he looks back at me as if contemplating if someone is impersonating me.

Maksim has been with me all his life, and he knows that I never bring drinks, hold them, or even offer to serve them. So this scene must look alien to him.

Once I make sure he's gone, I push the door to the sauna's locker room open, then place the drinks on the bench and turn the lock from the inside.

The locker room appears empty, but then there's a commotion in one of the bathrooms—a rustle of clothes and a low curse.

"One moment, Maks!" she calls. "I'll be out in a sec."

Maks.

That's what she calls him when they're alone.

Fucking Maks.

The only reason I don't break the door to the bathroom open is because I have a better plan.

I remove my shirt, shoes, pants, and boxer briefs, then hang them in one of the lockers. After I wrap a towel around my waist,

I head to the sauna and add more charcoal to the pit, making it unbearably hot.

Then I lounge on the wooden bench, watching the entrance. A few minutes later, Sasha appears at the door, wearing a bathrobe. Her hair is longer now, falling to her nape. Usually, she ties it in a small ponytail, but not right now.

Even with her head lowered as she focuses on tying the belt, she looks every bit the woman she's spent a lot of time and effort to hide.

"This is the first time I've done this. Promise it won't be too hot?"

"I'm afraid I can't."

Her head whips up, and I revel in the way her lips part and her skin turns a deep shade of red in a fraction of a second.

Patience is my strongest attribute, but that doesn't seem to be the case when it comes to this woman.

It's time she knows exactly why she shouldn't fuck with me.

TWENTY-THREE

Sasha

Violent shivers break out all over my skin in an unbearable chaos.

My first thought is to run.

There's absolutely no use in considering any other options when all of them will lead to the half-naked enigma in front of me.

Kirill lounges leisurely on one of the wooden benches, a towel wrapped loosely around his waist, hinting at the inked V line and teasing the toned muscles of his stomach.

His skin glistens with humidity, drawing more attention to his slick, defined abs. Despite the low orange light in the sauna, everything about him pops—his tattoos, his muscular superiority, and his monstrous strength.

Strands of his now longer hair fall haphazardly over his strong forehead, some of them camouflaging the inhumane color of his ice-cold eyes.

Dangerous, ethereal eyes.

There's nothing idle about Kirill, even if his casual posture aims to convince me of such.

He's just not someone to be taken lightly or easily. I've known him for months, and I still feel as extremely out of my depth in his company as I did the first day I met him.

Leaning back on his elbows, he tilts his head in my direction. "Are you going to stand there all day?"

"Where's Maks?"

"*Maksim* has an errand to run."

"I…will just come back after you're done."

"Nonsense. Come in."

I fidget on my feet, not wanting to move either in his direction or outside. I'm stuck in the middle where my mind and body war for dominance, and neither comes out victorious.

"That's an order, Sasha. Get in here."

I purse my lips, even as the weight lifts off my chest when he takes away the choice. I like to think that I didn't want this, but I have to do it.

It's completely out of my control now.

And for some reason, that makes my movements lighter and more at ease.

After closing the door, I sit a step below Kirill, doing my best to avoid being in direct view of his destabilizing gaze.

I'm not sure if it's the temperature or my overbearing company, but I start sweating profusely in the span of seconds. The bathrobe feels like a thick blanket, effectively suffocating my breathing. But I'm only wearing boxer briefs beneath it, so I can't, under any circumstances, take it off. I was going to keep my chest bandages on, too, but I thought that would be uncomfortable. The boxer briefs are already a pain. Are people even supposed to wear underwear in saunas?

The air thickens with tension and silence, both trying to overpower each other for dominance. My skin turns into lava, but I don't move, fearing the change of the status quo more than my being burned alive.

In a sense, my dramatic reaction to the current situation has to do with the fact that I'm trapped with him in a room, but I'd be naïve to consider that the only reason.

Kirill is a manipulative, emotionless monster with a skewed sense of morality, and yet I've never been so drawn to another person as I am to him.

It's illogical, it's madness, but I'm afraid I can't deny it anymore.

"Isn't this place too hot?" I ask in a half-assed attempt to murder the silence.

"Why do you speak English so well when you were born and raised in Russia?"

"I had a private American tutor." I bite my lower lip.

Was that giving away too much? It's a habit I developed in the army. Kirill was the only superior I considered worthy of respect, and, therefore, answering his questions has become natural. But, usually, I'd think carefully to avoid revealing anything about my background.

Maybe it's the heat or the fact that I can feel his presence behind my back, but something caused me to have a serious lapse in judgment just now.

Maybe he didn't notice or he's too busy enjoying the sauna—

"So you *were* a rich young lady."

The way he voices it means he's suspected it all along. Shit. *Shit.*

"I...wasn't."

"Sure thing, Sasha. Let's say a regular Russian speaks like nobility and has private tutors."

"And do you know a lot of Russian nobility?" I try to sound casual, even though I'm freaking out. Was I not careful enough? I thought I got rid of my old mannerisms in the years prior to joining the army.

But then again, Kirill isn't just anyone. He's so observant, it's scary.

"Yulia and her extended family are Russian nobility. Pretty sure you met her."

"I...don't act or speak like your mother."

"No, but you used to and, no matter how much you try to camouflage it, the traits are still there. So why don't you tell me your real last name?"

My body goes rigid and I think I'll throw up from the nerves ripping through the bottom of my stomach. The first thing that comes to mind is running away, but that would be no different than giving Kirill the opening he's been waiting for.

So I draw calming breaths and speak as confidently as possible. "You're right, my family was wealthy, and we were doing well in business, but we went bankrupt around my sixteenth birthday and I had to join the army to survive."

It's only half a lie, but it's believable enough that Kirill doesn't probe.

The silence feels like a weight on my chest, though. Not only is it uncomfortable, but I can sense that Kirill is doing it on purpose to make me spill my deepest, darkest secrets.

"This is my first time in a place like this. How about you? Do you often come to the sauna?" I blurt.

"Hmm." He sounds pensive, sleepy almost.

I glance back, only to find him leaning on both elbows, eyes closed, and legs nonchalantly parted, offering a glimpse of his cock through the opening of the towel.

And he's...hard. Or getting there, at least.

This is one of those times when I should look away. One problem, though—I can't bring myself to. In fact, my head tilts to the side so I can get a better view.

It doesn't help that I've been on fire since the moment I walked in here. The view turns the air hotter, boiling even.

"Like what you see?"

The raspy quality of his voice catches me completely off guard, and I gulp, choking on my own breaths. "N-no."

"You're still ogling my cock, Sasha."

I stare ahead, my cheeks feeling like they're on fire. Damn it. Why did I have to be so obvious?

"You look uncomfortable." His sinful voice carries in the air. "Are you perhaps hot and bothered?"

I hate how his voice is casual while I'm at the point of eruption. I hate how he can have this effect on me with the mere sound of his sinful voice.

There's rustling behind me before he appears beside me like a demon slithering out of Hell. I go still, my breathing getting stuck at the back of my throat.

Something cold meets my overheated skin, and I carefully look to the side to find Kirill placing a glass of alcohol against my cheek.

But that's not the problem. He's close, like way *too* close. *So* close that I can follow the droplet of perspiration sliding over his collarbone, to his chest, and then down...

I catch myself before I touch the droplet's resting place. I'm acting like a major pervert, and the worst part is, I can't stop it.

Must be because the heat is boiling my brain.

Usually, I have better control on my libido. Like back in that village. I rejected him then and again two weeks ago.

But why did it feel like I was rejecting myself instead? And maybe, just maybe, all those rejections are taking their toll on me and made me reach this state where I'm teetering on the edge.

"Want a drink?" His voice lowers, so sinister in nature, I actually swallow.

I reach for the glass, but he keeps it out of reach.

"Never said it'd be for free."

"I can go get my own drink."

"You can, but you won't, because I won't let you."

His free hand slides up the collar of my bathrobe, subtly

brushing his fingers against the skin of my breastbone. I shudder, my lips parting as I attempt and fail to subdue my reaction.

Then, in one violent go, he shoves the bathrobe down. My breasts bounce from their confinement, and the belt opens, revealing my black boxer briefs.

I gasp as the reality of the situation comes into focus.

Not only am I half naked, but I'm also not moving or attempting to cover myself. Why am I not moving…?

Kirill slides his finger from the pulse point of my neck, down to my collarbone, and then over the slope of my breasts.

A strange sound echoes in the air, and I realize with utter horror that it came from me. I've never been touched by this level of blinding control before.

There's no hesitation or slow exploration like I experienced with my high school boyfriend. And Kirill is definitely not a boy.

He's a man who knows exactly what he's doing and handles me with nonnegotiable firmness.

I'm paralyzed in the path of his madness. A part of me screams at me to stop this. There's a reason I shouldn't want this man, but I can't access my brain to fathom what that reason is.

I'm lost in a fog I can't escape. My heart and body attuned to the monster in the form of a man.

A monster I can't resist.

His fingers wrap around my taut nipple, and he pinches. A zap rushes through me, and I gasp at the mixture of pleasure and pain.

"You're so fucking beautiful." He twists my nipple again, harder, with sure intent that makes me want to cry. "Tempting." Another pinch, and more torture. "Irresistible." He pulls this time, adding a maddening friction that starts in my nipples and ends right between my legs. "And the worst part is, you have no fucking clue you are. That's why you keep flaunting yourself around so innocently, for anyone to see, but we can't have that, now, can we? I'm the only one who knows how beautiful you are, aren't I?"

He uses his hold on my breast to push me down so that I'm lying on the bench and the now open bathrobe.

I feel like I'll faint, but that has less to do with the temperature and more to do with the man who's hovering over me like a god. His knees are on either side of me and his face is much more handsome from this angle.

"Answer me, Solnyshko."

A fire burns inside me at that word, and I clench my legs as I nod.

His eyes rage into a darker blue, ethereal in color, molten in appearance. His attention never leaves me as he pours half of the drink over my breasts. I shudder when the cold liquid touches my hot skin and drips down the sides.

"I'm the only one who's seen these gorgeous tits, right?"

I'm lost for words because of one small fact. *Did he just call me gorgeous?*

"Does the silence mean some other bastard has seen your tits, Sasha?" His fingers dig into the sensitive flesh of my breasts.

I shake my head. "No."

"Only me?"

"Only...you." Sometimes, no, I *always* hate how he's privy to parts of me I have never and would never disclose to anyone.

But at the same time, I like this sense of...intimacy. There's something only the two of us know, and it will remain this way forever.

Kirill's head falls between my breasts, and he sucks a nipple into his mouth. My hands grip the edges of the bench to stop myself from falling over.

His knees tighten against my sides, trapping me between his large, muscular thighs. I'm light-headed but also...strangely protected.

Still pinching and twisting my other nipple, he bites, sucks, and toys with the one in his hot, wicked mouth. The cycle repeats again and again until I think I'm going to faint from the over-whelming sensations.

"You taste like an aphrodisiac," he says around my nipple, then his tongue chases the alcohol down to my stomach.

I try to clench my legs, but Kirill effortlessly parts them and pulls down my boxer briefs, then throws them aside.

The first thought on my mind is to hide, but I can't look away from the lust on his face. Or the way his jaw clenches upon see-ing me naked.

This man who usually feels so far away is the closest he's ever been, and he wants me. Not anyone else but me.

That knowledge makes the imaginary knot in my throat dis-appear. But just when I'm starting to relax, or at least, give into this madness, Kirill pours the rest of the drink over my pussy.

I hiss due to the difference in temperature, but it turns into a gasp when he throws my legs over his shoulders and dives at my core.

He doesn't nibble or suck, he straight out thrusts his tongue inside me.

My whole body recoils, and I'd fall off the bench if it weren't for his hold on me. Kirill tongue-fucks me, tearing me apart with each in and out.

The buildup startles me. I couldn't keep up even if I wanted to, and he doesn't give me any time to catch my breath.

His fingers dig into my thighs as he picks up the pace. My eyes go blurry, and I moan as I fall apart on his tongue. My legs shake, and moisture streams down my cheek, but I scream and thrust my hips.

Kirill doesn't stop with my orgasm. He doesn't take it slow, either. In fact, he licks every drop of alcohol off my folds and my clit. He bites my inner thighs and leaves marks that I can already feel forming.

The buildup doesn't prepare me for what's coming. This time,

I'm hit by a strong wave out of nowhere, and I think I'm going to faint.

It's an eruption.

It's complete and utter...*madness*.

Kirill's head peeks from between my legs and he licks my glistening arousal off his lips.

I don't know why I think he's never been as beautiful as he is right now. All tattooed and tall and handsome.

He's a monster, too, but maybe monsters do it better than others.

"Why...are you crying?" he asks with a note of darkness.

I dab at my cheek, and that's when I realize the moisture I felt wasn't sweat, but actually tears.

"I...don't know."

"Do you hate this?"

"It's not that I hate it..." *It's more that I love it too much.*

But Kirill doesn't wait to listen to the second part. He's back between my legs, his expert tongue fucking me into oblivion.

He does it over and over until I can't take it anymore.

Until I actually do faint.

TWENTY-FOUR

Sasha

IKE'S LITTLE FACE SLOWLY MATERIALIZES IN FRONT
of me. Young, sweet, and full of tears.

"Mishka, what's wrong?" I ask, my voice breaking.

"Help me, Sasha," he whispers. "Help us…"

I reach out a hand. "Slow down. Breathe. Can you tell me
what's wrong?"

The moment I touch him, he falls to the ground, and blood
explodes from his eyes, ears, nose, and mouth.

The gruesome scene from four years ago slowly comes into
focus. Mike's body lies in the middle of all the others.

Blood pools beneath them, and the corpses become identifi-
able one by one. My father, my mother, my cousins, my uncle, and
even my brother.

Anton lies on his side, bleeding from all his orifices like Mike.
Uncle Albert walks in the middle of all the blood, expression downward and tears streaming down his cheeks.

I call his name, but no words come out. Not even a sound or a cry.

His eyes meet mine, blood tears soaking them. "Are you happy, Sasha?"

I shake my head over and over. We can't be happy. I'm not allowed to be happy when everyone is buried six feet under.

And then my uncle falls down, joining everyone else on the ground, bleeding from all their orifices.

The blood pool gets deeper and colder, but I run in their direction.

I lose my footing and fall straight into the pool. "Nooo."

White light blinds out all the red, and I startle into a sitting position. That's when I realize I'm in a bed.

For a second, just a fraction of time, I think I'm back at home. I only had a nightmare, and Mama just woke me up because I'm going to be late for school.

But this is not home. And the nightmare wasn't completely inaccurate.

"It's ten in the morning."

My head whips in the direction of the feminine voice. Anna. She's the one who pulled the blinds, revealing the huge tree near the balcony, and is staring at me with those judgmental eyes that have never trusted me.

Her gaze bounces between me and the bed—Kirill's bed.

Shit.

Memories from the sauna slowly come to focus, and heat rises to my cheeks and ears.

Holy hell.

What on earth have I done?

I stop myself from thinking about that, or more accurately, Anna's unwavering attention forces me to.

She's watching me as if I'm the greatest threat to this family or something.

I'm thankful Kirill actually dressed me in a shirt and sweat-pants. But there's one tiny fact that I can't change.

Me in Kirill's bed.

What must she think of me?

"Uh, I..." I scramble from the bed, wincing at the ache be-tween my legs, but I wrap the blanket around me. I'm not naked, but I don't have my chest bandages on either.

Anna stands in place like a dictatorial headmaster who's a fan of dishing out punishments.

"I wasn't feeling well, so Boss must've...uh, carried me here." *I sound like a fucking idiot.*

The small woman's expression doesn't change. Whether in affirmation or the opposite. She's like a statue whose sole purpose is to judge me.

"I...I'm going to take a shower."

"Eat first." She motions at a tray that's overloaded with food. "Kirill told me to prepare him breakfast, and only after I brought it here did he mention that I have to make sure you eat."

Oh.

That must be why it looks like one of those luxurious break-fasts. Kirill must've known that she wouldn't have put any effort into the meal if it was for me, so he tricked her into thinking it was for him.

Honestly, manipulative should be that man's middle name.

"Thanks," I say.

She doesn't reply, but nods instead.

"Do you know where Boss is?" I ask in my most amicable tone.

"You should be the one to know that, considering you're the bodyguard."

Ouch. Okay.

I sit on the couch and sigh. "Look, Anna. I don't know why you hate me..."

"I don't hate you. I just don't trust you," she says simply. "Kirill is the only person who's able to lead this family, and to do that, he needs competent people by his side. Not people he has to save each and every time something happens."

Ouch again.

I can't even say anything in reply, because she's right. I'm supposed to be saving Kirill's life, not the other way around.

"I'll tell him you ate your breakfast," she says, then leaves the room.

I take a bite of toast and drink some orange juice, then wince when I shift in place. My pussy feels sore and achy, but for some reason, I'm desperate for more of the torture Kirill inflicted last night.

Once again, my cheeks heat.

I can't believe I fainted.

But then again, it was too hot in that sauna. Add his touch, and it was impossible to keep up.

It also doesn't help that I was overwhelmed with all the cryptic emotions that were going through me at the time. Even now, I can't put a name to them.

Except that I...probably enjoyed it more than I should have.

Maybe that's why I had that nightmare. Uncle Albert asked me if I was happy with the new life and setting I chose for myself.

It was also the second time Mike asked me for help, and I haven't been there to answer his plea.

My phone vibrates on the nightstand, and I manage to swallow the contents of my mouth before I stand, stumble on the blanket, then release it and go to check the text.

Something knots in my stomach when I don't find Kirill's name on the screen.

> **Viktor:** You're on the night shift at the club tonight. You have no orders until then.

I type.

> **Aleksander:** Am I not needed at Boss's side now?

I could've asked the man himself, but I'm too embarrassed

to talk to him after what happened last night. Especially since he didn't contact me first.

Viktor: No.

Aleksander: Do you know where he is?

Viktor: Nowhere you should concern yourself with.

I resist the urge to roll my eyes. Leave it to Viktor to be the most unhelpful person ever.

So I text my friend.

Aleksander: Morning, Maks!

The reply is immediate.

Maksim: Morning, Sash. I've been waiting for you to come back to the annex, but then I recalled you were on night duty. Was everything all right yesterday?

Aleksander: Yeah, why wouldn't it be?

Maksim: Boss looked kind of angry or annoyed. I couldn't tell for sure, and since he doesn't look like that most of the time, I was worried something had happened.

Aleksander: Nothing happened. Just the usual, I guess.

I'm such an excellent liar in texts. Which can't be said about real-life interactions, because I was so close to telling Anna everything if she so much as pressed me earlier.

Maksim: Thank God. It's never good to be on Boss's radar.

Tell me about it.

Aleksander: I know, right? Speaking of Boss, do you know where he is?

Maksim: He headed out with Viktor and Yuri last night and still hasn't come back.

I grow taller, my breath catching.

They can't be in danger, or else Viktor would've said something or called for backup. But for some reason, I still don't feel good about this whole thing.

After mulling over the information, I walk into Kirill's closet in search of something I can use as temporary chest bandages.

My jaw nearly hits the ground when I find my clothes in the corner—all my suits, shirts, and sweatpants. Not only that, but underneath them, there's a duffel bag with my bandages inside them.

Why did he bring them here…?

Not coming up with a logical answer, I wrap a bandage around my chest and get into a suit.

Since this is the perfect chance to try and find something in Kirill's belongings, I do the most logical thing for someone in my position—go through his closet. Ninety percent of his tailored suits are black, but they have different cuts.

The remaining ten percent are either navy blue or dark gray, but I've rarely seen him wear those.

He has drawers upon drawers of luxurious and special edition watches. Ten of the same set of black-framed glasses. Some sunglasses that he almost never wears. Italian shoes and leather belts, but that's about it.

There are no personal items or anything that helps with my search.

I'm about to put a bag back on the top drawer, when a picture falls. I grab the frame and pause.

There's no picture inside, just…a handkerchief with his first name embroidered in the corner.

My fingers tighten around the frame, and an alien feeling drops to the base of my stomach. Kirill is anything but a sentimental person. He's methodical, practical, and manipulative to a fault.

Actually, he uses people's emotions against them, so the fact that he kept a handkerchief, framed it even, goes against everything I know of him. This was obviously done by a girl. But who? An ex-lover?

"Sasha! Are you in here?"

Karina's sudden voice nearly causes me to drop the handkerchief. I hastily put the frame back exactly where I found it and step out of the closet.

Karina stands in the middle of the room, wearing an ample tulle dress, its black color contrasting against her skin.

Her face has some makeup on it, and she's let her shiny blonde hair fall to the middle of her back. She's crossing her arms and tapping her Louboutin heels on the floor. "Where were you? I was calling you for the past ten minutes."

"Oh, sorry." I grab my phone from the nightstand. "I left it here."

"Whatever. Let's go."

"Go where?"

"To have breakfast in my room, of course."

"I already had breakfast."

"Then you can just accompany me. What's so hard about that?"

"I'd love to, but I have work to do." Or, more accurately, I have to try to find Kirill. While we do stay overnight at the club sometimes, I'm usually there, so I know he's safe.

Now, I'm not sure. Even with Viktor and Yuri by his side.

Is it weird that I'm starting to genuinely care about his safety? But I'm only doing this because I can't get information if he's dead, considering he's the only one who has access to what his father left behind.

…Right?

"Liar, liar. I know you have the day off and don't have to work until this evening."

"Well…"

"Nope, not hearing it. You're coming with me."

She all but drags me and tells me to carry the breakfast tray, too, because it's apparently better than the one she got.

Her room is dark and gloomy, as usual. She has the candles lit and some dim lights on, though.

"It's breakfast, Miss. We should maybe have it on the balcony."

"I told you not to call me Miss. My name is Karina." She blushes. "Or Kara if you want. And nope, there's no way in hell we're going outside."

"The balcony is still attached to your room. It's not exactly outside."

"Still no. Nope. I'm not hearing you."

"I won't force you, but you look so beautiful today, and I thought the sunshine would make you look even better."

"I..." She purses her lips and studies her perfectly manicured nails that she does herself, as she told me. "Okay, I guess. Just fifteen minutes, though!"

For a sheltered princess, she really is adorable. And Kirill is right, she's neither violent nor messy. She's just scared of the world and prefers her little cocoon.

I pull back the curtains before she changes her mind, and she physically winces at the light. I clean the chairs and the outside table and then place the tray on top of it.

Karina remains in the shadows of her room until I gently pull her out. She holds on to my hand with her sweaty ones and watches her surroundings like a trapped animal.

"The food is so good. Anna is definitely talented." I bite with passion into the toast, trying to make her forget about where we are.

Her leg bounces on the floor, but when I offer her a cup of coffee with cream and sugar like she prefers it, Karina accepts it, her stance relaxing.

"Are the fifteen minutes over?"

"It's only been three minutes, Miss...I mean, Karina."

Her expression lights up, and she smiles. "You should totally become my guard, but that stingy Kirill was like, *no,*" she mimics his dispassionate tone.

"You asked him to make me your guard?"

"He didn't even let me finish asking and flat out refused."

I didn't know that.

"But you don't need a bodyguard, since, well, you're always in your room."

She purses her lips. "Of course I do. I can, like, try on clothes I order online, and you tell me what you think. I can do your nails and we'll have meals together like this."

That's not really a bodyguard's job, but I don't tell her that.

Karina traces the rim of her cup and sighs. "We never had meals as a family, you know."

"Why not?"

"Mama and Papa didn't like each other, and they made it their mission that the three of us would be filled with hate, too." She gulps a mouthful of coffee. "They made us compete against each other all the time."

I lean over in my seat. "Compete how?"

"Kirill and Konstantin were at it way before I came along. At first, it was childish things like racing and grades, but then it was martial arts, shooting lessons, and how to perform under pressure."

"Perform under pressure?"

The coffee cup shakes in her hand, some droplets falling all over the table. "Stupid psychological tests about mental endurance."

"You...did that?"

"I had no choice! It was mandatory because Papa was an asshole." Her eyes shine with tears. "I was thirteen, Konstantin was nineteen, and Kirill was twenty-one. We were dropped off on an isolated island and had to survive using whatever means necessary. I was glued to Kirill's side, but I was taken by some scary masked men. Kirill came to save me, but there were too many of them. He was pushed down, beaten, burned, electrocuted, and I had to watch all the torture in real time. I was crying and screaming so loud, I fainted. Konstantin was the only one who passed that test since he found a boat and escaped. Kirill and I failed because we were supposed to be detached and act like Konstantin did. I never left my room after that. Whenever Mama or Papa forced me out, I would vomit, have a seizure, or faint, so they gave up and thought it was better to hide me from the world. A few years later, Kirill left me, too, and went to Russia."

How…monstrous can a person be to do this to his own children? Karina isn't this way because she's mentally unwell. It was caused by trauma. That's why she's scared of being outside and is physically unable to handle the exterior world.

If that's the most traumatic thing that happened to Karina, I wonder how many times Kirill was tested by his father to turn out the way he is.

If he was beaten, burned, and electrocuted at twenty-one, what else did his father do to him prior to that?

"I'm so sorry, Karina."

She shakes her head and wipes the tears that have escaped from her eyes. "I already lost my parents a long time ago, but I thought I at least had Kirill. But he also left."

"Is that why you tried to kill him the day he came back?"

She sniffles and glares in the distance. "I will still kill him."

I smile. She absolutely doesn't mean that. In fact, I think a part of her is scared he'll leave again.

"If I kill him, you can be my guard!" She claps her hands as if she's come up with the most genius plan.

"I'll be your guard without that."

"Really?"

"Yeah, but as I said, you have to go out first."

"No, thanks."

"We can just start with the balcony like this."

"Just the balcony?" she asks with innocent eyes.

"Just the balcony is fine."

"I don't hate the balcony."

"I'm glad you don't."

"Thanks, Sasha." She smiles.

"For what?"

"If you hadn't come, I wouldn't have known the balcony isn't so bad."

"Anytime."

She slathers some jam on a piece of toast and offers it to me. "I can't believe that Anna. She made Kirill's plate so much better than mine. She's always had favoritism issues."

"She seems like she loves him, though."

"That she does." She stares off in the distance. "You know, she lost her son who was around the same age as Kirill due to drowning. Her life kinda went off the rails after that, and she was about to jump off a bridge. Viktor said he and Kirill were passing by when they saw her. Kirill caught her at the last second and told her if she had no use for her life, he could give her purpose. That was when he was, like, fifteen. He brought her back here, and neither Papa nor Mama liked her. Mama said he was picking up homeless people off the streets. But do you know how he forced them to accept her? He asked Papa for his prize after finishing one of his missions, and his prize was having and keeping Anna."

Karina smiles broadly, looking awfully proud of a brother she often threatens to kill. I can't help but mirror her smile. No wonder Anna is overprotective of Kirill. She must've raised him as her own son ever since he brought her here.

"We're gonna have to steal Kirill's breakfast every day!" she announces with determination. When she raises her cup of coffee, I clink mine against it.

Even though I want to go find Kirill, I take my time with the breakfast. Karina and I stay on the balcony for over an hour, and not once does she mention the fifteen-minute limit.

TWENTY-FIVE

Kirill

I SHAKE HANDS WITH IGOR AND HIS SON BEFORE THEY LEAVE my office.

Loud music slips from downstairs in the small time frame all of Igor's men leave my space.

This was the second night of incessant negotiation. It started last night, and when we didn't come to a full agreement, Igor didn't give up.

Instead, he brought his son, Alexei, and more men to convince me that we can help each other.

Yuri closes the door behind them and stands there with his arms crossed. Viktor finally moves from his statue-like position by the wall and stops in front of my desk.

"That's a good deal," he says.

"I wouldn't be so quick to conclude that." I drum my fingers on the desk. "Igor, and especially Alexei, don't do favors for no reason."

"Igor was friends with your father."

"That means nothing. He's not friends with me, and if he's offering to back me up, there's a price to pay. If not now, then somewhere down the line."

"Then you can use his influence and discard him later."

"That's a dangerous path to take," Yuri, who's been silent all this time, intervenes. "Just because Igor's unit doesn't flash victories like Damien's or Mikhail's doesn't mean it's weak. In fact, it's one of the strongest in the organization. Making enemies with him would be both foolish and suicidal."

"Correct." I snap my fingers in his direction. "But that doesn't mean I'm going to sit around and do nothing. If an alliance is what he wants…he'll think that's what he's getting."

My biggest ally, however, will always be Adrian. I stack cards on my desk and start to build my house as I pull out my phone and dial his number.

He picks up after a few rings. "Volkov."

"Morozov." I match his closed-off tone with a touch of mockery.

"If this is another one of your idle chats…"

"Now, Adrian. Why have you turned so heartless? We've known each other all our lives, overthrew our tyrant fathers, and took over their legacies. We should be closer than this, don't you think?"

"I'm hanging up."

"What if I tell you I have an in with the cartels?" I drop the amused tone.

There's a long pause, then, "Keep talking."

"I can't unless you give me your word for a partnership."

"I'll have to see results first. Which cartel do you have an in with?"

"I did say cartels, *plural*. I'll pick and choose when I get there."

"You're either a suicidal idiot or an unhinged genius if you think you can pick and choose with cartels."

I laugh, building my house at lightning speed. "When I bring in the first shipment, you'll call me a maestro."

"How will you do that?"

"Didn't you ask me the same thing when I got us that deal with the Yakuza? Not only are they our allies now, but they're also profitable."

"That was a stroke of luck."

I put the phone on speaker so I can focus on the harder parts of the house. "You don't even believe that, Adrian. But don't they say work hard enough that outsiders think it's easy?"

"So you did something right once. Now, what? You think you can handle another beast this soon?"

"And another and another." I stack two more cards in a perfect inverted *V*. "And another."

"I'm only warning you because I don't want the hassle of dealing with your brother if you somehow get killed, so listen carefully."

"Aw, worried about me, Adrian? I knew you had a place for me in your little black heart."

"If you don't shut the fuck up and listen, I'm hanging up." He pauses, releases a breath, then continues, "The cartels are different from anything we've ever dealt with. We've always had some relations with the Italians, Irish, Triads, and Yakuza, but a deal with the cartels always falls short before the execution stage. They're not good with newcomers or outsiders, and you look nowhere near Hispanic."

"That, I don't. But I do have my ways. I'll hit you up for intel soon."

"Your plan?"

"I don't ask you how you get information, so don't ask me how I come up with my plans. Let's both just do our own things."

He doesn't say anything more and we hang up on a cold note from Adrian, because he's an asshole.

But, anyway, it's a start.

"We have an in with a cartel?" Viktor asks. "*Cartels*, plural? When did that happen? In fucking Russia?"

"Of course we don't, Viktor. But we will. Soon."

"You just told Adrian that we do," he points out like an idiot.

Yuri steps forward. "If lying to Igor is dangerous, doing it to Adrian is nothing short of begging to be killed."

"I wasn't lying since I *will* have an in. I just failed to mention the timeline."

My father had an in with three cartels, but he always screwed it up due to poor decision making. Lucky for the organization, I'm better than him in picking and choosing people.

I stack the final two cards at the top and stare at my creation with a satisfied smile.

Everything and everyone are going according to plan. The organization doesn't know this, but they'll soon fall into my hands.

A commotion reaches me from outside—some bickering and fooling around. Then all the noise disappears, and a knock sounds on the door.

I don't have to guess who it is.

When Yuri opens it, it's Maksim and Sasha. They look serious now, but that doesn't conceal the fact that they were joking around just a moment ago.

"Reporting for night duty," Maksim says casually as if he's not climbing to the top of my hit list at lightning speed.

I push my glasses up my nose and catch Sasha's eyes following the motion before she subtly stares at the floor.

She's quick to hide her reaction, but not quick enough to conceal the red hue that covers her neck and ears.

Fucking adorable.

I have to adjust my position because my cock has chosen this exact moment to tighten against my pants.

Images of her body laid out for me, open and pliant and ready to be owned, play at the back of my mind.

I would've gone all night long if she hadn't fainted on me. That includes pushing out my meeting with Igor.

While I have been contemplating touching Sasha for months, it wasn't until I actually did it that I realized just how addictive she is.

Now that I've had a taste, I can't be stopped.

It goes against everything in me to tap an ass I know nothing about. It wouldn't have been worth it for anyone else, but for Sasha...fuck if that logic works.

"Everyone out," I announce in a clipped tone.

Yuri and Viktor nod before they comply. Maksim's brow furrows, but Yuri drags him out with him.

Sasha stares at me, or more like glares, before she lowers her head and starts to follow them.

"Not you, Sasha."

She stops in place, her shoulders tensing.

As soon as the door closes, she stares at me but doesn't say a word.

I beckon her over with two fingers. "Come here."

"I'm not your dog."

"I said, come here."

She practically stomps in my direction, and I resist the urge to smile. Her fire is a fucking turn-on, and I'm tempted to own that fire and cage it where I'm the only one who has access to it.

When she's within reach, I grab her by the wrist and pull her forward so that she crashes against my shoulder and gets trapped between my legs.

She pulls back, but she can't get away since I wrap my arm around her waist.

"W-what are you doing?" Her fearful eyes fly to the door. "Anyone could walk in."

"Not without my permission."

I inhale her scent—soap and a hint of...perfume.

"Were you with my sister?" I ask.

Her eyes widen. "How did you know that?"

"You have her smell on you."

"Oh, right. We had meals together. I convinced her to have breakfast on the balcony. Not lunch or dinner, though. I figured that would be too much for one day."

"Karina went out on the balcony?"

"Yeah, and I even have selfies to prove it."

"*Selfies*," I repeat. "Aren't you getting too cozy?"

"She's lonely and wants friends. I understand her feelings, so I'm trying to help. Is there something wrong with that?"

"Your tone of voice, for starters."

"Well, I'm sorry I'm not robotic enough for your liking."

I reach a hand out and stroke the cushion of her bottom lip. "This mouth is begging to be fucked."

"You…" Her hot breaths skim over my skin. "You said you won't fuck me until I give you something."

"Maybe I changed my mind." My finger strokes the skin back and forth, back and forth, making her breath choke on air. "You certainly need to be claimed, so you'll stop flaunting yourself around."

"I'm not flaunting myself…" she trails off when I thrust my thumb inside her mouth.

At first, she looks at me wide-eyed, her lips pulsing against my skin for a few seconds, but then she starts to tentatively dart her tongue around my finger.

"Do it properly," I order, pushing my finger farther against her tongue. "Suck like you mean it."

Her eyes, the color of a vibrant forest now, never leave mine as she licks and sucks, her determination bursting at the seams.

I can almost picture these lips around my cock, which is such a fucking bad idea because it's about to burst from my pants.

The more she puts her enthusiasm behind sucking, the closer I am to coming like a pubescent.

I yank out my finger. "On your knees."

"What…?"

"I said, get on your fucking knees, Sasha."

Her lips part, but she slowly gets into position, and she does it so naturally that I grow even harder.

While Sasha may seem inexperienced, she's a natural submissive. She might act like a brat sometimes, but she knows exactly when to lay off and do as she's asked.

Her eyes follow my hands as I take my time unbuckling my belt and then my pants. "You haven't been following orders, Sasha, and that needs to be punished."

"What…" She swallows, still not taking her eyes off my hands. "What orders?"

"I told you to stop being so friendly, didn't I?"

"But I wasn't."

"How about Maksim?"

"He's…my friend."

"He's *nothing*."

She opens her mouth, but no words come out as I free my cock and wrap the belt around her neck to pull her forward.

I hit her lips with my cock, and she complies, opening the widest possible. I thrust all the way to the back of her throat, but I still don't get all my length inside.

Sasha chokes, her pale skin turning red and the veins popping in her neck. I keep my cock in place, but she doesn't fight or push me away.

What she does do, however, is look me in the eye. Even as hers fill with tears that stream down her cheeks.

It's almost as if she…trusts me.

Fuck. I'm the last man she should trust.

I pull out, and she sputters and inhales deeply before I thrust in again. I use her tongue for friction, and I fuck her mouth.

No, I actually fuck her throat.

My belt around her neck keeps her immobile as a vessel for my pleasure. No matter how far or hard I go, she doesn't attempt to fight me.

Not even when I pick up the rhythm and fuck her mouth like I'm punishing her. Not even when spit, tears, and precum cover her face, and she becomes a painting of my own making.

"You're such a good girl," I grunt as I near my peak.

She crawls slightly farther in my direction and opens her mouth wider as if loving the compliment.

"You're taking me so well. These pretty little lips were made for my cock, Solnyshko."

Her eyes brighten, and I smirk.

"You love it when I call you that, don't you, Solnyshko?"

She doesn't answer with words, but she tries to lick my cock, offering additional friction that drives me over the edge.

I'm not the type who usually comes fast, but I'm reaching a record with my cock inside Sasha's mouth. It's still more time than anyone else could handle, especially someone who looks as innocent and as naïve as her.

I come down her throat, and she tries to swallow as much as possible while still looking at me.

Mine.

This woman is all fucking mine.

When I pull out, some of my cum decorates her lips and chin, and she licks them while still staring at me.

Ah, fuck.

Now, I'm getting hard again.

Using my hold on her with the belt, I force her to stand, and she does so on unsteady feet. Her expressive eyes brighten with anticipation, waiting and needing to know what happens next. When I continue watching her without taking action, she shifts and rubs her legs together.

She's wet and horny.

I can see it in the darkening color of her eyes. She doesn't even try to hide the signals her body is sending to my monster.

The fact that she got this way because of how I used her is even more thrilling.

"Looks like I'm going to have to fuck you, after all."

I shove her against the desk, sending the cards in all directions. Sasha gasps, then moans when I step behind her and grind my erection against her covered ass.

"You like being used by me, don't you?"

"N-no, I don't."

"Don't lie to me when you're dripping wet for my cock." I accentuate my words with a swipe of my fingers over her covered pussy.

Her moan echoes around us, and I smile. "Such a good girl, my Solnyshko."

That earns me a choked whimper. She does love the pet name, after all, my Sasha.

I grab the hem of her pants, about to rip them down, when the door opens, and the last person I'd expect barges inside.

Rai Sokolov.

And she has a complete view of the situation.

TWENTY-SIX

Kirill

I DON'T HAVE TO SEE HER FACE TO KNOW SASHA IS FROZEN. Her whole body stiffens, and she might as well have transformed into a stone in my hands.

Rai's unfocused eyes narrow on us as she sways on her feet, the sound of her heels scraping on the ground amplified tenfold in the imposing silence.

That seems to kick Sasha out of her stupor, because she responds to my tightening hold around her waist and abruptly ducks down and crawls under the desk.

The fucking cockblocker Rai doesn't look away from my half-nude state so, to be a dick—no pun intended—I look her in her dazed eyes and take my time tucking myself in.

Again, I don't have to look at Sasha's face to sense her distress. It's bleeding from her and bouncing off my skin.

Option one: shoot Rai between the eyes and think of a way to hide her body and any evidence that she came to my club.

Option two: torture the fucking piece of shit, and only when I'm satisfied do I kill her.

Choices, choices...

"Was that..." Rai points a finger between me and the desk, sounding drunker than a sailor in his victory parade.

I ignore her insufferable existence and lower myself to my haunches. Sasha is hiding beneath the desk, her legs tucked to the side and face so pale, it appears sickly.

Her parted lips are dry, eyes shifty and scared.

No, not scared. They're as terrified as if she's seen a ghost who's been haunting her for eternity.

"It's not that I don't want to be a woman, it's that I can't," is what she'd said back in Russia. It's also why she's tried her hardest to keep her distance from the other men.

For eliciting this fear in Sasha, I'm tempted to go with option one and shoot Rai. Fuck the fact that she's the Pakhan's grand-niece and he'd skin me alive if he found out that I'd hurt his precious relative.

My fingers find Sasha's cheek to try and calm her down. But not only does she flinch, her body also breaks into a shaking mess.

With an annoyed sigh, I drop my hand to my side.

"I'll take care of it," I say in my attempt at a gentle tone that still sounds firm. "Stay here."

She doesn't nod or show any signs of hearing me, but I don't have time to focus on that, because Rai is approaching us. Her steps are no different than those of a toddler who just learned to walk, and I hope she trips on her heels and breaks her ankles.

Or better yet, hits her head and dies. That way, I could confidently say that I'm not the one who did it.

Unfortunately, no falling happens, and I'm forced to intercept her so she doesn't witness Sasha's state.

I round the desk and grab Rai by the elbow. "Come with me."

"I'm going nowhere with you," she slurs and glares at me. "Do you want to die?"

"I assure you that you'll be the one to die if you don't follow me this instant."

She does try to push me away and even attempts to dig the pointy part of her heel in my shoe, but she's as drunk as they come, so I successfully drag her out of the office.

"Boss." Viktor watches the scene with wide eyes. "She threatened to have the Pakhan kill us if we touched her, so I couldn't stop Miss Sokolov—"

"Obviously." I glare at him. "No one is allowed in the office until I get back."

Yuri starts to say something, but I direct my glare at him. "I mean it. If I find out anyone went in there, they better not let me see them again."

"What is this about?" Rai grumbles like a spoiled rich kid, which she is, actually.

Not offering a reply, I pull her with me to a secondary office and shut the door behind us.

I might have accidentally—or intentionally—pushed Rai harder than needed inside, because she slams against the desk and hits her head on the lamp.

Propping herself up on the edge, she faces me with a death glare, a red bruise already forming on her forehead beneath the blonde hair.

She's wearing a knee-length black dress that's more suitable for a funeral than a club. White pearls don her neck, and she has on the makeup of a president's wife. I know she tries hard to look older than she actually is, and she might manage to fool an outsider, but not me.

Besides, I've known her since her grandfather, the previous Pakhan, brought her to the organization when she was a preteen. We've never gotten along.

She has some of Yulia's haughtiness, and anyone who resembles my mother, even the tiniest bit, has a special place on my hit list.

"What do you think you're doing, Kirill?"

I lean against the door, legs crossed, blocking the only exit. "I should be the one asking you that, considering you chose to barge into my club."

She folds her arms over her chest. "The club falls under the organization's jurisdiction."

"*My* jurisdiction."

"As a member of the financial report team, I'm here for revenue control."

"And when did you intend to do that? Before or after the hangover that's waiting to happen."

"I just…got a little carried away."

"A *little?*"

"Okay, a lot." She releases a breath, then narrows her eyes that look too much like her dead grandfather's. "But that's not what's important here, is it?"

A muscle clenches in my jaw, but my expression remains the same. "Care to elaborate?"

"What…was that I just saw?"

"You've seen something? You sure it's not just the alcohol talking?"

"I'm not drunk enough to start hallucinating. Are you perhaps…gay?"

Hmm.

From her point of view, I was bending over a man dressed in a suit on my desk. I was so busy thinking of how to make Rai believe she's fucking crazy that I didn't consider this angle.

It would be nearly impossible to make her go whacko, considering it would take effort, careful planning, and, most importantly, time that I don't have.

"What if I am?" I ask casually.

"Nothing to it, I guess." She lifts her shoulders, then smirks. "At least, that's what I think. Everyone else in the organization, however, tends to be old-fashioned and close-minded. I'm not sure they would treat this information as neutrally as I do."

"Your point?"

She uncrosses her arms and approaches me with confident 'I'm in control of this situation' strides, then stops a few paces away. "I can keep this a secret if you do something for me."

I adjust my glasses. "Which is?"

"Vote for me at the upcoming meeting to become the executive director for V Corp."

I burst out laughing. The sound is so intrusive and loud that Rai shifts from easy overconfidence to annoyed anger.

"What's so funny about that?"

I raise a hand, pretending that it takes me more effort than needed to stop myself from laughing. "You. Head of V Corp. That's what's funny, Rai."

"Granduncle is the head. I'll just be the executive director."

"Which is another word for the one who calls the shots. That can't be you."

"Why the fuck not? Because I'm a woman?"

"Because you still struggle with controlling your bursts of emotions, and the others don't respect you."

"That's only because I don't have a dick between my legs."

"That's part of the reason, but it's not all. You can still have an imaginary dick and balls."

"What is that supposed to mean?"

I resist the urge to throw her against the nearest wall or actually shoot her to get rid of her once and for all.

The alternative is that I have to help this woman reach her ambition in exchange for keeping this whole situation under wraps.

I don't even like Rai, not that I like anyone, per se, but the reason why I dislike her more than most is her holier-than-thou attitude and unbending personality that could be snapped like a twig.

It doesn't help that she has a lot of moral 'shackles,' and I can't possibly have her as an ally since we disagree on almost everything.

So now, I have to give up an important position at V Corp to her when I could've used it as leverage to gain a more valuable ally.

If Sasha weren't in the picture, I wouldn't have to take these extreme measures, but she *is* in the picture, and I couldn't remove her even if I wanted to.

I focus on Rai's expectant face. "You lack experience and allies, in that order. You need to work on that first before you ask for a vote. I assure you that even if I vote for you this time, everyone else, Sergei included, will shoot you down. The current executive director, one of Mikhail's men, has been bringing in a five-percent growth for three years. If you come up with a way to beat him, by all means, ask for a vote and demand that you're appointed. That's the only way for this to work."

"If I do that, do I have your word that you'll vote for me?"

I nod.

"If you don't, I'll tell everyone about what I just saw."

"By all means."

She offers her hand. "It was nice doing business with you, Kirill."

I shake it harder than needed. "The same can't be said about you."

I wait for her to leave, but she just heads to the bar for more drinks, so I go to the main office, in front of which are Viktor, Yuri, and Maksim.

"Monitor Rai," I tell them. "Don't let her out of your sight until she leaves."

"Yes, Boss," they say in unison.

Once they're gone, I step into the office. When I find no sign of Sasha, my mind goes to the worst scenario.

She got so scared about the possibility of her identity being revealed that she ran for it.

But if that were the case, surely Viktor would've told me.

Is she maybe…

I head to the desk and lower myself to my haunches. Sure enough, Sasha is still beneath the desk. Only now, she's hugging her knees to her chest, face red, and eyes brimming with unshed tears.

"Why are you hiding?"

"You told me to stay here," she says so easily.

"What the fuck am I going to do with you?" I say more to myself than to her. Then, seeing her expectant expression, I add, "It's all been taken care of."

"How?"

"Rai thinks I'm gay. She probably didn't even see your face, so you're fine."

The unshed tears fall down her cheeks in frightening succession, and she flat out breaks into sobs. The sound is so loud and haunted that I remain frozen.

To say I've never cared about people crying would be an understatement. My father made sure to rip that emotion out of me just like he did every other emotion.

But the sight of her rare tears reminds me of her desperation and deep grief when we left the old dead couple back in Russia. It reminds me of the time she started to hate me, put distance between us, and completely erased me from her immediate circle.

She might have followed me to New York, but that was for some other agenda, not for me. She might yearn for my touch and let me do what I want with her, but there's a wall that separates us.

These tears are a reminder of that wall. A *very* cruel reminder that I actually have no clue what goes on in this woman's head.

"I said it's taken care of," I repeat in a less gentle tone. "Why the fuck are you crying?"

The shadows from the desk cast dark edges on her pale skin. "Rai thinks you're gay and will certainly use it against you, right? She'll threaten you with it and might even put everything you've worked for in jeopardy. How is that taken care of?"

"Are you possibly crying because of the implications of this incident on me?"

She blinks slowly. "Why else would I be?"

"Didn't you say you can't have your real gender revealed?"

"Oh, yeah. That."

"Why did that sound like an afterthought?"

She lifts her shoulders and sniffles. "I guess it is. I don't want others to know I'm a woman, but I'm mostly worried about your position. If the Pakhan finds out you've been passing a woman bodyguard as a male or that you're homosexual, he probably won't let it slide, right?"

"Let me worry about that."

"But…I'm supposed to be the one who protects you, not the other way around."

"You have a point, but you don't always have to protect my physical body. Viktor and the others can take care of that."

"What can I protect then?"

"My cock that Rai blocked so hard that he's all blue?"

She snorts, smiling through the tears, and her cheeks turn a deep shade of red. It's the most fucking beautiful thing I've ever seen.

My fingers find her face, and I take my time wiping away the tears that cling to her cheeks, nose, lips, and chin.

She trembles in my hold, and more tears cascade down her cheeks. I pull her forward, then dart my tongue out to lick the tears that are forming a streak down her cheeks and over the edge of her lips.

Her lips shake and I can't resist the incessant need to ravage her. I remove my glasses and press my mouth to hers. My tongue thrusts inside her welcoming heat, and I kiss her with the savagery of an animal.

Sasha tries to kiss me back with tentative strokes, but it's impossible for her to keep up with my pace, not when I have every intention of devouring her whole.

Not when every particle in me demands that I absorb her so wholly, there will be nothing left of her when I'm done.

She whimpers against my mouth, her heartbeat clashing against mine and her body going pliant in my hold.

I kiss her as if I'll never stop kissing her, and she kisses me like she wants to break this twisted connection but can't.

TWENTY-SEVEN

Sasha

"**S**ASHA, IS THAT YOU?"

I hide farther behind the wall at the bottom of the club's stairs and tighten my grip on my burner phone. "It's me, Uncle Albert."

"What were you thinking?" His voice hardens with concern. "How could you leave Russia without telling me?"

"I'm sorry, but you said not to contact you unless it was urgent and absolutely necessary so…so…"

"So you decided to go without informing me after you promised to stay away from the Morozovs."

I fidget, more sweat trickling down my spine with every passing moment. He sounds calm, but there's an edge of disappointment behind his words like he trusted me with something, but I failed him.

"I just wanted to know what Roman Morozov's involvement

was with the death of our family. I deserve to know why I lost everyone in the blink of an eye."

"And? Did you get your answer?"

"No. He died as soon as we got here, but I'm getting closer to Kirill. If I prove myself, he'll give me access to the office in which his father kept files, and—"

"It's useless, Sasha. You're fighting a hopeless battle here."

"But why? I won't know until I try."

"Or get killed for crossing the mob." He releases a long sigh. "This isn't regulated military life, Sasha. You went ahead and inserted yourself into a lawless world that has zero tolerance for betrayal. You might think you're getting close to this Kirill, but the moment he sniffs something wrong, you'll be buried where no one can find you."

My breath catches, and I lean against the wall to regain my composure. Yes, I thought about this possibility when I first decided to come here, but that was before everything that happened with Kirill.

The truth remains, a small, probably foolish part of me thought that I could definitely separate business from pleasure. We're both using each other's bodies to satiate a carnal need, and that's it.

I don't have feelings for him, and God forbid he has feelings for anyone. Sometimes, I think he doesn't even like himself.

It's been a week since Rai caught us in his office. Every night, we come to the club, where he meets the people he deems fit for his manipulation, and then we go back to the mansion, where he eats me out and then makes me choke on his cock. Yesterday, this happened at the same time.

After we're done, he leaves me to sleep in his bed while he does more work on the sofa opposite the bed. Sometimes, he builds his stupid house of cards.

He never lies down beside me and sleeps. He doesn't sleep much in the first place.

I wish I didn't sleep either, because all my nights have been plagued with the same reoccurring nightmare where Mike asks for help and then dies, followed by Uncle Albert and Babushka.

So although I was scared of Uncle Albert's reaction to my trip to New York, I had to call him and make sure everything is okay.

"I can take care of myself. Don't worry about me," I say with confidence I don't feel. "How are Babushka and Mishka?"

"They're fine, Sasha. We're all fine. You're the one who got yourself in a dire situation."

"It's not really that bad, I have..." I trail off before I let out that I have friends.

Uncle Albert won't react well to that. Having friends is no different than putting my real identity and, therefore, all of them in danger.

"You have what?" he asks.

"Integrated well here. No one suspects me." Except for Kirill and Viktor. Anna, Yulia, and Konstantin don't like me either, but my uncle doesn't need to know about that.

"You can never be too careful in a place like that."

"I know, I know. I'm actually getting close to Kirill."

"You are?"

"Absolutely. I must be good at what I'm doing, right?"

"He's a Morozov, Sasha. I wouldn't be so sure about being close to him if I were you."

"I know that I'm getting there. Anyway, how is Babushka?"

"You're changing the subject."

"Can you tell me?" I ask in an innocent tone.

A long sigh comes from the other end. "She's getting old, but she's not suffering or anything. She's more energetic than me, actually."

I smile as relief washes over me. "That's good to know."

"Call me occasionally."

"I thought that was dangerous?"

"It is, but I would rather hear you're still alive once in a while."

"Will do. Can I talk to Mike?"

"One moment." His voice sounds far from the phone. "Mike, it's Sasha."

A boyish squeal comes through the phone before his short breaths follow. "Sasha, Sasha, is it really you, Sasha?"

My shoulders relax, and I soften my voice. "Hi, my love. I miss you."

"Miss you more than to the moon and back then up again, miss you, miss youuu, Sasha."

"Not more than me. I want to eat you up."

"What do you mean? I'm not candy!" He laughs, and I laugh, too. "When are you coming back?"

"I'm sorry, but I can't right now, Mishka. I'm in a faraway place and won't be able to come home for a while."

"As far as the moon?"

"No, but it's hard to come back right now."

"But you will one day, right?" There's a tremor in his little voice, and I want to kick myself for putting it there.

"Of course! I'm doing this to keep you safe, but one day, I'll come back and never leave, okay?"

"Okay," he says with little energy. "Here's Papa."

I look up to fight the tears and my eyes meet icy ones.

Kirill stands at the top of the stairs, leaning against the railing with a hand in his pocket.

Shit.

Fuck.

Please don't tell me he heard the entire thing?

No, I made sure no one was there when I started talking to Uncle, so he couldn't have...

I try not to be jerky when I hang up the burner phone and slip it into my gun holster. "Were you looking for me?"

His expression is neutral, but that's by no means a good thing. I've learned that Kirill hides his emotions, or whatever emotions he has left, frighteningly well.

You can never see his anger or contemplation when he so successfully tucks them where no one can see.

When he doesn't answer, I walk to the stairs, summoning a sense of ease that's opposite the anxiousness knotting my stomach.

Every step feels as if I'm dragging a dead body.

"Boss…"

"Who were you talking to?" His question is casual enough, but an edge lurks beneath it.

"No one—"

"Don't fucking lie to me."

The commanding tone of his voice renders me speechless.

It takes me a few moments to summon my courage and whisper, "Since when have you been listening?"

"Why is that important with regards to divulging the identity of the person you called?" He takes one step toward me. "I'm not asking because I can't find out on my own. I'm asking to give you a chance to tell me yourself."

My heartbeat thunders in erratic intervals, not allowing me to think properly. It doesn't help that Kirill is approaching me in even, steady strides that mess with my line of thinking.

For the first time in a long time, I'm acutely aware of how big and imposing he is. There's a predatory quality to the way he walks. It's similar to a fire that's about to burn everything in its wake.

When he stops in front of me, it's no different than being sucked into another person's orbit and having the air stolen from me.

He looks down at me with his freezing eyes, and I'm slammed by the difference in our height. Only now, he seems to have gotten bigger and taller.

Intimidating.

Dangerous.

"Who was it, Sasha?"

The more I stare into his unforgiving eyes, the dryer my mouth gets. The harsher and deeper they swallow me into their depths.

"Last chance."

One second passes.

Two.

Three.

He reaches for me, and I squeal when he wraps his arm around my waist. In the beginning, I thought he was done with verbal intimidation and was moving to the physical, but he doesn't pull me to him or shake me as I expected him to.

Instead, his hand reaches for my gun holster. I only realize what he's doing when it's too late. Kirill grabs hold of my burner phone with baffling ease, then steps back to inspect it.

Every cell in my body goes on alert, and I leap up to grab it, but he effortlessly keeps it out of reach.

With the phone in the air, he stares at me with his cold gaze. The one that every member of the organization and even his household dreads to see.

"Please give it back," I implore, my voice shaking.

"I've given you multiple chances to divulge what you're hiding from me. My patience in itself is a chance. But since you refuse to take it, I have to resort to this method."

"So I'm not allowed privacy?" I ask in a biting tone.

"No, you're not. I told you that your life is mine, and I specifically said that I wasn't joking, but you apparently chose to believe the opposite."

In a last attempt to fix the situation, I pull out my gun.

Kirill doesn't change his stance and merely stares at me in the same manner he has all along. "Are you going to shoot me, Sasha?"

I don't allow myself to think as I aim and shoot.

The phone flies out of Kirill's hand and clutters to the ground with a hole right in the middle.

I release a breath. Uncle Albert's phone number is safe now. Kirill can't, under any circumstances, get a hold of that part of my life.

Not only does he have no loyalty to anyone but himself, but

he's still his father's son. He's clearly overachieving what his father failed to do, so what if he also decides to exterminate the rest of us like his father wanted to?

One moment I'm standing, and the next, my feet leave the ground as Kirill grabs hold of my neck.

His fingers dig into the sensitive flesh, and I can't breathe as he tightens his hold. I thrash, scratching at his wrist, but I might as well not be touching him.

His voice darkens, sounding like it's underground due to the buzzing in my ears. "Who is he that you'd go to this length to protect him, hmm?"

I pat his wrist, my eyes begging him to let me go. "Ki…rill…"

"Who the fuck is he, Aleksandra?"

His voice booms in my ears. It's the first time I've ever heard this angry, frightening tone that could crumble mountains.

Tears rim my eyes, and I'm not sure if it's because of the way he yelled at me or the fact that I'm suffocating.

Just when I think I'll lose consciousness, Kirill releases me. I stumble to the ground, coughing and massaging the handprints he left on my throat.

My shoulder hits the wall, and I'm thankful for the support as I topple over and nearly throw up from all the coughing.

When I'm calmer and breathing more easily, I stare at the monster standing over me. His eyes are a raging color that resembles a stormy sea that's out to drown me.

"I'm going to need a name."

I slowly shake my head. "I…can't."

"You can't or you won't?"

I rise to my full height. "Why should I be obliged to tell you anything when I know nothing about you?"

"I own you, not the other way around."

"No one *owns* me."

He gets closer, his expression more frightening than before. I step back.

BLOOD OF MY MONSTER | 269

I don't mean to. It just happens.

Kirill is a scary man. Some would argue he's not a man, but half man, half beast. Right now, he looks fully monstrous.

This isn't methodical like on the battlefield or when he's plotting something. He's neither calm nor collected.

This is personal.

It's clear in every step he takes that this situation will end badly for me. The problem is, there doesn't seem to be anything I can do to dissipate the raging volcano that's about to sweep me over.

I can't even escape with him blocking the only exit.

Maybe if I distract him—

A commotion comes from the stairs, and I freeze. Kirill doesn't; his entire attention remains on me. He's like a giant black cat who won't stop until he catches his prey.

"Boss!" Maksim calls from upstairs. "There's been an intrusion."

TWENTY-EIGHT

Sasha

DESPITE THE STATE OF EMERGENCY, IF I COULD HUG
Maksim for interrupting Kirill's destructive plan, I
would.

But then again, that might have the exact opposite desired
effect and put Maksim's life in danger, which is why I refrain from
acting on that impulse.

That, and the fact that the club's security might be in jeopardy.

In situations like these, anyone would expect chaos to ensue,
but that's impossible in an establishment run by Kirill.

There isn't even an alarm asking people at the club to leave.
The music continues, and everyone keeps dancing and drinking,
completely unaware of the severity of the situation.

Kirill heads straight to the control room. I take a few moments
to compose myself before I follow after.

But even when I reach the area, I remain in the shadows, at
the farthest point, while still standing in the same room as him.

BLOOD OF MY MONSTER | 271

For my survival, I need to avoid being the center of his attention as much as possible.

We find Yuri watching the security footage with some other guards. On one of the screens, Viktor is inspecting a package that was left at the doorstep of the staff entrance. A large duffel bag, to be specific.

"Rewind the footage to the beginning of the incident," Kirill orders, then clicks the intercom that connects to the speaker outside. "Don't touch that yet, Viktor."

"Yes, sir," comes the guard's reply.

Yuri clicks a few buttons, and the images go back to five minutes ago. A black van screeches to an abrupt stop near the club, then accelerates to the entrance. A few guards shoot at it, but nothing penetrates it. Which means the vehicle is bulletproof.

The people inside the van shoot their own bullets, hitting two bouncers before the side door opens and the duffel bag is thrown out. Then they rev down the street at high speed.

Kirill perches beside Yuri and rewinds the footage a few seconds, then pauses at the moment the door opens. He does it a few times, watching and rewatching the moment the duffel bag was thrown out.

He lets it play again and clicks the intercom that connects him to his senior guard. "There's a person inside the duffel bag, Viktor. If he's not dead, kill him."

"Yes, sir." Viktor slowly opens the zipper and everyone, including me, focuses on the picture that Yuri projects on three large monitors.

Viktor pauses when he gets a view of the person. The only thing we see from the camera's angle is a head and short bloodied hair.

"Is he dead?" Yuri asks.

"No," Viktor replies.

"Why aren't you shooting then?" Kirill asks.

Viktor looks at the camera with a bemused expression. "It's Mr. Konstantin, Boss. Should I kill him?"

Kirill actually pauses as if he's really thinking of finishing his younger brother's life. Then he casually says, "No need. Take him to my office, and make sure he's conscious when I get there."

He doesn't wait for Viktor to reply and stares at Yuri. "I want you to strengthen the security while you figure out who's behind that van."

"I don't think they will come back…" Yuri trails off when Kirill looks at him pointedly. "On it, Boss."

He starts to leave the control room, but he stops at the door. "You're coming with me, Lipovsky."

My heart tightens with a strange sense of pain. It's been ages since he called me that—since the army, to be more specific. I don't care if Viktor does it, but it's different with Kirill.

I don't like to be called by the fake last name. It feels distant. Almost as if we're strangers.

Still, I follow after, even while keeping a distance. I expect Kirill to pick up where he left off earlier, but he doesn't even address me during the walk from the security room to his office.

The only part of him I can see is his back—broad, imposing, and…far.

He seems so far away right now. There's always been a wall between us. Though it's not disruptive, it's there, highlighting the difference between us.

Kirill Morozov is a man of no morals. A monster with no limits. A beast in the form of a sophisticated gentleman.

There were times when I thought the wall was shrinking in size, specifically on the rare occasion when I thought Kirill was being kind. When he saved me and took care of me. When he protected my identity. When he looked at me as if I were the most beautiful thing he'd ever seen.

I actually believed him when he told me I was gorgeous.

Now, I realize all of those moments could've been me trying

to rationalize the hole I've been digging for myself, just to make myself believe that I'm different to him.

That maybe I hold a special place in his cutthroat life.

But right now, that wall keeps getting taller, crushing my futile hopes and every rosy thought I ever had.

When we arrive at the office, we find Viktor lowering an unconscious Konstantin onto one of the chairs. Blood trickles down his temple. His usually impeccable dark brown suit is crumpled, and his white shirt is soaked with blood.

His right eye and his lips are swollen, one of his shoes is missing, and his chest is smattered with cigarette burns.

There's no doubt about it—he was tortured.

Despite his thirst for power and lack of practical decision-making skills, Konstantin isn't actually a bad person. I think he's just jealous of Kirill and hates his mind games. He's also too influenced by Yulia's hatred to see straight.

Ever since that incident in the Pakhan's house where he was kicked out and thoroughly humiliated by Kirill, he's been either avoiding him or glaring at him from afar.

Somewhat like Karina.

Yulia has been taking him to her family's conventions, probably trying to build his power again. Kirill completely ignored that fact when Viktor brought it to his attention.

"They're weak and won't be able to accomplish anything. Let them entertain themselves by trying," was the reply he gave.

Right now, however, Konstantin looks to be in critical shape.

"Should I call the doctor?" I ask.

"No," Kirill says. "Wake him up, Viktor."

"But he could have an infection," I argue. *He's his brother, after all, no?*

"I don't have all day," he addresses Viktor, completely ignoring me.

The burly guard nods and pours a bottle of water on

Konstantin's head. He startles awake, inhaling sharply, then breaks out in a fit of coughs.

His good eye widens, but the other remains half shut as he takes in the sight of Kirill standing in front of him.

"Who did this?" Kirill asks. "Who's trying to send me a message through your useless life?"

Konstantin's eyes ignite with anger so great, it burns through his whole frame. "Why...would you fucking care?"

"I don't." Kirill grabs him by his hair that's soaked in blood and wrenches his head back. "But you happen to share my last name, and I don't appreciate people sending me messages through the weak links in my life."

"*Fuck you.*"

"That doesn't answer my question." He slaps him on the cheek twice, then grabs him by the hair. "Focus."

I don't know how or why I do it, but I step to his side. "Please stop that. His eyes are unfocused, and he's probably feverish. He needs medical help."

"This is none of your business. Back off." He doesn't even look at me. "Who was it, Konstantin?"

His brother breathes harshly, but it's irregular, and his tongue gets stuck on the roof of his mouth. "Fuck you...you fucking bastard."

Kirill shoves him away, but he raises his fist to punch him.

I stand in front of him, arms on either side of me, and shake my head. "Don't."

"Which part of back the fuck off do you not understand, Lipovsky?"

Usually, I would shake like a leaf in front of those intense eyes, but I force myself to stare straight back at them. "Brothers aren't supposed to hate each other."

"I'll let you know when I need your unsolicited advice."

"Please..." I soften my tone since hardening it had the exact opposite effect I was hoping for. "You want answers, right? I'll get them for you. If you leave me alone with him…"

"Leave you *alone* with him?" His voice drops to a frightening range.

"Okay, don't leave me alone with him. But can you at least back off for a moment?"

"No."

"Just…" I release a harsh breath so as not to lose my cool. "I only need ten minutes."

"Five."

"Seven."

"Five."

"Fine." I look him up and down. "You're still standing here."

He takes a step back. No kidding, just one.

"You need to go farther."

"No."

"At least stand beside Viktor."

He narrows his eyes, and for some reason, they appear colder than usual, which is terrifying in and of itself, but he does go to stand beside Viktor.

It's not that far, but they're at least behind Konstantin, so he can't see them. He can probably sense the hostile energy radiating from them, though.

I slowly turn to face him, and he glares at me with his one good eye. "Whatever the fuck you think you're doing—"

Kirill steps forward, and I lower myself so that my face is level with Konstantin's. "It's okay, you don't have to tell me anything."

I grab a box of tissues from the coffee table and wipe at the blood on his temple. I can sense Kirill's stare—or more like glare—but I ignore it and focus on Konstantin instead.

He curses under his breath with each of my ministrations, and his breathing turns shallower. He definitely has a fever, too.

"They really did a number on you," I say with enough nonchalance to sound concerned, but not like I'm pitying him.

"Wait until I get my hands on those motherfuckers." He coughs and wheezes. "I'll drill their brains with holes, I swear to fuck—"

"Isn't it too late after they already got you?"

"What the fuck do you know, asshole? Were you there?"

"No, but if I had been there, none of this would've happened to you."

"You think you're all that?"

"No, but I'm probably better than your useless guards who allowed this to happen."

He purses his lips. "They were shot down. We were ambushed, so they couldn't have done anything."

"Doubt it. If they'd had the right security plan—"

"It was a setup!" he strains. "We were supposed to meet a contact from the Chicago branch, but it turned out they were out for me."

"You mean me." Kirill strolls to my side. "Your only power is being my brother."

"Fuck you, motherfucker."

I glare at Kirill for ruining the semblance of an agreement I was trying to build, but he merely ignores me. "Who was the person you were supposed to meet?"

"Ivanov," he spits out.

My legs go weak. Did he just say Ivanov? No, surely this is a coincidence. There are a lot of Russian people with our last name. Maybe even from other nationalities as well, so it's not like this person is related to me.

Besides, the only Ivanovs I know are back home.

"First name?" Kirill asks.

"Don't know."

"Description?"

"A burly blond guy who loves torture."

"No shit." He runs his gaze over Konstantin's multiple injuries. "Are you making fun of me?"

"I don't know. Have you done something I should be making fun of? Getting yourself ambushed by some guy whose background you haven't even checked does sound amateurish."

"You fucking—"

"Let's get him a doctor," I intervene to avoid whatever war is about to start.

Kirill turns to leave, not bothering to consider my suggestion. "Boss!" I call.

"Viktor, take him somewhere else so he'll stop bleeding on my floor," he announces, then leaves.

"That son of..." Konstantin wheezes, sounding delirious with fever.

"Let's take him to a doctor," I implore Viktor.

"Boss didn't say that."

"He also didn't say to leave him to die. Come on, help me."

He grunts, glances at the door as if he wants to be beside his tyrant boss, but then, he picks up the phone.

"Get the doctor to the house. We're arriving in twenty with Mr. Konstantin. He's injured and needs medical care."

Then Viktor helps me carry a semiconscious Konstantin to the car. To be completely transparent, he holds most of the weight.

As we make our way out, there's no sign of Kirill, Yuri, or Maksim in the halls or in the club's VIP booth.

We arrive at the house five minutes after the scheduled time, and we're greeted by a pacing Yulia. She's in her sophisticated satin robe. For the first time, her blonde hair is gathered in a bun and her face is free of makeup, allowing some wrinkles of age to show through.

Upon seeing us, she pales, but her expression doesn't change as she hastens her pace toward us. "What...what happened? Oh, Kostenka! Who did this to you?"

She pushes me away, and I nearly drop her son. "You...and you!" She punches Viktor's chest. "Did Kirill tell you to do this?

That…that devil isn't satisfied with everything he's done, so he's now taking my son from me?"

"It's not like that," I say in a gentle tone. "Mr. Konstantin was tortured and thrown in front of the club, so we—"

"Mother…" he croaks, his voice breaking.

"Yes, dear? Mother is here now. Everything is going to be okay." Her tone changes to that of motherly affection. A tone I've never heard her use on either Kirill or Karina.

She stops pushing and punching us, just so we can get him to the clinic. Once the doctor arrives, she kicks us out.

Still, I remain outside.

"What the fuck do you think you're doing, Lipovsky?" Viktor asks when I don't follow him.

"I'm going to stay here in case the doctor needs anything."

"Who the fuck are you? Mother Theresa?" He gets closer. "We got him help. He's going to be fine. Other than that, we don't mingle with him or his mother."

"She's Kirill's mother, too."

"Does she look like his mother to you?"

"Well—"

"Get the fuck out of here."

"But—"

"I said *out*. Go wait for Boss in front of his room for night duty."

I want to punch Viktor square in his stoic face, but something tells me that wouldn't go over so well.

Begrudgingly, I tell one of the maids to notify me about Konstantin's condition, then I go up the stairs to wait for his majesty the tyrant Kirill. Maybe I should pretend to be sick so that I'm not trapped with him in the same room.

I consider asking Maksim for help, but I don't want him to get suspicious—

"Sasha!" a familiar voice calls me as soon as I'm up the stairs.

Karina clutches my wrist, drags me into her room, and closes the door. As usual, it's filled with candles and weird mojo, but she at least has the curtains drawn back.

"What happened?" she asks in an alarmed voice. "I heard the maids talking about the doctor and medical care. Is…is Kirill okay? Is that his blood on your clothes?"

"He's as good as the devil." I clamp my lips shut, forgetting that I'm actually talking to his sister.

"Oh, thank God." She releases a breath.

"It's Konstantin. He's the one who was hurt."

Her shoulders drop, but she says nothing.

"Don't you want to see how he's doing?" I ask.

She shrugs. "Yulia is probably by his side, right?"

"Yeah."

"It's okay then. I'll just hear about it from the maids."

"He's your brother, Karina. You're not supposed to hear about it from the maids."

"I would rather do that than see Yulia fawning all over him." She purses her lips. "He's the only child she ever cared about, you know. The only one she treated as her own. Bought him things, took him on trips, and gave him words of affirmation. She looked at him with love, worried about him, and offered him the whole parental package. She only ever looked at Kirill and me with disgust. Contempt, even. When I started having panic attacks and anxiety, I went crying to her and asked for help like any scared daughter would ask her mother. But when I hugged her, she pushed me away as if I were revolting and told me I got exactly what I deserved. She's like our stepmother."

"I'm so sorry, Karina."

She wipes away the tears clinging to her eyes. "Stupid water coming out when it's not needed. Don't worry. I'm totally over that."

"Okay."

"I'm not scared or anything, but just in case, can you stay here until I fall asleep?"

"Sure."

I remain by her bedside as she tells me stories and cool tidbits she's learned online. She's a serial comic writer and said maybe one day she'd tell me her pen name. While she struggles with the world, she's managed to build her own miniature world where she feels more at ease.

After she falls asleep, I cover her with a blanket and silently step out of the room.

I get a text from a maid informing me that Konstantin is out of danger and asleep. Yulia is staying by his side tonight.

Releasing a relieved breath, I go to Kirill's room. I've got Konstantin's blood all over me from when I carried him earlier, and I need a change of clothes before I report to night duty.

The moment I open the door, black energy grabs hold of me before a hand wraps around my mouth. A muffled squeal leaves me as I'm dragged inside.

A dark, ominous voice whispers in my ear, "Shh. I need you to shut the fuck up, Sasha."

TWENTY-NINE

Sasha

M Y MIND GOES BLANK.

The worst part isn't my lack of reaction or thinking. It's how suddenly my body takes charge of the situation.

The moment I'm pulled inside, I don't go into hyperaware mode or tense for a fight. It's far from that.

I recognize the touch and drown in the familiar masculine scent that I couldn't grow immune to even if I tried.

The door closes with a quiet click, and then I'm pushed inside. The feral power of his strength leaves me breathless and with no choice but to match his steps.

Or try to.

He's too fast, too unpredictable, and that awakens a dormant beast inside me.

My calf hits a hard edge, and I gasp as I stumble straight onto the soft surface of the mattress.

Then he's on me.

His hand imprisons my wrists over my head, and his knees lie on either side of my stomach.

I get the first look at his face since he ambushed me, and I wish I hadn't.

It's tight but blank. Dark but emotional.

There's nothing scarier than a calm Kirill. He becomes a force to be reckoned with, lacking any restraint or moral codes. Not that he ever had either of those, but he at least makes the effort to pretend that he does. Right now, though?

There's no hint of that part of him. He's fully set on destruction, and I happen to be in the wrong place at the wrong time.

"What..." I trail off when he shakes his head once.

"Shhh, don't talk. I'm this close to becoming a pure fucking animal, and if you keep talking, this situation will turn very ugly, very fast."

I swallow, but a ball gets stuck at the back of my throat. This is the first time I've heard him use that low tone of voice. It's firm and collected, but a frightening hurricane lurks beneath the surface.

"Now, Sasha..." His voice deepens further to a subtle threat. "Have you finished being the benevolent one and making sure Konstantin is all safe?"

"Yes, I have, actually." No clue how my voice sounds so neutral under the circumstances. "One of us had to do it since he's your brother."

"Have I asked you to look after my brother?" His menacing tone shakes me to the core.

I probably should keep quiet, but that doesn't guarantee he'll stop this.

No matter what I do, if Kirill has something in mind, then he'll get to it. So I might as well get these chaotic emotions off my chest.

"I don't need your permission for everything I do." I try to wiggle my wrists free, but it's impossible to loosen his iron-like hold. "Unlike what you like to believe, you're not my keeper, Kirill."

A cruel smirk lifts the side of his lips. "If you find solace in these delusions, then, by all means, keep believing them, but the reality is the following: you are mine to do with whatever I please. You're my fucking property, Sasha. Is that clear?"

Hot moisture stings the corners of my eyes, but I refuse to show him the damage his words inflict on me. While I've always known Kirill to be a methodical, cold-hearted monster, this is the first time I've witnessed it firsthand.

Everything that happened in the past and the semblance of safety I felt in his arms was nothing more than my wishful thinking. He's only ever thought of me as something he can own. An addition to his collection. I'm not, by any means, part of his ambition. Hell, I might as well be the toy he wastes time with until he takes over the position he's working to obtain.

"I'm not your *anything*," I say with a calm I don't feel. "And I'm certainly not yours."

A muscle clenches in his jaw and his eyes darken behind the glasses. "Is that because you already belong to someone else?"

"Someone else?"

A long pause drifts between us as the dim nightstand light creates shadows over his sharp features. "I'm picking up where I left off earlier. I need a name."

"I don't know what you're talking about."

"You know exactly what I'm talking about. I need the name of the man you were talking to on the phone earlier."

My heart pounds, and I think Kirill might have the ability to pry my skin open to get his answers. I have to constantly remind myself that no matter how godly he is, that's not something he can actually do.

"That part of my life doesn't concern you," I say simply, softly enough for the words to come out as a plea.

"A name, Sasha. I won't repeat myself another time."

I purse my lips.

Tension drifts off Kirill in waves, accentuated by his tightening grip on my wrists. For a moment, I think he'll break them or something, but then he lifts me up by them.

I'm stunned into silence when he releases my hands, removes my jacket, and rips open my shirt. The buttons scatter on the bed and roll onto the floor.

My breasts tingle beneath my chest bandages, and my nipples harden to painful buds.

There must be something wrong with me, because even though I know he's mad, I still like his rough side. A part of me yearns for it while another part is scared of it.

The fact remains, if this will keep his mind off the current topic, then all I can do is let it happen.

Soon after, my bandages are gone with a fast maneuver of his strong, veiny hands. My breasts bounce free, and my nipples pulse with need.

He then unbuckles my belt and pushes away my pants and boxer briefs so that I'm sitting completely naked on the bed.

This isn't the first time I've been naked in front of him, but I still get that pang of doubt around him. I've always wanted someone, *anyone*, to see me as a woman. Sure, I didn't sign up for it to be this unfeeling monster, but he happens to be the only one who discovered my identity.

And for some reason, I want to be beautiful to him. I want him to kiss me like he can't get enough of me, like he did in his office the other day.

I love when Kirill kisses me. That's the only time he feels more like a man than a monster.

My thoughts scatter when he grabs me by the wrist and hauls me off the bed. I stumble and nearly fall, but his grip keeps me upright. I have to jog to keep up with his wide strides as he leads me to the en-suite bathroom.

The strong white light blinds me as the sparkling marble counter and giant mirror come into view.

He pushes me against the sink and stands behind me with the eeriness of the Grim Reaper.

His eyes flash to a scary darkening blue that resembles an angry ocean. I don't even focus on the fact that I'm stark naked while he's fully clothed. All I see in the mirror is an entity of violence.

He releases my wrist just to close his hand around my throat from behind. The grip is firm enough that I go to my tiptoes, but it's not meant to steal my breath.

This is a grip of control. So I know exactly who's in charge of this situation.

His other hand drifts over my hip, leaving goosebumps in its wake, then disappears between my throbbing thighs. Two of his fingers thrust inside my core, and I go still.

My skin turns red, and I'm forced to see every detail of my embarrassment in the mirror in front of us.

I have to see the two whitening scars on my side from the massacre and the ugly hole in my shoulder from when I was shot.

When I try to shift my attention to the floor, Kirill uses his grip on my neck and lifts it up.

"You're going to watch me own every part of you so you understand that you're completely mine."

He thrusts a third finger in, stretching me so fully that I can't focus on anything but his touch. He scissors his fingers inside me, and a burst of pleasure floods through me. My toes curl, and my heart beats so fast, it's scary.

Kirill's pace verges on madness as he pounds his fingers into me with heightened intensity. My eyes close halfway, and I want to look away from the storm that's about to take me over, but I can't.

The longer I'm swallowed in his icy eyes, the more light-headed I become. He teases my clit in two expert strokes, and I'm a goner.

I come with a deep moan and would fall forward if it weren't for Kirill's hold.

"That's it, Solnyshko. Show me how much you want me." His voice falls against my ear in a grunt before he bites down on the flesh.

My thighs shake, and the orgasm seems to heighten and draw out in both length and intensity. It's like his words are an aphrodisiac.

And maybe, just maybe, I'm too conditioned to the way he calls me his sun.

Why would a monster need a sun?

His hand disappears from between my legs, and before I can mourn the loss, he unbuckles his belt, and I feel his erection brush against my backside.

A shudder goes through me when his cock nudges against my ass cheek. Once, twice.

The pleasure that I thought would finally dim rises and grows.

I gasp. "Kirill…"

"I'm so tempted to stuff my cock into this hole." He pushes his huge cock against my ass again. "I'd fuck you until you realize that every part of you belongs to me. Not anyone else. *Me.* This is my ass, my property. Fucking mine."

My hand finds his thigh, and I try to push at him, but he imprisons my wrists behind my back and uses both his hands to wrap his thick leather belt around them. I'm completely immobile, and I couldn't move if I wanted to. Then his fingers go back to my throat.

"But tonight…" He slides his cock between my legs. "I'll start with my pussy."

He thrusts inside, and I gasp as pain explodes all over my core. Kirill is just too huge, and despite the orgasm I just had, it hurts to have all of him in me.

"You're so tight. Mmm. So fucking right." His grunts fill my ears, and even though it hurts, I try to fall into the rhythm.

I don't have to try for long.

After a few thrusts, pleasure starts to war with the pain, and my moans echo in the air. Kirill uses his hold on my neck to make me look in the mirror.

I'm startled by the sight in front of me. He looks larger than life behind me and no different than a beast who's devouring me alive. My skin is sweaty, flushed, and molded to his rhythm.

With his hand around my throat and my wrists bound, I'm completely at his mercy.

"Look at who owns you, Solnyshko. Look at how your body submits to me as if it was made for me. You are mine, and you will always be fucking mine. You'll never belong to anyone else but me."

The dark possessiveness in his words should scare me, and it does to an extent, but I can't think straight with him pounding me to within an inch of my life.

His rhythm is as intense as he is. He fucks with his usual control, but sometimes, he goes so fast and so hard that even he can't control it. His glasses fog up from sweat and exertion, and he throws them aside and then ramps up the intensity.

My breasts bounce and ache from the arousal, and my hips hit the marble counter a few times. The sting of pain adds to the savage pleasure building in my core.

All of a sudden, he tightens his grip on my throat and cuts off my oxygen.

I can't breathe.

I can't...

Just when I think I'm going to die, I come.

And then air and ecstasy rush through me all at once. I start to fall over, but Kirill pushes me down against the counter. The shock of cold hits my heated skin, and my hard nipples scrape against the marble.

But those bursts of discomfort are forgotten when he grips me by the back of my neck and fucks me through my orgasm. He goes deeper, pulls out, then drives back in again and again.

Then he rams into me with the lethality of an animal. He *is* an animal.

A monster who can't get enough.

Not even when I start crying from how intense it gets. Not even when I think I'll actually pass out.

Kirill doesn't stop or slow down, and he certainly doesn't finish. He fucks me on and on, until pleasure begins to blend with pain. Until I don't know if I ever want him to stop.

The way he takes what he wants and uses me for his own pleasure makes my thighs messy and sticky with arousal. Another orgasm builds in my core and spreads all over my body.

That's when Kirill growls, pounds harder for a few strokes, and then warmth fills my insides.

He pulls me up by my throat so that my back is glued to his clothed chest. His hot breaths fill my ear before he growls, "Mine."

A frightening shudder goes through me when I realize that he means that and will probably stop at nothing to really make me his.

THIRTY

Kirill

THE MOMENT I OPEN MY EYES, I REALIZE TWO THINGS.
One, I fell asleep.

Ever since my father started his torture sessions, my type of sleep has been only resting my eyes. I'm always fully aware of my surroundings and ready to spring into action at any moment.

I haven't had a deep night's sleep in…maybe twenty years or so, to the point that I've forgotten what it feels like. The army made my sleeping habits even more erratic. What's the point of resting my eyes when I could be using that time to do something constructive?

Consequently, my sleeping time has gotten shorter and shorter over the years. The only exception was that night in the village. I found it concerning then, and it's even more troubling now, considering I actually fell into a deep sleep for…over six hours.

This brings me to the next thing I've realized.

Sasha is gone.

The bed is crumpled where she slept, and her scent lingers in the air, but that's the only evidence that she was ever here.

I look down and find a blanket has been thrown over me, surprisingly managing to cover almost the entirety of me.

After I put her to bed, I sat in my usual spot on the sofa, meaning to do some work, but apparently, I fell fucking asleep. Not only did I not notice her waking up, dressing, and leaving, but I also didn't sense her touching me.

Fucking fuck.

I spring up and head to the bathroom to see if she's there, despite having the feeling that she's not. I stop at the threshold as memories from last night hit me. The fucking, moaning, slapping, grunting, and crying.

There was a lot of crying when Sasha couldn't take being fucked anymore, but sometimes, there was begging, too, so I let her come.

The more the tears streamed down her cheeks, the harder I got. The longer she begged, the more I needed to own her so thoroughly, no one would be able to take her away from me.

I wanted to stop after that first time since she was clearly spent and probably sore, so I tried to be a gentleman and took her into the shower. But the moment her body fell against mine in a half hug because she couldn't stand properly, all gentlemanly thoughts flew out the window. Not that the role had come to me naturally in the first place.

As my nature dictated, I fucked her against the shower wall until she had no choice but to hold on to me. Until she nearly fainted from how many times she came, and I had to use her mouth to finish off.

She did smile, although faintly, and murmured, "Thank you." Now, I'm not sure what she was grateful for, but I still reveled in the fact that she was thankful to me.

If anyone were to ask what's come over me, I wouldn't have

BLOOD OF MY MONSTER | 291

an answer. Even I don't know what the fuck happens to me when Sasha is around.

In the beginning, it was mere curiosity as to why she pretends to be a man, but then I got to know her determination and tenacity, and it grew into a form of respect.

That says something since I only hold respect for a select few people and it took them a long time to earn it.

Soon after, I was irritated that she had the audacity to hide secrets from me when I own her life.

Now, it's fucked-up desire. The type that's impossible to satisfy, no matter how long or hard I fuck her. As if to prove my words, my dick strains against my sweatpants, demanding another round in her tight cunt.

No, it's not *her* cunt. It's *mine*.

Everything Sasha has to give is mine to own, no matter what she says about it.

I head to the closet and change into a suit, still speculating about why the fuck I fell asleep. And why Sasha disappeared while I was sleeping.

She ran away, and you know it.

I button my shirt with controlled movements in spite of the fire that's turning my insides to ashes. I've always been the type to turn calmer but deadlier in situations that go against my desires.

It allows me to see the picture from all angles and come up with the perfect plan to eliminate the problem.

Right now, that problem isn't the assholes in the organization whose graves I'm slowly but surely digging. It isn't my idiot brother or my useless mother.

It isn't even Karina's wasted life.

It's the reminder that Sasha has a man somewhere.

I didn't hear the entire conversation last night, but I heard enough to know she misses him, loves him more, and she'll soon go back home for good. Oh, and she was smiling like an idiot and kicking imaginary rocks with her foot.

That's the first time I've seen her that happy. It's also the first time I've wished I had the power to pull someone from the other end of the phone and shoot him between the eyes.

But I can't even find out who he is, because she shot the phone. To protect him.

From *me*.

My fingers tighten around the button, but I release it before I break the thing off.

She can try to hide him, but she's underestimating my abilities to find anyone I set my mind on.

After I'm finished dressing, I leave my room and send her a text.

Kirill: My office. Now.

She doesn't read it. I glare at the phone as if that will make her magically appear.

"Boss."

I lift my head to find Viktor standing by the stairs and watching me peculiarly. "What is it?"

"The situation is a bit complicated."

"Out with it, Viktor. Don't just stand there staring like an idiot."

"You're probably not going to like this."

"In that case, spare me the details." I pause. "Where's Sasha?"

"Lipovsky is involved in the situation you're probably not going to like."

I narrow my eyes. "What's he done now?"

"You better see it for yourself. It's all happening in the clinic where Mr. Konstantin is resting—"

Before he's finished his sentence, I'm already storming outside. I'm going to break Konstantin's neck and lock Sasha the fuck up. It's not enough that she pulled the whole stunt about saving him yesterday, but she also had the nerve to run away from me to go to him first thing this morning.

When I arrive at the clinic, one of the nurses bows her head in greeting. "Mr. Konstantin is in the second room on the left."

I give a curt nod, and she smiles as she continues on her way. She must think I'm here to visit my useless brother, which is far from being the case.

I'm ready to send him to the grave he escaped from last night—

My thoughts come to a halt when I reach the door to his room. Konstantin sits in bed with a hideous-looking face that has more blue and purple than normal skin, but he's grinning from ear to ear.

None other than Karina helps feed him some soup while smiling. She doesn't do that, or she stopped for years, and I almost forgot she has deep dimples in her cheeks.

The fact that my recluse sister actually went out of the house and walked the length of the garden is a feat in and of its own. Not only that, but she's also visiting Konstantin. I always got the impression she didn't like him, despite his attempts to take her under his wing.

Another surprising fact is the absence of Yulia from his bedside. In the past, if he so much as fell and scraped his knee, she'd fawn over her golden son for days, always blaming me for not taking care of 'my brother.'

The funny thing about Yulia is that Konstantin becomes my brother when it suits her. When it doesn't, I'm just the devil who took 'her' son's rightful place.

Sasha stands by Karina's side, smiling softly, and the whole picture starts to become clear. She must've convinced my sister to visit Konstantin and accompanied her on the journey from the house to here.

Judging by Karina's long-sleeved dress and boots, she was mentally prepared to go outside.

"She wanted to come last night," Sasha tells my brother. "But she was wary of your mother's presence."

"I see," he says. "It was good that you texted me. I told Mother

294 | RINA KENT

I needed another doctor, and she went to personally make sure she gets the best."

Did he just mention texting? As in, Sasha is *texting* him?

I'm seriously contemplating why I didn't let Viktor shoot him last night in that fucking duffel bag.

Sasha nods. "I really wanted to bring Karina here when your mother wasn't around, hoping to make it easier for her."

"Good call," says Konstantin.

"Thanks, Sasha." Karina takes her hand and offers her a dimpled smile. "I couldn't have done this without you."

"Well, isn't this lovely?" I stride inside. "A family reunion that's only missing cake and champagne."

"Kirill!" Karina says excitedly and jumps up, nearly spilling the contents of the bowl. "Look, I'm outside! I came through the garden and only had one panic attack and…"

She trails off, realizing that she's talking to me when she swore she'd hate me for eternity. Then she flops back to Konstantin's side, hugging the bowl.

"Am I dreaming, or are you here to visit?" my brother asks with a hint of annoying gloating.

"Definitely dreaming. I'm here to inspect the situation, not visit." My attention slides to Sasha, who seems to find the top of Karina's head interesting.

"Would it kill you to be a decent human being for once?" A tinge of venom spills in his tone.

"Very rich coming from you, Konstantin, considering how you wanted to get rid of me the moment I returned. Who's the subhuman between us, I wonder?"

"You fucking—" He starts to lunge forward but pauses, then winces and breaks into a fit of coughs.

Karina goes still, her eyes turning shifty. She was never good with stressful situations or anything sensory in nature.

It's Sasha who delicately rests him back in place. "You're still recovering. Don't push yourself."

My jaw tightens, and I resist the urge to haul her up by the waist or throw her over my shoulder. I don't, though. For the simple reason that I don't want Konstantin in my business. If he gets wind of how infuriatingly Sasha affects me, he'll use it to his advantage. No doubt about it.

"Don't get involved in this," Konstantin warns me, still speaking with difficulty. "I'll find out who did this to me and make them pay. This is my fight, stay away from it."

"No can do. You and I both know this hit was directed at me, not you. So just stay put and sleep on your mama's lap like the golden child you are."

"Kirill, I swear to fuck—"

"Stop it," Karina whispers, her voice trembling and barely audible. "Just stop this, please, both of you. It's been years since we were willingly in the same room, so let's not fight. Please?"

My brother glares at me, but he keeps his mouth shut. I meet his eyes that are a carbon copy of Yulia's.

He got her looks. I had her character.

Once upon a time, I tried to protect him from whatever internal wars our parents had. I shielded him from the ugliness of our family and took his punishments.

I tried to mentally prepare him for Roman's inhuman tests and treated him like my best friend. My *only* friend.

But then a wall grew between us, and that wall is called Yulia fucking Morozova.

The day she helped him off that island, and he chose to ditch me and Karina was the day I lost any affection I had for him.

That incident completely fucked Karina up, and he knows it. He could've stopped it or pleaded with his mother to actually save her *other* children, but he didn't.

I will never forgive him for that. He'll never forgive me for enlisting in Russia after he begged me not to.

Now, we're just enemies. It's as simple as that.

"We're leaving, Sasha," I announce and turn toward the door.

"I'll join you after I take Miss Karina back to her room," the little shit says as if I didn't just give a direct order.

But since it's about Karina, it's fine.

Just this once, though.

I find Viktor waiting in front of the clinic, arms crossed, and brows raised.

"Don't," I say as he falls in step beside me.

"I wasn't going to say anything." I'm almost sure I catch a smile on his stoic face, but he does keep quiet and tells me about the plans for the day. He finishes with, "Damien called me. He said you're not answering his calls and that you still owe him a fight."

"Ignore him."

"He might show up like he did the last time."

"Continue to ignore him."

Damien is no different than a rabid dog. He has this fixation on fighting anyone he deems worthy enough, and since I managed to punch him that time, that someone has become me. He won't stop until I get into some form of a primal bout with him.

After Viktor finishes his daily report, we head to the car. He rides with Yuri in the front, and I get in the back, but I order them to wait.

And we do for over fifteen minutes until Sasha finally jogs toward us, her face red.

She slides in next to me, panting, but she doesn't look at me. "Sorry I'm late. Miss Karina wanted me to remain by her side until she calmed down."

"Go, Yuri," I order, then I click on the button that rolls down the black isolating screen. "I have files to review, so none of you speak to me for the entire ride."

Viktor and Yuri nod as the screen closes.

I can feel Sasha stiffening before I see it as the car leaves the driveway. When I do look at her, I'm struck by the unnatural paleness of her skin. Her face is soft and so fucking beautiful. Even her now longer hair gives her a certain glow. Maybe it's that or the fact that I know how beautiful she actually looks beneath that unflattering suit, but she appears so feminine right now.

She stares at her linked hands in her lap as if that will miraculously make me lose interest.

"Now that you have nowhere to run to, care to explain why you disappeared this morning?"

Her head whips in my direction, and red blotches cover her skin as she hisses, "Yuri and Viktor are here."

"They can't hear with the screen shut. Answer my question."

She steals a glance at the front, as if not believing my words, then murmurs, "I didn't really disappear. I just...woke up and went to see Karina for breakfast."

"Bullshit." I grab her by the wrist and waist and then pull her onto my lap. Her head bumps against the roof before she settles in place, hands on my chest and eyes wide.

But there's another look there. It's subtle, almost undetectable, but a smidgen of excitement lurks beneath the apparent horror.

"Kirill...what are you doing?"

"What does it look like I'm doing? I'm trying to get you to admit to the reason behind your escape."

"But...we're in the car. Your men are just on the other side. They could lift the screen any second."

"Then you better start talking, no?"

"I..."

"Yes?"

Her eyes meet mine, sharp, mostly green, and full of light. "I don't see what the problem is. We used each other, and that's it."

My hand starts to tighten on her hip, but I force myself to stop before I break her bones. My tone comes out calm and light, almost nonchalant. "So we're using each other, huh?"

"Well, isn't that the case? It's not like we're in any form of a relationship. You've made sure it's strictly physical."

"Shouldn't it be the other way around?" My face gets so close to hers, my lips hover over her parted mouth. "You're the one who's hiding your lover from me."

"Lover?" she asks in a low, surprised tone and I almost fall for her spectacular acting skills.

"Don't fuck with me, Aleksandra. You shot the phone, so I couldn't find out who he is. But mark my words, I will bring him out from whatever nook he's hiding in."

Fire ignites in her eyes, ferocious and deadly. It's the angriest I've ever seen her. Even her expression when Nadia and Nicholas died doesn't compare.

"If you go after him, I'll be your enemy, Kirill. And I will kill you without giving it a second thought."

My jaw tightens. It's not the threat, per se, it's the fact that she threatened me because of *him*.

"You can't even punch me, but you think you'll kill me?" The more I talk, the more eerily calm I become. "You seem to have a mis- conception about me or else you wouldn't have said those words. I could and I would squash you as if you never existed."

"Then why aren't you doing it?" Her eyes brighten with an un- natural shine. "Why aren't you getting rid of me, Kirill?"

"Because, as you so eloquently put it, we're using each other." I pull on the button of her pants, and she goes still, her skin turn- ing red.

I unbuckle my own belt and release my cock that's been in a state of hardness since I woke up this morning and she wasn't there.

I lift her up, pull down her pants until they hit the floor, then jam my cock against her boxer briefs. The friction turns me on more than anything I've ever experienced.

"Wait..." Her hands curl into my jacket.

"If you want me to stop, say it. Otherwise, stay fucking still."

She gulps, but she doesn't speak. She also doesn't uncurl her fingers that remain still on my shoulders.

I only mean to shift her boxer briefs to the side so that I can have access to her cunt, but I end up ripping them. My fingers get coated with her arousal, and so does the crown of my dick.

"You claim to not want an audience, but you're soaking wet at the idea of it." My fingers play with her clit, and she gasps, sinking her teeth into her bottom lip. "You're my dirty little fuck hole, aren't you?"

She starts to say something, but it ends on a moan when I lift her up and then bring her down on my cock. Her head falls back, and she slaps a hand on her mouth to stop the sound, but that does nothing to conceal the erotic noises she makes.

"See? Your cunt is stretching and welcoming me home." I grip her by the hips and thrust inside her at a pace that's more savage and unhinged than last night. "Your cunt knows exactly who owns her, so how about you follow her example?"

Sasha's only answer is whimpers and the occasional gasp whenever I hit her G-spot. So I do it again and again until her pussy tightens further and strangles my cock.

The slap of flesh against flesh echoes in the car, and so do her moans. When she loses her balance and is about to fall off, she wraps her arms around my neck and looks down at me with those half-lidded fuck-me eyes.

I go crazy, ramming inside her with brutal urgency. She bounces off my cock, then her lips form an O as her thighs shake against me.

But I don't stop.

And I certainly don't take it easy.

I release a hip and wrap my fingers around her throat. I love the way her pussy tightens around my cock whenever I'm strangling her. The way she takes me deeper and harder, allowing me access to the most secret part of her.

"So this is what you like being, Solnyshko? My little fuck toy?"

Tears shine in her eyes, and I'm not sure if it's because of my words or her ongoing orgasm. She does tend to cry whenever it gets too intense.

"You'll let me stuff my cock into this cunt and use you whenever and however I please, won't you? You'll come for me, too, because we're *using* each other."

My strokes get faster and shorter, making her head hit the roof of the car. I pull her against me as I go on and on. Her wild heartbeat falls against mine, and her sniffles fill my ears and then spread to the darkest part of my soul.

When she hides her face in the crook of my neck, I come in her warm pussy. My release is long and hard, and cum smears all over her thighs.

Sasha doesn't move. Her frail hands are thrown on my shoulders, and her teary face is hidden in my neck. We remain like that for a few moments. Me catching my breath from the most powerful release I've ever had. And she... Fuck knows what she's doing.

After a few moments, she pulls back, her face streaked with tears, eyes red and glittery, but her expression is unreadable. She awkwardly tries to lift herself up so she can make me pull out.

I help her, and she winces, probably sore. Since she was moving just fine earlier, I didn't consider that she might be sore from last night.

My cum smears down her thighs as she tries to settle in the seat beside me. I grab some tissues and start to wipe her off, but Sasha attempts to take them away.

I fixate her with a look, and she stops, but not before glaring at me as if I murdered her favorite puppy.

After I finish cleaning her up, she adjusts her pants and I do the same, then buckle my belt.

When I look at her again, she's staring out the window, her arms crossed over her chest. I let my hand rest against my thigh for a moment, seriously considering why the fuck I'm not close to being satisfied with what just happened.

I want to do it again and again and again.

Better yet, I want to lock her up where only I can have access to her, and that's a fucking dangerous thought.

I've never wanted to keep someone before. Never thought about fucking them again the minute I was done.

"You didn't use a condom," she murmurs, still staring at the streets. "You didn't last night either."

"And?"

She whips her head in my direction, a line appearing between her brows. "Ever thought of the possibility of impregnating me? My cycle has been all over the place since I joined the army, and I'm not sure the shot works."

"It probably does."

"Probably? That doesn't sound very convincing."

I lift a shoulder even as I completely pause on the inside. I've never had sex without a condom or without a professional cleaning the premises soon after.

That started after a gold digger nearly made me impregnate her, and another tried to sell my cum.

So why the fuck did I completely forget about that angle when I was fucking this woman?

Her brow furrows. "Still, you should use a condom for safety."

"I'm clean. I'm sure you are, too, considering how tight you felt the first time. You probably haven't had sex for a long time."

Her cheeks redden, but she stares out the window again.

"You haven't had sex for a long time, right?" I ask again.

"Why is that important?"

I wrap my fingers around her wrist and squeeze until she finally faces me. "Were you perhaps...a virgin?"

The red that spreads from her neck to her cheeks and ears is all the answer I need.

Fuck me.

When I found her impossibly tight last night, I honestly thought she'd been celibate for some time. She also didn't bleed, but then again, not all women bleed.

"I'm your first?"

She visibly shivers, and I don't know if it's due to the way I dropped my voice or the question itself.

"It's not that important, okay? Besides, I had a boyfriend when I was a teen and we did stuff and—"

"Don't. One more word and I will make it my mission to find this ex-boyfriend of yours and fuck up his life."

Her shoulders drop. "Do you have to be like...this?"

"This?"

"Antagonistic for no reason."

"Obviously, there's a reason, but that's not important right now, is it? The fact that you chose me as your first is."

"I didn't *choose* you. It was just convenient."

Convenient. Hmm.

So I'm reduced to convenient now. That's certainly the first time anyone has ever used that word for me. I'm many things, but fucking *convenient* isn't one of them.

It doesn't matter.

If using each other physically is what it takes to keep her by my side and away from whatever motherfucker she's protecting, then that's exactly what will happen.

I'll trap her so deeply, she'll have no way out.

Sooner or later, she'll have no choice but to forget about her lover and be with me.

THIRTY-ONE

Kirill

ONE MONTH LATER, I DO WHAT I PROMISED EVERYONE.
I'm now the only one in the Bratva who has an in with two infamous cartels. Sergei threw a party in my name. Adrian, Igor, and the boring Vladimir told me I was playing with fucking fire. They said, one day, this unorthodox relationship will backfire and I'll have to stick with one of them.

Damien said he'll punch some people for me if I agree to fight him.

Mikhail looks at me with newfound respect.

Rai is more wary of me, as she should be.

Point is, I did what none of them has accomplished. Two shipments have passed through and I'm here tonight with most of my men for the third.

Adrian tells me that if I keep going down this unsure road, I might lose everything. That motherfucker cares about my safety. He just refuses to admit it out loud.

At any rate, even if I lose these cartels, I will just have to secure others. The leader of one of them did suggest I could strengthen our relationship by marrying Karina to his son, and I resisted the urge to bash his head in.

I don't like the fact that he knows she exists, let alone thinks that I'd marry her off for this. I like to think that no one deserves my sister, but even if such a motherfucker does exist, he won't be in our world.

She needs a normal life after all the fuckery she lived through.

But I digress, only slightly.

Viktor, Yuri, Maksim, and Sasha are scouting the premises of the dock to make sure the rest of the men are in their positions and that no surprises lurk between the containers.

I look out the window of the car at the cloudy sky, then check my watch. It's been exactly three minutes since I texted Sasha to get back to the car. Minutes that she could've used to get her ass here.

To say I can't get enough of her would be a fucking understatement. I often find myself cornering her anywhere possible, just so I can have access to her.

Is her pussy addictive? Fuck yes.

I still find it infuriating that she has this type of hold on me, especially since I've never been as attuned to another woman's body or needs as I am to hers.

The moment I'm done fucking her is the exact moment I want her again. I actually have to physically restrain myself from ramming into her all night long just to put some form of distance between us.

Then I recall that she said we're only sex buddies, so I drive her to the edge without mercy.

Now, since we have about two hours until the arrival of the shipment, I can fuck her in the car while everyone is doing their business. Sometimes, Viktor asks, "What the fuck do you need Lipovsky for when you have me?" and I resist the urge to face-palm him.

Sasha finally shows up in the distance, checking her watch and quickening her steps. She cut her hair again because the length was making her so 'girly' that even the other guards started teasing her about it. She hated doing it. I could tell because she was in a sour mood all day long.

She opens the car door, panting. "You asked for me?"

I pull her inside so that she's sitting on my lap, then slam the door and wrap my arm around her lithe waist. "Took you a minute too long."

"I was on the other side of the dock, double-checking my position." She tries to push away, but my hold around her waist forbids her from getting free.

"Stay still." I start to unzip her pants, but she jerks and slips from my hold, practically throwing herself across the seat and against the door before she sits up.

My hand flexes and unflexes as I contemplate the best way to haul her back where she belongs. "Care to explain what the fuck you're doing?"

"We're not having sex while waiting for an important shipment, Kirill. That's just not going to happen." Her confident way of speaking makes my dick fucking hard.

"Why wouldn't we? We have two hours to go."

"I'd lose concentration," she admits in a lower tone. "And I'd have shaky limbs, which wouldn't help in the least when I'm supposed to be a sniper."

"Then you can just rest here. We'll take care of the mission."

"So now I'm only useful for sex while you and the others *take care* of the mission?"

"I never said that."

"Well, that's what I'm getting. I'm telling you, Kirill, my job is more important than sex."

Did this fucking woman just say that being a bodyguard is more important than fucking? If this is her way of further insinuating that I'm 'convenient,' I swear to fuck—

306 | RINA KENT

"Well, not more important," she blurts, her cheeks reddening. "They can't be compared, I guess. All I'm saying is that we can't have sex. It's distracting and I'm trying to stay focused."

That makes me smirk. "I'm distracting?"

"Of course you are."

Distracting is better than convenient, so I let it go. For now.

"What am I supposed to do for two hours if I'm not fucking your brains out?" I ask.

"You can sleep for once." She steals a look at me. "You haven't done that for weeks."

"I don't sleep."

"You did…that other time."

"When you ran away to meet Konstantin, you mean?"

"When I took Karina to see Konstantin, yes."

"That was an anomaly."

"How about when we were in Nadia and Nicholas's house? You slept then."

"Another anomaly." I close my eyes and lean my head against the window in a hopeless attempt to calm my raging hard-on. We only need to get this fucking shipment out of the way and then I'm fucking her to my heart's content.

That barely offers my starving cock any consolation, though.

"Want me to help?" Her soft voice drifts through the car like a lullaby.

I like the way she speaks like a woman when it's only the two of us. No matter how much she pretends to be a man on the outside, she completely loses that persona around me.

"Don't waste your time. I've made peace with not being able to sleep. It's better this way."

"No, it's not. It'll affect you badly in the long run. Can I try something?"

"Be my guest."

A gentle hand wraps around mine and lifts it up. I open my eyes as she lays my palm on her chest.

I grin. "Have you changed your mind? Should I start by giving your tits more attention?"

"No," she says like a stern teacher.

"Then do you prefer to sit on my cock?"

"I said, no. Now, close your eyes and try to focus."

"That's hard to do that when all I can think about is twisting your little pink nipples."

"You're impossible." She shakes her head. "Just do as I say."

Begrudgingly, I close my eyes and lean back against the seat. "This is nothing short of a cocktease. If this doesn't work, mark my words, I'll fuck you."

"It's a deal. Now, focus on my heartbeat instead of your dirty thoughts. And, seriously, stop squeezing!"

"Fine."

The beat beneath my fingers is calm, regular, and delicate, too.

Her breaths fan my ear and my nostrils flare.

"Are you sure this isn't some sort of foreplay, because it's only managing to get me hard."

"Shh." Her low voice slips through my ear, followed by a slow hum.

Then Sasha does something I would've never expected. She starts singing in a soft, melodic voice. The Russian lullaby mothers sing to their children filters through my ears and reaches a place I didn't know existed inside me.

Her voice resembles a warm breeze on a freezing winter night. The strange pull calls for me like some enchanted instrument that's snatching my physical being from the real world and transporting it to a mythical dimension.

Then, all of a sudden, the voice stops and I open my eyes to find Sasha shaking my shoulder. My hand that was on her chest is now on the seat beside me and she's smiling. "It's time to go. The shipment arrives fifteen minutes from now."

I rub my eyes. "Why did they come early? We still have two hours."

"No, we don't." A proud, wide smile covers her face. "You slept for about two hours. See? I told you I could help."

Is this some sort of a fucking joke? I only closed my eyes for a minute.

I look at my watch and, sure enough, about two hours have passed.

Fuck me.

I fell asleep around her. Again.

I didn't feel any-fucking-thing going on around me. *Again.*

Someone could've shot me during that time and I would have been none the wiser. She could've shot me, but she looks more proud about managing to put me to sleep with her soft fucking singing and some heartbeat magic.

I need to put an end to this situation before it gets any worse.

THIRTY-TWO

Sasha

"I F IT ISN'T KIRILL'S WEAK BODYGUARD."

I straighten and turn around at the familiar deep voice and nod.

Damien studies me in that calculative way that always looks like he's up to no good. He's been constant about his intentions to fight Kirill, going as far as crashing dinners at the main house, announcing a fight to the death in front of the Pakhan, and everything in between.

He still hasn't gotten the okay from Kirill, and while that would've made anyone else give up, that's not the case for Damien.

If anything, he's become even more insistent about getting what he considers is his 'rightful fight.'

This morning, we're at the Pakhan's house for the weekly meeting, an occurrence that I heard Damien never gave a fuck about but has been attending religiously ever since his imaginary rivalry with Kirill started.

He came out of the meeting before everyone else, though, since he gets bored of these things, which is why he's talking to me.

He retrieves a cigarette and stuffs it in his mouth, then lights it as he sizes me up. "Though you're not as weak as when we first met. You training those muscles, Sasha?"

My lips part. How does he know that when I wear clothes that are a size too big?

After that two-hour nap in his car six months ago, Kirill abruptly stopped the one-on-one training sessions. But I've continued training every day, sometimes with Maksim and Yuri, sometimes alone.

"You're still weak, though," Damien continues in his one-sided monologue. "Weak getting strong, so there's an improvement. Here's a piece of advice."

He gets closer, and I'm assaulted by the smell of cigarettes. "You're a good sniper, eh? Train those arms and stick to that."

That's the same thing Kirill told me a long time ago. Do they really think I can't get physically stronger? In that case, I would be happy to prove them wrong, even if it's the last thing I do.

"Now pay me for that advice," he says with a grin that would look charming under different circumstances.

Damien is a very attractive man with a shock of dark hair, dark brows, and piercing green-gray eyes, but the charm stops there. His personality doesn't make up for it, and I'm apparently broken, because I keep comparing every man's looks to Kirill's.

No one even comes close to that monster's intense attractiveness.

"Pay you?" I echo his words.

"Yeah, I gave advice, and I expect payment."

"I never asked for advice and, therefore, refuse to provide any type of payment."

"Now, now." He wraps an arm around my shoulder. "Don't be so stiff, Sasha. That's your problem, you know. You take everything way too seriously. Be like your boss and start being a little laid-back."

Kirill is anything but laid-back. He's ruthless. He's calculative. And most importantly, he's merciless.

I've seen him kill people without a second thought and order his men to do it for him because he can't be *bothered*.

But because he's methodical and gives off a playful, somewhat chill public persona, everyone, including those in the organization, think he's easy to approach and deal with.

Which I'm sure is a tactic he's using to bring their guard down and hit them when they least expect it. Damien and Mikhail are the only ones who fall for it readily. The others might not show it, but they're wary of Kirill. Especially Rai, which is concerning since she's holding a 'secret' over his head.

Damien brings my attention back to him when he tightens his hold on my shoulder. "I won't ask for a lot for payment. Just forward me Kirill's schedule for the week."

"With all due respect, I decline."

"Oh, come on, that won't cost you anything."

"I'm forbidden to reveal anything about Boss's schedule. Besides"—I give him the side-eye—"don't you think this is a little excessive and stalker-ish?"

It *is* very stalker-ish, but I refrain from saying that out of respect for his position.

"Blame your fucking boss. If he agreed like a normal human being, I wouldn't have to do this."

The door of the conference room opens, and Kirill comes out first, talking with Adrian. He casts a mere glance toward us, but it's enough to make me breathe heavily.

I thought that with the passage of time, I'd become immune to the hold Kirill has on me. I'd learn to be less self-conscious around him, and he'd stop affecting me with a mere look, but I was miserably wrong. Not only is the effect there, but it's also grown.

We've been in a sexual relationship for months, *using each other*, as I so stupidly said that day he fucked me in his car. I didn't mean to, but I was hurt by how he chose to sleep on the sofa instead of the bed that first time.

Before that, I genuinely thought he stayed up all night working, but he slept just fine, just not beside me.

So I assumed we were using each other for sex, and apparently, I assumed correctly. He fucks me like a madman every day, sometimes a few times a day—in his office, in the car, or while waiting for a drug shipment. Wherever he deems fit.

But he still has never slept beside me on the bed. Not even once. I've tried telling him I'll help him sleep, but he vehemently refuses. My pride is a little wounded since I seriously thought I'd accomplished something by helping him fall asleep that time before the drug shipment.

For some reason, however, he's felt a bit more distant since then.

When I asked him why he moved my clothes to his closet, he said it was more 'convenient' that way. I really hate the apathetic tone he speaks with sometimes.

So, as a form of revenge, I've developed the habit of staying up late with the guys and crashing at their place whenever I feel like being a brat.

That usually only increases his already insatiable sexual appetite, though.

And just like that, we've fallen into this life of sexual gratification, physical attraction, and mad lust. It'll eventually come to an end—I know that. But I still don't want it to stop just yet.

Maybe it's useless selfishness, but Kirill, or more like this mythical attraction to him, is the only thing I've done for myself in a very long time. If I were to let it go, I'd feel like I was being forced back behind the bars of my previous prison.

Not that the prison is entirely gone, but it feels less

restrictive now. I don't only exist to exact revenge for my family. I'm also doing something for myself.

I feel like a woman in his arms. I feel beautiful and wanted and…right. It's weird, but it's right.

Adrian and Kirill separate at the entrance. My monster, who looks more gorgeous than a god, backtracks and tilts his head in Damien's direction.

"Are you nagging my people again?"

"Come on. Sasha and I are friends." Damien squeezes my shoulder tighter as if driving the point home.

"Are you now?" Kirill's calm voice makes me nervous for some reason. I've always hated how expressionless he is. How he can conceal himself beneath layers no one can catch a glimpse of, no matter what they do.

"Do you want to take him, then?" he asks Damien. "Since you're friends, you'll be able to employ him, no?"

My heart falls, and I stare at him. Is he…really pushing me toward Damien? Just like that?

Has the time come when he's gotten sick of me and wants to dispose of me in the most practical way possible?

"How can I know your schedule if I employ him?" Damien releases me with a click of his tongue. "How about you give me that fucking fight so we can get this over with?"

"How about you stop being annoying, and all of this will be over," he snaps in his face, "just like that."

"I refuse." Damien pushes Kirill's shoulder on his way out. "I swear to fucking fuck, I'll get you one of these days."

"Sounds like a clingy wife," Kirill calls after him with a slight smirk.

"Fuck you." Damien flips him off without turning around.

Kirill's smirk abruptly disappears as he stares at me. No, he glares before he heads to the car without a word.

I'm left there, partially breathless, partially not knowing what to do. What the hell was that all about?

It takes me a few moments to collect myself before I follow after. I find Yuri waiting by the car, brow furrowed.

"Did something happen inside?" Yuri whispers.

"Not that I'm aware of. Why?"

"Boss seemed displeased, but Viktor shrugged when I asked him if something went awry in the meeting."

I swallow as I go to the passenger door, only to find fucking Viktor already seated there.

Shit.

Now, I have to be beside a clearly pissed-off Kirill. Well, not clearly, since he's scrolling through some files on his iPad. But then again, his calmness is never good news. Besides, his jaw is tense, which is usually a bad sign.

I keep to my side of the seat, quietly counting the seconds until we get to our next stop.

After a few moments, I'm reminded of why I'm also on edge, and I start getting mad at the way he treated me.

"What's on the schedule this afternoon?" he asks without looking up from his tablet.

"Not sure. I erased it, thinking I was being transferred to Damien."

He adjusts his glasses as his intense eyes fall on me. "Was that sarcasm?"

"Were you really going to let Damien have me if he wanted to?"

"I don't know. You tell me. Since you're friends, I thought it might be a good idea to give you a change of scenery."

"I wouldn't want that, and I would appreciate it if you'd check with me before making these decisions."

His eyes narrow, but he reverts his attention back to his tablet and says nothing.

Since he seems to be in a better mood, I straighten. Originally, I'd planned to ask this later tonight, maybe after sex since he seems the most amiable then, but I don't trust myself not to fall asleep.

Besides, it's better if we have an audience so he doesn't question me for long.

"Boss..." I start.

"Hmm?"

"Can I have three days' vacation?"

At that, he looks up from his iPad and even tilts it to the side. "Why?"

"It's...private."

Silence falls between us for one second.

Two.

Three.

Then, without a change of expression, he says, "Fine."

"R-really?"

"Yes."

I narrow my eyes. To say this is highly suspicious would be an understatement. I was mentally prepared to fight tooth and nail for this while undergoing his unforgiving questioning. I even thought of how to survive if I cracked and told him everything under torture.

True, Kirill hasn't asked again about the 'man' he thought I was talking to that one time, and I somehow thought maybe he'd really taken my threat seriously. But that's just not his style.

The fact that I need to go home is making me even more nervous. I've rarely talked to my uncle since that day I almost got caught, and only when I'm off duty and away from the house. He quit asking me to end my mission to get close to Kirill. In fact, he seemed glad when I told him that I'm part of Kirill's inner circle now.

So I've been slowly working on my initial plan to eventually gain access to the office. I've been there a few times alone, but Kirill updated the security, so all the critical files are now protected by his thumbprint. I'm still trying to figure out a way around that issue without triggering his suspicion.

On the other hand, neither Uncle Albert nor I have received any news of my brother. Sometimes, I go to sleep with tears in my eyes, thinking he's already dead, but most of the time, I refuse to believe it.

Yesterday, I learned that Babushka is ill and that it's bad. Uncle Albert said he'd take care of her, but I have to go home, just in case. I'd never forgive myself if this were the last chance I had to see her alive and I chose not to go. So I told my uncle that I'll be returning to Russia in the next few days.

Which is why I came up with this vacation request. That Kirill so readily approved.

He'll probably send someone to follow me.

But that's fine. I'll just have to beat him at his own game this time.

‮⁓‬

"You don't have to drive me to the airport," I tell Kirill, who's personally driving the car.

He never does that.

His face is unreadable, not that he is readable most days, but it's been shrouded in more mystery since I announced I needed a vacation.

While he readily agreed, his attitude has changed. He's spent most of his time running external errands and has often ordered me to stay on house guard for Karina.

We haven't been alone in a room like he used to make sure we were in the past. And as for his room, he's only used it to shower and change clothes.

As a result, there's been no sex for three whole days.

Which hasn't happened in months.

Kirill has never gone an entire day without pulling me into a dark corner to fuck me until I have trouble standing.

So the recent change of attitude has left me baffled. I haven't been able to sleep or eat properly thinking about the meaning behind all of this.

Considering his nature, Kirill doesn't do anything without a purpose. Everyone and everything is part of a greater plan for him.

Maybe he did get tired of me and is now throwing me away. Except...

If that were the case, why would he personally drive me?

"How did you know I was flying out?" I ask when he doesn't answer my previous question.

Again, no reply.

My hands tighten in my lap, and a mixture of dark feelings—hurt, pain, and dissatisfaction—start to burst at the seams.

"If you were going to be this silent, you could've at least let Maksim or Yuri come along."

Zip. Zilch. Nada.

I stare out the window to stop myself from being overly emotional and probably saying things I shouldn't.

By the time the car stops in front of the airport, I'm ready to kill the crazy tension that's been suffocating me for the past hour.

"I'm off." I don't look at him, because that will make me want to hug him or kiss him, and we're simply not in that type of relationship.

A strong hand grips my wrist, wrenching me back, and I gasp as I turn and face him.

A shadow covers his face, and a weird expression I've never seen before takes over his sharp features. It's a mixture of pain and rage, accentuated by the deathly hold on my wrist.

"What?" I ask in a small voice, scared of speaking any louder.

"Don't go." It's two words, but they're so charged that they hit me in the chest.

"I...will come back in three days. I promise."

"Don't. Go." It's an order this time, fused with every ounce of authority Kirill is capable of.

"I have to," I whisper.

He pulls me over so that I'm half lying on his lap, removes his glasses, and kisses me. No. He doesn't only kiss me. He devours me, his tongue feasting on mine and his teeth nibbling and biting. He shows me instead of telling me that all my dark thoughts during the previous three days are null and void.

It's not that he's lost his desire for me or that he doesn't want to touch me anymore.

Because it's still there. I can feel his desperation that mirrors mine, and I can tell, without a doubt, that he probably wants me as much as I want him.

He kisses me with a fervent passion that seems foreign to him. It's chaotic, unplanned, and doesn't feel like he even knows what he's doing. But it's all him.

When his lips leave mine, I want them back.

No, I need them back, even if my mouth is too swollen and achy.

"Don't go, Sasha," he asks this time, softly, pleadingly even.

And I melt.

Every fiber in me breaks, willingly offering itself to this monster.

My monster.

I want to nod, to agree to his plea. I want to throw away that other part of my life and just remain here.

In his arms.

I want to keep looking at his icy eyes and fantasize about softening them one day.

But I can't. Because this isn't only about me. This is about my family.

With superhuman effort, I pull away from Kirill's grasp, still dizzy from the passionate kiss, and shake my head. "I'll be back in three days."

His expression doesn't change, but a muscle tightens in his jaw.

Before I change my mind and actually stay, I grab my backpack and leap out of the car.

The moment I'm in front of the entrance, I chance a look behind me to take my fill of Kirill, but he and the car are gone.

My shoulders hunch as I disappear into the airport. The flight is uncomfortable, not because of the length but due to the thoughts plaguing my mind.

I can't stop thinking about Kirill's expression when I refused to stay after he asked me for the third time.

Also...that kiss. It makes my head swim just thinking about it.

When I reach Russia, I change clothes in the airport bathroom so that I look different from when I left. I pull on a hoodie and hide my gun in my waistband. Then I turn my backpack inside out so it's blue instead of dark orange.

Though Kirill was mad at me when he dropped me off, I can't be too careful since he could've sent someone to follow me.

I even hide my phone in a locker at the airport since I'm sure it has some sort of a tracker on it.

It takes me more time than needed to exit the building, but I leave fully satisfied that no one is tailing me. And if they were, I already lost them.

Still, I take careful routes, hitching rides on some large utility trucks until I get to the faraway village where my family's located.

I leave the last truck and walk about five miles in the middle of the thick snow and freezing cold, just to make sure no vehicles or people are after me.

By the time I reach the location Uncle Albert gave me, I pause. I expected it to be a village, but there's only a warehouse.

It's hidden by a hill, looking way too similar to the warehouse from our last mission here...

This can't be right.

My senses go on full alert, and I retrieve my gun as my steps become careful. Uncle Albert wouldn't have brought Babushka here. It's not a place that's fit for an old woman or a child like Mike.

There must've been some sort of a mistake in the coordinates he gave me—

"Sasha."

I spin around, and sure enough, my uncle is standing there in the snow. But he looks...different.

My peaceful uncle is dressed in combat boots and has a firearm slung over his shoulder.

And he's not alone. A few other men appear, all dressed in fighting gear and black masks.

Mercenaries?

"What's going on?" I ask, my finger still on the trigger. "Where's Babushka? Who are all these people?"

"All in good time, Sasha." My uncle wraps his arm around my shoulder. "You did so well."

"I still haven't done anything." I stare at him quizzically.

"Oh, but you have. Here, put this on." He hands me a mask that's similar to the ones the others are wearing.

"Uncle Albert, can you tell me what's going on? I thought I was here for Babushka."

"Oh, you'll see her eventually." He puts the mask on me, then dons his own and hugs me. "I'm so proud of you, Sasha. You know that, right?"

I nod, even though my chest is tightening with every passing second.

He's saying I did so well, but why do I feel like I made a terrible mistake just by showing up here?

A noise echoes in the air before a snowmobile appears. I pull back from Uncle Albert, thinking this is one of their companions.

"You managed to get him to come alone," Uncle Albert says in a proud voice.

"Who…" I trail off as the rider of the snowmobile comes into view.

My heart drops. My legs shake, and the world starts spinning.

I would recognize that build anywhere. In a crowd. Or even in snow clothes.

"Uncle Albert," I whisper. "What…what are you planning?"

"Revenge, my darling. That man was the mastermind behind our family's massacre."

I watch in horror as my uncle opens fire on Kirill.

TO BE CONTINUED…

The story continues in *Lies of My Monster*.

You can check out the books of the characters that appeared in this book.

Adrian Volkov: Deception Trilogy.
Rai Sokolov: Throne Duet.

WHAT'S NEXT?

Thank you so much for reading *Blood of My Monster*! If you liked it, please leave a review.
Your support means the world to me.

If you're thirsty for more discussions with other readers of the series, you can join the Facebook group, *Rina Kent's Spoilers Room*.

Next up is the second book of the Monster trilogy, *Lies of My Monster*.

ALSO BY RINA KENT

For more books by the author and a reading order, please visit:
www.rinakent.com/books

ABOUT THE AUTHOR

Rina Kent is a *USA Today*, international, and #1 Amazon bestselling author of everything enemies to lovers romance.

She's known to write unapologetic anti-heroes and villains because she often fell in love with men no one roots for. Her books are sprinkled with a touch of darkness, a pinch of angst, and an unhealthy dose of intensity.

She spends her private days in London laughing like an evil mastermind about adding mayhem to her expanding universe. When she's not writing, Rina travels, hikes, and spoils cats in a pure Cat Lady fashion.

Find Rina Below:
Website: www.rinakent.com

Newsletter: www.subscribepage.com/rinakent

BookBub: www.bookbub.com/profile/rina-kent

Amazon: www.amazon.com/Rina-Kent/e/B07MM54G22

Goodreads: www.goodreads.com/author/show/18697906.Rina_

Kent

Instagram: www.instagram.com/author_rina

Facebook: www.facebook.com/rinaakent

Reader Group: www.facebook.com/groups/rinakent.club

Pinterest: www.pinterest.co.uk/AuthorRina/boards

Tiktok: www.tiktok.com/@rina.kent

Twitter: twitter.com/AuthorRina

Made in the USA
Middletown, DE
18 August 2024

59395964R00201